N. G. OSBORNE

RELEASE

N. G. Osborne grew up in Angus, Scotland and graduated in 1995 from Oxford University with a B.A. in Politics, Philosophy & Economics. At the age of eighteen, Osborne spent twelve months as a volunteer for Project Trust working in a school and the Afghan refugee camps of Peshawar, Pakistan. This experience was the inspiration for his novel Refuge. Release is the third and final book in the trilogy.

Release

The Third Book of Refuge

A Novel by

N. G. Osborne

Cranham & Keith Books

FIRST EDITION, AUGUST 2015

Copyright © 2015 by N. G. Osborne

ISBN-13: 978-0-9884371-4-2

To Harry and Frankie

I love you more than the entire universe

It seems to me we can never give up longing and wishing while we are thoroughly alive.

George Eliot

PART I

exit

ONE

Tora Bora, Afghanistan

December 13ᵗʰ, 2001

THE CAVE WALLS shudder. Stone pellets rain down from the ceiling. Dust fills the air. The booms are so intense that even with his shawl wrapped around his head and his hands squished up against his ears, it feels like his eardrums are set to perforate.

Tariq glances at the hazy silhouettes of the other six fighters. Their eyes are shut, their arms are wrapped around their knees. Usman, a freckle faced Uzbek fighter, screams. At least that's what Tariq assumes he's doing. Usman jolts to his feet and staggers towards the entrance. Tariq doesn't shout after him. After an hour of constant bombardment, Usman has lost the plot. Tariq wonders how long it will be before he does too.

O Allah, I beg you. Please let it stop.

And just like that it does. The other five fighters open their eyes. It doesn't seem plausible. They wait, not trusting the silence. Tariq checks his gun is still in its holster. They all stand. They creep past the stained mattresses that hang over the cave entrance and come upon a steep slope. They edge down it and are met by a haze of dust even thicker than that which infiltrated the cave. It clears and Tariq makes out a dirt brown landscape pockmarked with craters. An hour ago it was a plateau with tall pine trees and a blanket of crystal white snow. Most of the trees have been split in two by the bombs. Pages from al Qaeda training manuals waft in the acrid air. Bomb fragments litter the ground. A couple of unexploded ordnances lie amongst them. On one someone's scrawled in black marker - "Fuck you, Osama!"

Usman emerges from the haze like a biblical prophet. He grins maniacally. A myriad of fighters emerges from other caves and make their way towards him. They are all hardened jihadis but even they are stunned by the totality of the destruction. Tariq hangs back. The fighters gather in a circle around Usman. Usman shoves his AK-47 in the air.

"Allah Akbar," he shouts.

The fighters shout the refrain over and over, and drown out the sound of a mammoth bomber circling overhead. Tariq arches his neck and stares at the four, wispy contrails that trail behind it like a bridal train. Its bomb bay opens and a huge grey object plunges out of it.

Why are they dropping a tank?

Someone else spots it.

"Bomb," the man screams.

Desperate cries go up. Tariq turns tail and scrambles up the steep slope towards the cave's entrance. Behind him comes a piercing whine. Tariq stumbles past the mattresses and ammo boxes.

Please, Allah …

The ground gives way. The granite walls crackle with searing heat. The roar is so monstrous it's as if a fire-breathing dragon's outside the cave. Tariq is launched into the air and his body comes to a sickening crunch against the back wall. For a while he thinks he's dead. He can't see or hear a thing. But then he tastes the dust in his mouth and feels warm blood pouring into his eyes from a gash on his forehead.

I'm alive. I'm still alive.

His right shoulder throbs. He suspects it's dislocated, however, since he doesn't possess a right arm it's not a total loss. The darkness persists. Tariq wonders if he's gone blind. He crawls on his knees. He coughs madly. His ears ring. His left hand waves in front of him trying to discern what's up ahead. He cuts his hand on the jagged edge of an ammo box and is unable to hear his own wails. He carries on and in his muddled state forgets about the steep slope. He topples down it and lands on his dislocated shoulder. He screams again and this time he faintly hears their sound.

Tariq staggers to his feet. The first light materializes, the air now a thick, brown soup. Eventually it dissipates. Little exists other than black scorched earth. The broken trees are barely even stumps. In front of him is the edge of a massive bomb crater. He sidles up to its edge and peers into its abyss. He spies the odd hand, a torn off foot, a skull with the barest shred of skin still attached.

"Hello," he shouts. "Is anyone there?"

No one replies. He realizes all two hundred men must have been incinerated. He weeps. Only a few hours ago, as they had retreated up the freezing mountainside, he had thought it could get no worse. Yet it has.

And then he hears a voice. He recognizes it as bin Laden's. His heart swells.

He's come to save me.

Tariq spins around to face him but he isn't there. Tariq skirts the edge of the crater.

"Hello? Hello?"

He comes upon the burned and mangled body of a faceless jihadi. In his outstretched hand is a cheap Chinese radio.

Bin Laden's voice is emanating from it. Tariq bends down to listen.

"Dear brothers, I'm afraid to say that Allah, the most Compassionate, the most Merciful, hasn't answered our prayers. These are terrible times. If we'd gotten the support from the apostate nations, who profess to call themselves our Muslim brothers, things might have been different. But we didn't. I'm sorry to all of you for getting you involved in this battle. It was a mistake. If you can no longer resist, you have my blessing to surrender. May God have mercy on you."

A horse neighs.

"Let's go," someone else says and the radio goes silent.

Tariq stares at it in horror.

"No wait."

Tariq whirls around in the desperate hope that he might still spy bin Laden and his Arab bodyguards. Yet all he sees is a series of snow covered mountains. Tariq knows bin Laden is most likely miles away by now.

He's gone.

Down below, Tariq makes out a bevy of dots scrambling up a slope like an army of ants. He knows they are Northern Alliance fighters. He feels an overwhelming urge to sink to his knees and wait for them to arrive.

You've got to keep going.

Once more he takes in the snowy peaks above him. On the other side is Pakistan. It's his only chance.

Allah let you live for a reason. Now seize it.

With one unsteady step after another, Tariq forces himself up the mountain and heads for what he prays is refuge.

TWO

CHARLIE ALWAYS HEARS the crackle of the speaker however asleep he is. After eight years, nine months and twenty-two days of calling this cell his home, his very being is attuned to anticipating it. More often than not, and on this day it's no exception, a couple of vigorous coughs emanate from the imam before he wails the words of the adhan. Charlie lies on his back as the imam extolls Allah as the greatest, Muhammad as his messenger and urges the prisoners to make haste towards prayer because prayer is better than sleep. Charlie always takes issue with the last part. Charlie tucks his threadbare blanket under his body. It makes little difference. He shivers as Kadhim undoes the piece of cloth that they tie to each other's ankles before going to sleep. He hears Kadhim scuttle about looking for his sandals. Charlie opens his eyes and forms smoke rings with his frozen breath in a futile attempt to divert his mind. Here, deep in the desert, it's always cold at night, but in December the early morning temperatures get so low you think you're perched on the face of a Himalayan mountain.

As the only kafir, non-Muslim, in the prison, Charlie is exempt from fajr, the dawn prayer. It gives him an extra thirty minutes before he too must rise. When he first arrived he'd taken full advantage and lain there in self-pity. However, after he got his mind straight, he came to realize that these thirty minutes were too valuable to waste. They are, after all, the only minutes in his day when he's truly alone. Charlie glances across at his forty cellmates. They huddle by the cell door. Kadhim catches his gaze and nods. Charlie nods back. A buzzer sounds and the door trundles open. The prisoners trudge off towards the courtyard and Charlie plants his feet on the icy floor. By now he has his routine down pat. He places his mat on top of Kadhim's to create some space and then, despite the back spasms he's been experiencing of late, he does twenty push ups and thirty sit ups. He feels the blood flow through his body and he isn't so cold. Afterwards he goes to the toilet that juts out at the far end of the cell and does his business. He returns and places his mat back on the ground. He kneels on it in preparation for his morning prayer. This is something that Kadhim had instilled in him. For months, like any good Muslim, Kadhim had tried to convert Charlie to Islam but after six months of stubborn resistance Kadhim had compromised.

"You need to pray," he said one day in the quarry.

"Get off my back."

"Not to Allah necessarily."

"Then who to?"

"To whomever you wish."

"How about Grishna?"

"Who's that?"

"A seven headed Goddess who bestows virility on all who pray to her."

"I've never heard of her."

"That's because I just made her up."

Kadhim scowled.

"You're an idiot," he said.

"You just said I could pray to whomever I wish."

Charlie glanced over at Kadhim and Kadhim held his

gaze. Charlie often felt like a child in his presence, despite Kadhim being a couple of years younger.

"So are you going to do it?" Kadhim said.

"Of course not, it's a waste of time."

"What if it's not? Allah may hear your prayer."

"Ah, so it was a trap. You're trying to convert me."

"You know you're truly stubborn."

"Exactly! How do you think I got myself thrown in here?"

Most times Kadhim would have laughed but not on this occasion. He threw his hands up in disgust and muttered that Charlie was a *ghrabi*, a dumb ass. The next morning, however, when everyone went off to pray Charlie couldn't get their exchange out of his head and before long he was on his knees. As the minutes passed a certain peace came over him that he hadn't experienced since he and Noor had fallen asleep in each other's arms at the Holiday Inn. It took the sound of Kadhim returning to jolt him out of his state. He threw himself on his mat.

"Enjoying yourself?" Kadhim said.

"You know I'd have joined you if I could."

"The door is always open."

It would be another three months before Charlie swallowed his pride and told Kadhim he'd begun praying. Seven years later his prayers still do not vary that much, and today is no exception.

"Dear God," Charlie says. "Thank you for my life. I'm grateful for the air I breathe, the food you put in my stomach and the knowledge you've given me. Forgive me for all my sins especially my self-pity which I found rising up in me in the quarry yesterday. I know it's an addiction I cannot let myself succumb to. Give me the strength to hold it back. Look after my friend Kadhim. May his load be lighter today and the food he receives more plentiful. Look after Wali and Bushra, wherever they may be, and take care of my father,

Malaya, Aamir Khan and most of all Noor who reside with you in heaven. I'm forever in your debt, O God, for the time you allowed me to spend with Noor and I leave it to you to determine when we'll be reunited. Amen."

Charlie lets his mind go, sweeping the thoughts out of his brain as an old woman might dirt off her front steps. Some days this is easier than others and on this particular morning it is near impossible. A minute in he begins to shiver and within two he is back on his feet and moving about. He hears the communal prayer break up and Kadhim returns. They head to breakfast together as they have done almost every day since Kadhim arrived.

"It hasn't been this cold in a long while," Kadhim says.

"It reminds me of 97," Charlie says.

"Oh, it's way worse."

"That's because time's made you forget."

"Just you wait and see."

They come to a set of doors. As soon as they step outside Charlie understands what he means. An icy wind furrows its tentacles up his painfully thin cotton pants. To their left a dozen prisoners are kneeling on the ground. They listen attentively to a Wahhabi cleric. The cleric marks himself out as being particularly devout by the prayer bump in the middle of his forehead. In Arabic it's called a *zebiba*, which means raisin, a purplish oval of hardened skin brought about from years of grinding one's head on the ground. As far as Kadhim's concerned it's a mark of vanity. You have to put in a lot of effort to get one; merely praying five times a day is not enough. The cleric fixes them with a stare as frigid as the dawn air. His congregation all turn their heads.

"Best be moving on," Charlie says.

They hurry to the dining hall on the other side of the courtyard. Inside they get in line. No one acknowledges them. If anything they shrink away as if they're diseased. They are the two most despised men in the prison, Charlie the only kafir in the place and Kadhim the only Shia. Kadhim is from Najran, a fertile area in the south of the country that borders Yemen. Most of the people who live there are Sulaimani Ismailis, a moderate Shia sect, while most Saudis are Wahhabis which is a fundamentalist Sunni one. Wahhabis hate Shias more than they do Christians and even Jews since they believe the Shias have distorted the teachings of the Prophet Mohammed, and since the Royal Family are entwined in a mutually beneficial alliance with the Wahhabi clerics, it goes without saying that the Ismailis down in Najran are systematically oppressed. To be Shia in Buraydah prison is the equivalent of being black in an American prison infested with Aryan Nation. To make matters worse, in 1993 some extremist Wahhabi clerics in Buraydah forgot the bargain their forebears had struck with the Royal Family. They took to the streets to protest government corruption and the loose morals that in their minds were destroying Arabian society. In return the government gave a number of them five-year jail sentences and their virulent views still pervade the prison. For Charlie it couldn't have been a worse place to be sent. In Saudi Arabia, the Westerners are held in either Al-Ha'ir prison in Riyadh or Buraiman prison in Jeddah. There they lead dull but safe lives, if you discount any torture they may have been subjected to before being sentenced. They are visited once a month by consular officials and have occasional access to family. Buraydah prison is a wholly different place. Unlike Al-Ha'ir, it is decrepit and overcrowded, and since it's out of the way he's had only four consular visits in eight years. He is, in fact, the first Western prisoner to ever grace the inside of its walls, and when he arrived it was like a lamb wandering into a pack of wolves.

Three days in they raped him for the first time. It was in the middle of the night. He awoke to find a hand clasped around his mouth as someone else grabbed his arms and twisted them behind his back. A third assailant then ripped down his pants, and before he had a chance to react, the man was inside him. There was nothing he could do. Given the man's weight and the actions of his colleagues Charlie might as well have been in a vice. When the first had finished, the men switched positions as if they were playing a game of musical chairs. Afterwards they skulked off into the dark, their identities unknown. Charlie lay there not moving a muscle. It was strange; for something so physical it was a wholly out-of-body experience. He didn't call out for help. No one would have come but more pertinently he didn't feel like he deserved any.

This, Charlie Matthews, is your punishment for failing Noor. For letting her die.

To this day, Charlie cannot rid of himself of the image of the Prince holding Malaya's dripping head. 'This will not only be your fate but Noor's once my son is born,' the Prince had told him, and while the Prince had been wrong about Charlie's fate, Charlie saw no reason why he should have been about Noor's. She had no foreign government to intercede on her behalf, no one, like his father, who could push for a reduced sentence. Noor, most likely, never even went before a judge. She would have been beheaded somewhere private, perhaps the exact same stables the Prince had brought him to. To this day, Charlie still dreams of Malaya's execution except, when the Prince picks up her cleaved head, it's Noor's face that stares back at him.

From then on the rapists would come every night; at most four at a time, never less than two. Charlie would hear them approaching; the shuffling of their feet, the occasional stumble, the excited whispers. There were seven in total. Charlie was soon able to tell them apart by the stench of their breath, the hair on the back of their arms, each man's particular technique. He continued to endure the pain like a convicted martyr might the fires of The Inquisition. Around five weeks in the nightly visits became less frequent. First the men took a day off and soon it was unusual if they came by once a week. Within six months he was getting a visit once a month at best and that it's how it had remained till Kadhim showed up seven months later. The only explanation Charlie could come up with was that he was a lousy fuck. Where's the fun when your prey doesn't put up a fight. If he hadn't been American they might have gotten bored even earlier. One thing's for sure. They didn't give up their nighttime activities for there was hardly a night when he didn't hear the sound of muffled struggles or furtive fucking.

Breakfast is a pitiful meal; one piece of naan and a cup of tea. It is never enough. When Charlie and Kadhim get to the front of the line they take what's on offer and carry it to the far corner. There they chew their naan over and over whilst keeping an eye out for any discarded leftovers. If they're lucky one of the prisoners might get up with a quarter, even half a piece of naan left at his place. (Most prisoners, after all, are well fed due to the food packages their relatives bring to the prison.) Once spotted, unless the prisoner's whole table gets up as a group, they have to wait. If you scurry over and take the piece of naan whilst the prisoner's companions are still seated you get pushed away at best, beaten up at worst.

"Three o'clock," Kadhim says.

Charlie glances at Abdul, a fat, ugly bastard in on a smuggling charge, who's waddling away having left three-quarters of a naan at his place.

"Jesus," Charlie says. "You think he's on a diet."

"He's got diarrhea," Kadhim says. "He was up every fifteen minutes last night."

One of Abdul's friends leans in and rips the piece in two. He takes half for himself and hands the other half to the man across from him.

"I hope they get the shits too," Charlie says.

A couple of minutes later Charlie spots another prisoner stand up and leave a good third behind.

"Eight o'clock," he says.

They watch as the prisoner's table follows him out.

"Anyone else seen it?" Charlie says.

"Yeah. Shifty."

Charlie spots Shifty edging towards the table. Shifty is a bottom-feeder because, unlike the men who raped Charlie, he's considered a homosexual. Ironically in most prisoners' minds, the person doing the pitching and not the catching isn't; he's just someone looking to let off a little steam. The perception is that if you allow it to happen to you then you are, in essence, looking for it. But in a whole category of their own are men like Shifty. They are the ones who actively offer themselves up. They are truly despised, destined for ill treatment as bad as that meted out to Charlie and Kadhim.

"I'll block him," Kadhim says.

Shifty quickens his pace. Kadhim breaks into a run and body checks Shifty just as he reaches for the piece. Shifty tumbles to the ground. Charlie swipes the naan and slips it under his shirt. Shifty jumps up and screams at Kadhim. He attempts to slap him with the palms of his hands. The remaining prisoners cheer and bang on the tables. Charlie stomps on Shifty's shin. Shifty goes down wailing. Charlie and Kadhim step over him and slip out the door just as a guard comes barreling in. Charlie breaks the piece in half and hands Kadhim his share. They wolf it down. A siren goes off and with all the other men in their section they line up in the courtyard. There are about five hundred of them in total. By now, thankfully, it has gotten a little warmer. The sun is peeking over the whitewashed roof of the main building. The wind is still strong, however, and Charlie can only imagine what the conditions will be like at the quarry that day.

There are two types of prisoner at the prison; those who are favored and those who aren't. No members of the elite ever end up in jail, (their families make sure of that), but there are men in here who are never placed on work duty. Usually they are members of certain tribes or a relative is a government bureaucrat. Rather they wile away their sentences in the same lethargic manner they have spent their days on the outside. The disfavored includes everyone else; the bottom-feeders, the political prisoners, and the poor who have no connections. Every day the guards march them to the far edge of the prison where piles of television sized rocks await on a hard scrabble piece of land. Armed with sledgehammers the prisoners spend the next eight hours breaking them up into gravel. Their guards, almost to a man, are bastards. Unlike in Riyadh where the majority are African Muslims imported into the Kingdom, here they are all members of local tribes. At times Charlie wonders whether the job notice asked only for psychopaths and uneducated illiterates for that's the only type of guard he has ever encountered.

The guards have a love affair with the lash and when the courts don't give them enough victims they'll manufacture charges to create more for themselves. Along with Charlie's sentence of life in prison, the judge had tacked on two-hundred-and-fifty lashes. In Saudi Arabia that's a relatively moderate amount to hand out, (Kadhim received five hundred along with his eight years in jail and some men have been known to receive over a thousand). The guards usually mete them out fifty at a time. The lashings occur in the courtyard after Friday afternoon prayers. In front of the rest of the prisoners the unfortunate are called forward. There is usually a dozen or so of them. One after another their wrists are tied to the ends of a T-shaped wooden pole that's fixed in the ground and the lashing begins. There are two types of lashing; whipping in which the prisoner's shirt is raised above his head and the guards strike his back with a leather whip, or caning where they take a bamboo cane to the prisoners' buttocks and the back of his upper legs. Each has its own peculiar disadvantages. Whipping almost always draws blood and stings like hell. Afterwards you have to make sure you clean out the wounds otherwise you run the risk of developing an infection. Caning, on the other hand, never draws blood but creates such gargantuan bruises that it makes it impossible to sit down for three days afterwards. Each is equally painful to receive and if a prisoner ever cries out the favored prisoners howl with derision. Charlie never gave those bastards the pleasure. He received his punishment over the course of five weeks. Two guards would go at him, exchanging one blow after another in an almost rhythmic dance, and by the fortieth lash Charlie would always think there was no way he could endure another. Yet somehow he did and when they untied his wrists he had to do everything in his power not to collapse on the ground for that always brought the greatest howls of all.

Charlie and Kadhim trudge towards the quarry, more sensitive than usual to the guards' presence. A few days earlier Pockmark, a guard with an avid love of the lash, had charged the two men in front of them with talking in line and in turn the prison warden had doled out twenty-five lashes to each of them. Tomorrow the men will be receiving their punishment and from the way they are slumping along it's clear neither of them are looking forward to it. One thing it doesn't do is stop Charlie and Kadhim from talking once they get to the quarry. The guards soon get bored of watching them and retreat to a tent on the far side of the quarry. Since each prisoner has a set quota of rocks to break down with twenty-five lashes the punishment if they fail to meet it, there is no real need for the guards to monitor them.

By now it's warm, the temperature pleasant. The wind, however, is strong and sand peppers their faces. It's nothing they can't deal with. In the summer, however, when the midday temperatures reach a hundred-and-twenty degrees, the quarry becomes a suffocating oven where every rock can scorch your hands and every breath seems to singe your lungs. There is a water tap off to the side but in the summer its contents are as hot as freshly brewed coffee and while the rag over your head might protect you from direct sunlight there is nothing to protect your eyes from the piercing glare. Give it a couple more summers and Charlie's convinced he'll have cataracts. In the summer, everything bleeds together and from afar the prisoners look like a bunch of drunks stumbling outside a bar after closing. The only consolation is that the conditions inside the tent are only moderately better. At some point the guards can't take it themselves and a whistle blows and the prisoners are marched back to their cells. There they lie half out of their minds as they wait for the sun to set and for the temperatures to lessen. However much Charlie hates the cold nights in December they don't even begin to compare to the misery of summer.

"So you know what tomorrow is?" Kadhim says as he brings down his sledgehammer.

"Enlighten me?" Charlie says.

"Our anniversary."

"You're losing your mind. You're nine months off."

"Not yours and mine. Mine and Tahiran's."

Charlie grins at Kadhim. He was screwing with him.

"You're an asshole, you know that?" Kadhim says.

"So how many years is it now?" Charlie says.

"Ten years."

"That truly ages me."

"Did I tell you how I first met her?"

"Yeah, Egypt right? Still I'm fuzzy on the details."

This is an out-an-out lie. Charlie could relate the tale as accurately as Kadhim. However, in prison all a prisoner has to cling to is his memories and who is he to rid Kadhim of an opportunity to luxuriate in his own. After all, Kadhim does the same for him.

"I had gone to Cairo to do my residency," Kadhim says.

"In pediatric medicine."

"Precisely."

"I had only been there a week and already my mind was a blur. You must remember Cairo was the first place I had journeyed to outside of Saudi Arabia and the oddity of seeing unveiled women all around me was, I have to say, somewhat overwhelming."

"New York would have given you a heart attack."

"Anyway the first week was all about administrative affairs. Moving into my dorm room, filling out paperwork, you know how it is, so the next week when the pediatrics program started, well you must understand, I was stunned when I discovered that seven of the twenty students were women."

"You thought there'd be fewer women or none at all?"

"I assumed they would be receiving their instruction in a separate area, as it is done here. Anyway I have to admit, and Tahiran knows this too, that I wasn't immediately struck by her. There were a couple of very striking women in the program; both tall and slender. Tahiran is somewhat the opposite of that. Short, not fat, but definitely, I would say, ample in figure."

"So your dreams were filled with images of those two hotties?"

Kadhim blushes.

"You are going to hell, Charlie Matthews."

"For some reason I think I'm already there."

"No, my dreams did not concern those two women. The program was incredibly rigorous and by the time I went to bed I was so exhausted I didn't dream at all."

"So when did you fall in love?"

"Over the next few months Tahiran came increasingly to my attention. She was so bright. Her questions in class the most penetrating, her answers invariably the most incisive."

"So you fell in love with her mind?"

"No. I admired her mind. I fell in love with her soul. It was near the end of our first year. The two of us were assigned the same overnight shift and on that particular night a three-year-old girl called Mona was brought in. Her parents were squatters from one of the poorest areas in town and their stove had fallen over and fire had consumed their hut. One of their children had died and it was a miracle that Mona had survived the journey to the hospital. She had third degree burns over half her body. Anyway when we first examined her it was the contention of the attending physician that there was no hope. The most humane thing we could do was place her on a morphine drip and let her die in peace. Well this enraged Tahiran. You see, Mona had not come by ambulance. Her father had had to use what little money he had to bring her on a two-hour journey by taxi and as Tahiran put it if he went to that amount of trouble to try and save his daughter's life then the least we could do was expend a similar amount on Mona's behalf."

"Let me guess the attending physician overruled her."

"Absolutely. He was very irate. To be lectured by an internist and a female one at that was beyond the pale. But luckily for that little girl it was a slow night. When the attending physician went upstairs, Tahiran set about cleaning and debriding her wounds."

"Debriding?"

"You know getting rid of the dead skin."

"Okay, got it."

"It is a painstaking task. But after a few hours Tahiran was done and moved on to applying an antibiotic. When our shift was over she didn't leave. In fact, she didn't leave the hospital for a week. During the day she would observe the poor child and then at night would do her shift, looking in on her as best she could. There were a couple of nights when I didn't think Mona was going to make it but somehow at the end of the week she went from critical to stable and Tahiran set about lobbying the hospital administrators to approve skin grafts for her. Everyone told her that a child from the slums would never get such an operation but I watched in awe as Tahiran organized a fundraising drive. Two weeks later, to universal astonishment, she had the money and it was approved. Four months later, Mona walked out of the hospital with her father looking like any other little girl in Cairo for thankfully the flames had spared her face. I had volunteered to drive them home and Tahiran came with me. The poverty they came from, I have to tell you, I have never witnessed such a thing. As we were about to leave I took the father aside and handed him a hundred Egyptian pounds. The crazy thing is, despite how desperate they were, he wouldn't accept it. He said we had done more than enough."

"So you drove back with Tahiran?"

"Yes, I did. I was to drop her off at her home, and as we drove through the clogged streets of Cairo I realized I'd fallen utterly in love with her. We arrived at her family's apartment building, I think it was six in the evening, and I made some excuse that I needed to use the toilet. Tahiran invited me in and once I used the facilities I introduced myself to her father and asked him for Tahiran's hand in marriage."

"He must have been taken aback. He didn't even know you."

"Oh no, he was overjoyed. The whole family was. You must remember Tahiran was twenty-five. In Arab countries a woman is considered over-the-hill by that age and the parents, the mother especially, despairs that they'll ever find a husband."

"And how about Tahiran?"

"Well to my astonishment she was furious. To her family's dismay she turned me down on the spot and refused to look at me, let alone talk to me, for a whole month."

"Why?"

"Later she told me that she had thought me presumptuous, arrogant and unprofessional."

"I get the first two, but unprofessional?"

"She thought I was intruding on our work as doctors."

"So how did you break her down?"

"I just did my job. What else could I do? Following her example, I gave everything I had to every child who came through the doors and one day I looked up and there she was and she said, 'My answer's yes if you'll still have me.'"

"I hope you made her sweat it out."

"We were married three months later on three Shawwal, 1412."

"April 7th, 1992."

"If you say so, yes."

Kadhim smiles. The rest of the morning he doesn't say a word and Charlie doesn't offer up a story of his own. Just as one must respect a fellow prisoner's right to retell his stories, one must also respect their right to wallow in their memories. Charlie tends to do less of that than Kadhim. Kadhim has a future. He can dream about what his son and daughter will look like when he gets out of jail in nine months and of the life he and Tahiran will lead in Cairo. Kadhim had conceded long ago that there was no life left for him in Najran. In 1997 the government had annulled his marriage forcing Tahiran and their two children to return to Egypt. In the government's contorted view, since Ismailis weren't Muslims and Tahiran was Sunni, there was no way their marriage was legal.

It was these types of practices that had led Kadhim to write his petition to the King eight years earlier. Led by the governor of Najran, the government had excluded Shias and Ismailis from government posts, taught their children that their faith was sorcery, shuttered their mosques, which the Wahhabi clerics considered temples, and placed their spiritual leader under house arrest. Being a pediatric doctor, Kadhim was mostly concerned with children's health, and he wrote a petition to the King demanding the same level of medical care for Ismaili children as Sunni children. A few months later a bunch of Ismailis protested in front of the Holiday Inn, where the governor had decided to live, and government soldiers fired on the crowd. Kadhim was swept up in a wave of mass arrests. Suddenly that innocuous petition was deemed incendiary. They threw numerous charges at him, the most serious being incitement against the Wahhabi school. Like most, who were arrested, Kadhim was offered a deal. He had to sign a pledge renouncing everything he had written and promise to refrain from any further criticism. In return he would get a shortened sentence. Kadhim refused. He was happy to refrain from any further criticism, after all his life's mission was curing the sick not political agitation, but he could never renounce something he believed to be true.

"I would never renounce my faith so why would I renounce any other beliefs that are built on its foundation," he once told Charlie.

For his obstinacy, he received eight years in jail, five hundred lashes and his exiled imprisonment in Buraydah. Some days when Charlie sees him toiling under a particularly fierce sun, Charlie senses pangs of regret. It's not like Kadhim had achieved anything, discrimination is as rampant in Najran as ever, but then their day will end, Kadhim will head off to do what he does best, doctoring, and whatever regrets have been hanging over him will disappear as quickly as a rain shower in this parched land. For unlike the people who rule this country, Kadhim has never compromised himself and when he goes before Allah, as he so firmly believes he will one day, he will do so with his head held high and his honor intact.

By noon, Charlie's back has begun to ache. It's always his goal to finish two-thirds of his quota by lunch. It allows for a more leisurely afternoon, if one could call it that, and removes any fear that he might not make his quota. But today he's not even fifty percent of the way there. His back has gotten progressively worse over the last month. After a hard morning, if he bends over too far, a spasm will shoot up it and he'll freeze in whatever position he's in until it passes. Any one spasm is worse than a single stroke of the cane and at the quarry Charlie lives in dread of setting another off. He has limited his range of motion and as a result his productivity has plummeted.

A whistle sounds and they put down their sledgehammers. It's time for *dhuhr*, the noontime prayer. Charlie would like to continue while the others are praying but that would only create a riot amongst the prisoners. So instead he goes over to the prison's outer wall and sits in the shade. The prayer is always over quicker than he hopes. He pushes himself back up and heads towards his and Kadhim's piles. An hour later a pickup truck trundles up with two large pots sitting on its flatbed. It is a welcome sight. Until two days ago, the truck and its contents had disappeared for a month as Muslims around the world observed the month of Ramadan. Not a single morsel of food could be eaten and not a drop of water drunk between sunrise and sunset. Kadhim endured it every year with a religious zeal. He insisted to Charlie that it brought him closer to God. Charlie tended to believe it brought everyone closer to insanity especially when it occurred at the height of summer. In those years everything was turned upside down, with the work at the quarry done at night under floodlights. Everyone, including the guards, would have died otherwise.

Kadhim lines up. Charlie will only go up when he returns. One of the hazards of lunch is that while you're getting it someone will steal some of your gravel. Before Kadhim arrived it was a constant worry for Charlie and on many an occasion he would return from the lunch line to find his pile severely depleted. A hellish afternoon would ensue as he pushed himself to the limit to make up for his losses.

Kadhim walks back with his plate. Charlie heads towards the line. He is the last to be served yet there is still enough for one of the kitchen staff to fling a baseball sized blob of rice on his plate and deposit a couple of chicken legs beside it. There is no drink to speak of. If he wants water, he can go over to the tap by the wall. They eat in silence. Charlie eats the rice first then turns to the chicken. His chicken legs are so devoid of meat that he assumes the poor chicken died of anorexia. After he cleans the legs of every scrap of flesh he sucks the bones dry before searching for any morsels of rice he might have dropped on the ground. Lunch might be their best meal of the day but it's still never enough. There are nights when he dreams of being back at a restaurant in New York with waiters bringing him sumptuous dish after sumptuous dish until he cries out that he can't take any more.

"I would like to feel full just once," he says to Kadhim.

"I know, but on the flip side you will live longer."

"That's the stupidest thing I've ever heard."

"No truly. They have done many experiments on mice and whenever they substantially reduce their caloric intake their lifespan almost doubles."

"Ah, now I get it. This is the Saudi government's sick way of getting twenty more years out of me."

Kadhim smiles but in a mournful way. Charlie's life sentence is something they rarely talk about, the infinite nature of it too awful to contemplate. With Kadhim's release less than a year away Charlie is starting to have panic attacks. He has no clue how he's going to continue on without him.

Kadhim has had a profound effect on Charlie. Kadhim's first day at the prison was a Friday and when Kadhim walked into the courtyard Charlie could tell from the way people treated him that he was in for a hard time. He elicited poisonous glares from the Wahhabi clerics and general disdain from everyone else. Even the other bottom feeders didn't want anything to do with him. Whenever Kadhim tried to sit down a prisoner would walk over and kick him till he got up. He ended up walking aimlessly around the center of the baking yard. After prayers, the guards called up the men who were to be whipped. Kadhim was amongst them. The guards left him until last. They always liked to make the 'virgins' watch the other recipients first. When it was Kadhim's turn, one of the guards tied him to the post and pulled his shirt above his shoulder blades as another read out the reason for his lashing. If anyone at the prison didn't know Kadhim was an Ismaili they did now. Then a couple of fresh guards stepped up to the plate. It was obvious they wanted to inflict as much pain as possible since they had chosen a right handed guard and a left handed guard who could come at Kadhim from either side of the post. As each stroke sliced across Kadhim's back the prisoners let out a roar of approval. Kadhim didn't emit even a single moan and by the end of his hundred lashes his back was a flayed and bloody mess. The guards untied his wrists and to the immense satisfaction of the crowd he collapsed onto the dusty ground. Everyone slunk inside to escape the heat, and if it had been anyone else Charlie would have done likewise. In the year and three months he'd spent at the jail he had lost all ability to empathize with others. Yet something in the way Kadhim had endured his punishment sparked the smallest flame inside of him. He went over and knelt down beside Kadhim.

"Are you okay?" Charlie said.

It was a dumb question. Of course he wasn't but what else do you say to a man in such a situation. Kadhim didn't reply and Charlie assumed that Kadhim, like most of the prisoners, didn't speak English. Charlie tried to pick Kadhim up by placing his arms around Kadhim's chest but he ended up rubbing against the wounds on Kadhim's back and now, without the crowd present, Kadhim let out an agonized scream. Charlie's only recourse was to drag Kadhim inside by his feet, his face trailing along the hot sand. Once inside Charlie pulled him into the shower room and let water rain down on his back. Apart from cleaning the wounds, Charlie thought the water might revive him but if anything Kadhim seemed groggier than ever, so Charlie dragged Kadhim back to his cell and lay him down on a floor mat.

The rapists came for Kadhim that night and from the sounds of the brief scuffle Charlie deduced that Kadhim had come around. Charlie listened to them have their way with Kadhim and an anger grew inside of him. When he saw Kadhim the next day at the quarry, his eyes haunted, Charlie's anger only grew. At lunch Charlie approached him but Kadhim would have none of it. Kadhim knew that Charlie knew and that only made him more ashamed.

That night Charlie waited for the rapists to visit Kadhim. Once again there was a scuffle and when he sensed they had subdued Kadhim, he rose from his mat with two rocks he had sharpened at the quarry. He crept over and made out three figures; one covering Kadhim's mouth with his hand, another holding back his arms and a third on top of him, his pants around his knees. Charlie plunged one of the rocks into the man's ass cheek. The man let out an unholy howl and rolled off Kadhim, his hands searching frantically for the rock. The second man let go of Kadhim's arms and lunged at Charlie. Charlie stabbed him in the thigh and the first man in the shoulder. They too screamed and along with the other man they staggered off into the dark. Not long after the lights burst on and a pack of guards came running in. Charlie stood there with one of the rocks still in his hand, blood all over his shirt and his heart beating like he had just completed a four hundred-yard dash. For the first time in a long while he felt alive. The guards dragged him from the room, sucker punching him along the way. Yet however painful their strikes were they couldn't eradicate that rediscovered feeling.

For the next six days Charlie occupied the *hajuz*, a six by six-foot cell in the basement of the prison. Before they threw Charlie in, they stripped him naked and doused him with water. Soon after he heard an electric hum and cold air began to circulate. Before long Charlie was shivering uncontrollably and he panicked that they were going to freeze him to death. He found the air conditioning unit on the far wall and kicked it over and over with his right foot. It wasn't easy – it was at waist height and on more than one occasion he went crashing to the ground. The cold air kept on coming and after a while his right foot was so bloodied and bruised he had to use his left. That foot had as little effect as the right one and soon he was smashing the unit with his fists more out of frustration than hope. And then a miracle occurred. With a deep-throated groan the unit died. Charlie screamed in triumph. Not long after the guards barreled in and dragged him out for another round of beatings. After a while their enthusiasm waned and he lay there on the floor while a custodian tried to fix the unit. After half-an-hour he got into a shouting match with the guards and stalked off. In frustration the guards gave Charlie a fresh beating before throwing him back in. After a few hours how Charlie wished the air conditioning unit was still working. The cell had slowly warmed up and now was doing its best impression of a sauna. How he survived the following six days he's still not sure. It was more than just the heat. The pitch darkness made him lose all sense of time and space. Apart from the occasional bowl of rice and cup of water delivered through a hatch he had no contact with the outside world. A crushing fear began to pervade his soul. Perhaps he'd been sent here on the Prince's orders, con-demned to live out the rest of his days in this box. And then, just as he was at the very edge of his sanity, the doors were flung open and he was dragged outside. The sun blinded him but from the cheers of the crowd and the slash of the whip he realized it had to be Friday. This time he was to be the finale yet when the first strike sliced across his back rather than yelling out in pain, he screamed with joy.

I'm alive, he thought.

The blows rained down harder and harder and around the fortieth strike he fell unconscious. When he awoke, he was lying face down on his mat, a wet rag on the back of his neck. He turned over and saw Kadhim kneeling over him.

"I'm Kadhim," the man said.

"Charlie," he replied.

Their friendship was born.

Back at the quarry a guard blows his whistle. Charlie gets up and takes their plates to the truck. There isn't much conversation that afternoon. Charlie knows he can't let up yet every swing of his sledgehammer sends shards of pain through his upper back. Charlie looks over at Kadhim. Kadhim's brow is furrowed, his forearms straining as he brings his sledgehammer down again and again in an attempt to finish his quota so he can help fill Charlie's. They catch each other's gaze.

"Thanks," Charlie says.

"No need. You'd do the same for me."

He would. It is the founding credo of their friendship. Without Kadhim, Charlie suspects the men he'd attacked would have killed him the night he returned to the general population. He was way too weak to be able to fight back. However, when they came for him with their homemade shivs, Kadhim was waiting with a rock wrapped inside a homemade pillowcase. Kadhim swung it around his head like a knight brandishing a mace and after a couple of crunching blows Charlie's assailants went scurrying off into the dark. Courage was never the rapists' strongest attribute.

From that night on Charlie and Kadhim slept side by side with Charlie's mat up against the side of the wall and Kadhim's beside his. This ensured they could only be attacked from one direction. They initiated the ritual of tying Charlie's right ankle to Kadhim's left one. It meant neither of them could be dragged away in the middle of the night without the other being alerted. Kadhim never had to suffer the horror of being raped again, and by extension neither did Charlie. They were still universally despised but they were now, to a certain extent, feared, Charlie even more so than Kadhim. In the prisoners' eyes the placid, almost catatonic foreigner had morphed into a deranged lunatic, and Charlie saw no upside in disabusing them of that notion. In line he would mumble a litany of American swear words. If he sensed anyone coming up behind him he would spin around and swing his fists. It was effective, other prisoners learned to keep their distance. He caught one of the guards on the chin once and received another week in the hole. He didn't mind. If anything it only enhanced his reputation. If he was prepared to hit a guard, God knows what he might do to a prisoner.

They had created a zone of security for themselves though they soon learned that they could never get complacent. On one occasion when Charlie went for a piss in the middle of the night a bunch of men jumped him. By the time Kadhim came to his rescue, Charlie had a broken nose, a left eye that was rapidly swelling shut and blood streaming from a shiv wound to his neck. Kadhim told him that God must be looking out for him. He estimated the shiv had missed Charlie's carotid artery by a fraction of an inch. From then on, however asleep one of them was, they would always wake the other if they needed to go and relieve themselves.

Their bond grew and they spent whatever free time they had chatting with each other. (That is when Kadhim wasn't studying his Koran – the only book that was allowed in the prison.) Charlie felt that he got more out of it than Kadhim. To begin with Kadhim taught him Arabic, correcting his pronunciation over and over until even he professed that he couldn't tell Charlie apart from a man on the street. Kadhim persuaded Charlie to pray and with that came Charlie's first ever real connection to God. It was Kadhim's fervent belief that there were two great struggles in this life; one to rid yourself of impurity and sin and the other to realize the intimate balance and connection between spirit and matter.

"If you pull off the first," he once said, "you will obtain Allah's benevolence. If you manage the second you will gain an elevated understanding of God."

"And what's so good about that?" Charlie said.

"Only the greatest feeling in the world."

"Which is?"

"The blessing of perpetual closeness with God."

Charlie will never pretend he has come close to succeeding in either of these struggles, but he has gotten closer and in so doing regained a certain measure of life. For over a year, his soul had acted like an emotional black hole. Now, every time he prays, a small amount of life ekes out again. He feels things, good things like friendship and trust, harsh things like sorrow and fear. There are nights when he feels such anguish that he will bawl, calling out for Noor and for God to save him and Kadhim will kneel beside him stroking his hair or holding his hand till he falls asleep. When Charlie wakes up the next morning he senses that a part of his shattered persona has been rebuilt, not to what it was before but in a new arrangement that is neither better nor worse, just different. He has begun to accept.

"Allah has a reason for everything in this life," Kadhim told him one night.

"So what do you think was God's reason for Noor's capture," Charlie said. "For her death."

"I don't know, but it was a good one."

This was the only time Charlie ever thought of punching Kadhim. Somehow he managed to restrain myself.

"And we just have to accept that God somehow knows best."

"Charlie, if we don't believe that then this world makes no sense at all."

Charlie prayed to God and asked His forgiveness. He asked Aamir Khan, Malaya and Noor for theirs too, and after a number of months he sensed that he had received it.

There was a reason the Wahhabis hated the Ismailis so much. For the Ismailis the personal struggle, the jihad-e-Akbar, was far more important than the jihad-e-Asghar, the struggle against the enemies of Islam. For them the jihad-e-Asghar was an afterthought and if it had to be waged it should be purely defensive and include humanitarian service and volunteerism. Kadhim never tires of telling Charlie that it was during the Ismaili Fatimid empire in the tenth and eleventh centuries that Islam was at the zenith of its power. It was an empire where science and ideas were open to rigorous debate, where merit beat out nepotism and where Jews and Christians were welcomed and their communities allowed to flourish.

"Look at us now," he'll say, "look at this country. We may have all the wealth in the world but we are as backward as we have ever been."

By now, Charlie's back has all but seized up. Over the last hour he has managed to produce one more bucket of gravel and when he looks at his pile his practiced eye tells him he's at least seven short. He looks at Kadhim's pile. He has done well but it isn't enough to make up for his own shortfall.

This isn't good.

"How long do you think we have left?" Charlie says glancing at his shadow.

"Not long," Kadhim says.

In the Sunni tradition, *asr*, the late afternoon prayer, occurs when the length of any object's shadow equals the length of the object itself.

"Fuck," Charlie says.

He hoists his sledgehammer up above his head and a spasm grabs a hold of his upper back. He muffles a cry. The sledgehammer tumbles from his hands.

"Stop," Kadhim says. "I'll get it done. I promise."

Charlie lowers himself to the ground. Incredibly Kadhim ups his pace. Chunks of rock go flying as Kadhim brings his sledgehammer down over and over again. The whistle blows. The prisoners down their tools. Kadhim bends over and gasps for air.

"You think we got enough?" Charlie says.

"Just," Kadhim pants.

Another whistle blows. It's their cue to bring their daily production up to the dump truck. Kadhim grabs a bucket and shovels it full of gravel.

"Here," he says, "you go first."

Just as at lunch Kadhim and Charlie arrange it so one of them is always standing beside their pile. Charlie carries the bucket towards the line. He feels a couple of twinges but these are manageable. As long as he keeps his arm locked and his back frozen he should be able to do it. The truck is parked beside a raised platform. On both ends is a set of steps. Pockmark stands there with a clipboard. He looks inside Charlie's bucket to make sure it is full and puts the first checkmark beside his name.

"Yalla," he says.

Charlie climbs the steps and pours his gravel into the bed of the dump truck. He trudges down the other side and returns to Kadhim who is already waiting with a bucket of his own.

Eight buckets in Charlie gets a sinking feeling that they don't have enough. Three buckets later it's clear they're screwed. Kadhim stands with his eleventh bucket ready to go. The pile contains five more buckets at most. They need eight.

"Don't fill the next one so close to the brim," Kadhim says.

He sets off. Charlie gains renewed hope. Maybe they can pull a fast one. Charlie gathers the gravel in his bucket. A litany of swear words explodes from the front of the line. He turns to see Pockmark hitting Kadhim over the head with his clipboard and sending him back the way he came with a kick.

"I guess some plans work better than others," Kadhim says on his return.

Charlie fills Kadhim's bucket to the brim.

"There you go," he says.

Kadhim shakes his head.

"No, you take it."

"There's only enough for one of us to make their quota."

"Exactly. That's why you need to go."

Kadhim holds Charlie's gaze.

"No," Charlie says. "Not gonna happen."

"You're in no condition to take a lashing."

From the front of the line, Pockmark shouts at Kadhim to get going.

"I won't let you do this," Charlie says.

Kadhim picks up his bucket and pours its contents on the ground. He heads in the direction of the truck. When he gets to the front of the line, he shows Pockmark that it's empty. Nothing can disguise Pockmark's glee. He writes Kadhim up and sends him back.

"You better get going," Kadhim says.

Charlie has tears in his eyes.

"I owe you one."

"Don't worry, I know."

After asr prayers the guards take Kadhim to the Warden's office where his punishment of twenty-five lashes is confirmed. On his return Kadhim goes out on his rounds. He started doing them a couple of weeks after he got to Buraydah prison. The vast majority of prisoners turn their backs on him, many convinced that he's out to cast spells on them. Yet the very sickest never do. After all they have nothing to lose, and while Kadhim may not have medical supplies what he can do is give them instructions to hand to the prison doctor. Doctor Jaber, or Doctor Death as Kadhim calls him, is a seventy-year old Yemeni whose medical knowledge seems rooted in the seventeenth century. Kadhim will assess the sick prisoner and write down precise instructions as to the type of drug or test he needs. Doctor Jaber, to his credit, accommodates these instructions. The prison is loathe to let the prisoners leave for medical treatment but if a blood test comes back positive for Hepatitis A, for example, they have to act on it, and in so doing Kadhim saves a life. It is a thankless task. One might think after Kadhim helps someone they would at least show him a little respect. However, such is the sway of the fundamentalist preachers, that it never happens. Kadhim never complains.

"However badly they may treat me they are still my brothers," he explained to Charlie one day. "And so every evening I will keep trying to care for them as I hope they would care for me if I ever got ill."

"But they won't," Charlie said.

"Probably not."

"Definitely not."

"Then that's all right too."

In nine years Charlie has been to see Doctor Jaber only twice. The first time, after he'd been stabbed in the neck, he thought Doctor Jaber was going to prescribe leeches. Instead, per Kadhim's instructions, he grabbed a needle and thread and a container of antibiotics, and Kadhim did the necessary repair work. The second time had been a month ago. For a while Charlie had had an ever-worsening tooth ache. Kadhim took a look and concluded that one of his back molars had gone rotten. Getting it out was a procedure Kadhim wasn't capable of doing and so Charlie petitioned the guards to see a dentist. Nothing came of it so he petitioned them again and again until the pain in his tooth was so excruciating that he begged Kadhim to take it out with whatever crude instruments they could lay their hands on.

"You don't want to experience that much pain," Kadhim said.

"I'm already in pain," Charlie wailed.

Kadhim procrastinated and it was a good thing too. A day later a guard came up to Charlie at the quarry and escorted him to Doctor Jaber's examination room. There Doctor Jaber was waiting for him with a put-together man in his thirties. The man introduced himself as Doctor Mahmoud and explained that he was a dentist.

"It is better that I do this procedure than Doctor Jaber," he said.

Charlie could have cried. Doctor Mahmoud examined Charlie's tooth and winced.

"It's badly infected," he said. "I'll need to put you to sleep to extract it."

Charlie had no objections. Doctor Mahmoud connected Charlie to a drip and the next thing Charlie knew he was waking up in his cell, the wail of the muezzin blasting from the speaker on the wall. He opened his eyes to find Kadhim bent over him.

"What time is it?" he said.

"Just before dawn," Kadhim said.

"Shit."

Charlie tried to sit up but Kadhim laid a hand on his chest.

"It's all right. They said you could take the day off."

"You're screwing with me."

Kadhim shook his head and Charlie collapsed onto his mat with relief. The back of his mouth throbbed but on the Richter scale of pain it was a two compared to a nine.

"Tooth's gone?" he said.

"Yes. A nice blood clot's already formed in the socket."

"Guess things are looking up around here."

Kadhim smirked.

"Who knows maybe they are."

That night Kadhim's rounds take so long that Charlie doesn't see him until after *Maghrib* prayer. Charlie has spent the intervening hours lying on his back.

"Come on," Kadhim says. "Let's go."

"It's okay. I don't need to eat."

"Yes, you do. And besides lying still is the worst thing you can do."

Kadhim extends a hand and Charlie grabs it. Dinner is similar to breakfast and comprises a piece of naan and tea. It is generally when Charlie and Kadhim speak the most. However, tonight Kadhim has little to say. Charlie doesn't try to force the conversation. When facing the lash, you prepare for it mentally like a boxer might for a fight.

It was at dinner a little over two months ago that Charlie had learned of the attacks on the World Trade Center. Kadhim and Charlie had been eating their evening naan when a guard rushed in and jumped up on a table. He shouted out that a group of *shahids* had flown two planes into the towers of the World Trade Center. There was a moment of stunned silence then someone screamed out 'Allah akbar' and soon everyone but Kadhim and Charlie had joined in. There were hugs, tears, clapping, impromptu dancing and of course insults and jeers thrown in Charlie's direction.

"You want to get out of here," Kadhim shouted over the din.

Charlie shook his head. He wasn't too perturbed. He doubted a couple of Cessnas could have done much damage. Just as the excitement was dying down, the guard came running back in, his face beetroot red. A hush descended over the room.

"The shahid have hit the Pentagon," he said.

A roar went up. Charlie looked at Kadhim. This didn't sound good. The guard blew his whistle.

"That's not all, my brothers," he shouted. "One of the towers has fallen. All hundred stories. Gone. Into dust."

For a moment even the prisoners were too stunned to say anything, and then the loudest roar of the evening went up.

"Let's go," Kadhim shouted at Charlie.

Kadhim grabbed Charlie by the arm and as they passed through the crowd a prisoner's fist came out of nowhere and landed square on Charlie's nose. Charlie flew backwards, blood spurting from his nostrils. He lay on the floor trying to gather his wits and this gave the prisoners the opportunity to stomp on him.

So this is it, Charlie thought. *This is how I die.*

Kadhim wrestled his way through the scrum.

"Grab my hand," he shouted.

The first time Charlie tried, his arm got smashed aside by a vicious kick. The second time it was Kadhim's turn as a punch connected to his ribcage. On the third attempt their hands joined and Kadhim managed to pull Charlie through the cyclone of feet and fists. They began running. A fist exploded against Charlie's ear. Another crunched against the small of his back. A metal plate nailed Kadhim in the forehead. Yet somehow the two of them stayed on their feet and once out the door they sprinted across the courtyard, the baying mob close behind. When they reached the door of their cellblock a miracle occurred. The call to prayer rang out and the mob halted. Kadhim and Charlie continued on to their cell and sat with their backs to the wall, blood streaming down their faces. They knew there was nowhere to hide. Kadhim found his large stone and placed it in his pillowcase. Charlie located a jagged rock he had hidden inside the stuffing of his mat. They both assumed that this was it; their last stand. When prayers ended the celebrations started up again. A huge roar went up as a guard announced the destruction of the second tower. However, instead of forcing the prisoners to go to their cells, the guards let everyone stay outside. By the time everyone ambled in their energy was spent. It didn't stop Charlie and Kadhim taking shifts that night. During Charlie's he couldn't help but think that if this was the reaction of a thousand Saudi prisoners what must it have been like across the rest of the Arab world. Worse what was America's reaction going to be in turn.

Nothing good's going to come of this, he thought. *Nothing.*

The muezzin calls the prisoners to *isha* prayer and interrupts Charlie from his recollections. While everyone else heads to the courtyard, Charlie returns to the cell and gets down on his knees to say his own prayers. It isn't easy. Despite Kadhim's recommendation, his back pain is worse than ever. He keeps them short and prays that Kadhim's blows are light tomorrow. He lies down on his mat, wraps his blanket around him and entertains himself by creating smoke rings with his freezing breath. Not long after the rest of the cell's inhabitants come traipsing in. Kadhim finds the piece of cloth and ties it around Charlie's right ankle before tying it around his left one. The cell door trundles shut and the overhead lights go out.

"Charlie," Kadhim whispers.

"What's up?"

"Is everything fine with you?"

"I'm the one who should be asking you that question."

"Oh, don't worry about me. This isn't my first flogging and I'm sure it won't be my last. I'll survive."

For a moment neither of them speaks.

"So?" Kadhim says.

"So what?"

"Are you all right?"

In so many ways Charlie isn't. His back is killing him and though he has tomorrow off he doubts it will be in much better shape by Saturday. He continues to lose weight, however much naan they manage to snag at breakfast, and when he last gazed in the mirror in Doctor Death's waiting room he hardly recognized the man staring back at him. He is thirty-three years old yet he looks like he is forty-five and feels like he is seventy. Yet this is his life and he accepted that long ago. He has a newfound faith in God and a belief that this life isn't it. There's something else to come afterwards and thus there's no reason to get down. However tough life is, it can and will be endured until the day God so elects to take you from this world to the next.

"You know what, I am," Charlie says.

"Truly?" Kadhim says.

"Truly."

They lay there in silence and Charlie finds himself transported to the night he and Wali lay next to each other in their tent in Afghanistan. It was right before Wali lost his legs and Charlie still remembers the intense closeness he felt towards Wali at the time.

Who'd have thought that the two men I've felt closest to in this life are both Muslim.

"Kadhim," he says.

"Yes."

"Don't take this the wrong way …"

"You may want to stop there."

"No, let me just say something."

"Go ahead."

"I love you."

Kadhim doesn't reply and Charlie worries he's gone too far. Perhaps after eight years, nine months and twenty-two days, this is one of the few things one should never say in prison.

"I love you too, Charlie," Kadhim says.

Charlie smiles. Soon after he falls asleep.

THREE

THE SPEAKER CRACKLES and the call to prayer rings out. Charlie groans. It feels like only a minute ago that he fell asleep. Kadhim unties the cloth connecting their ankles.

"See you in a bit," he says.

"Not too soon, I hope," Charlie says.

The cell doors open, and Kadhim and the other prisoners head off to pray. Charlie sits up and his back spasms. He moans and waits for the pain to pass. There's no way in hell he's going to be able to do his exercises this morning. He gets down on his knees and takes a deep breath.

"Dear God. Thank you for my life. I'm grateful for the air I breathe, the food you put in my stomach and the knowledge you've given me. Forgive me for all my sins. Forgive me for—"

"Matthews."

Charlie twists around. A pot-bellied guard stands at the door. He jerks his head and indicates that Charlie follow him.

Shit, what have I done?

Charlie catches up and they make their way out of the cellblock and across the courtyard past the praying prisoners. Charlie tries to catch Kadhim's eye, however, Kadhim is too absorbed in his prayers to notice him.

Oh well, if nothing else, I'll have a story for you later.

They enter the administration building. They trudge up a flight of stairs and down a long corridor. Charlie knows where he's going. The warden's office.

This ain't good.

The only other times Charlie has visited the office were to receive his lashing sentences and when he was informed that his father had died. He doubts he's there to receive a lashing sentence. A prisoner is generally reprimanded before he's brought before the warden. No, the more likely explanation is that someone's died. Charlie is at a loss as to whom it could be. Perhaps it's his stepmother or one of his half-sisters.

Dear God, I hope not.

They enter the warden's empty anteroom. The guard gestures for Charlie to sit on one of the leather couches that run along two sides of the room. Charlie suspects it's going to be a long wait. No one gets into work early in Saudi Arabia; not unless they have to. At nine-thirty the warden's secretary ambles in. He sits down at his desk and busies himself with paperwork without once looking in Charlie's direction. At ten o'clock the first thobed man enters and after that others begin arriving at regular intervals. They stare at Charlie as if he is an exotic species. Tea and pastries are served and the men light into them as only men can do after completing a month of daily fasts. Cigarettes are lit and the men gossip amongst themselves. One bemoans the expense of the wedding he is throwing for his third daughter. Another boasts about the extravagant celebration he laid on a couple of nights earlier for Eid al Fitr. Charlie tunes them out. There are only two reasons why they are here. Either they are local businessmen bargaining for prison contracts or they are influential relatives asking for special treatment for one of their kinsmen. Around eleven o'clock the first guards appear, and it's not long before one yanks Charlie from his spot. The guards aren't fools, they know what transpires up here, and like dogs lying under their master's table, they linger knowing that scraps are sure to fall on the floor. It's not long before Charlie's back starts throbbing.

Thirty minutes later the warden breezes in. He stops to kiss and exchange pleasantries with a couple of the men and soon after the secretary escorts them into his office. Some time later they come out sporting broad grins and the secretary guides another man in to meet the warden. Charlie counts the men still in the room and does a quick calculation. If the warden sees him last, as is likely, he won't be out of here until five o'clock at the earliest.

Shit, I've missed breakfast already, am certain to miss lunch and there's a distinct possibility I might miss dinner too.

Charlie's stomach rumbles. It only gets worse when lunch is brought in on large trays and placed on the coffee tables. The supplicants guzzle down soda and overload their bellies with rice and chicken, falafel balls and pita bread. Charlie doesn't dare take any. God knows what punishment that might incur. The call for salat al-Zuhr, the early afternoon prayer, rings out and everyone, the warden included, lumbers out of the office to pray.

Oh my God. It's a miracle.

Charlie forces himself to count to sixty, before stealing over to one of the tables. He shovels chicken and falafel balls into his mouth. He moans with delight as their juices saturate his tongue.

I'd endure a hundred lashes for this.

He continues on to the rice before returning to the falafel balls. Unlike the chicken, there are so many of them that their disappearance will never be noticed. He eyes a Coke but steals himself. The last thing he can afford to do is burp and give the game away. He even has the presence of mind to halt his gorging. He can only imagine the effect this rich food will have on his stomach if he keeps going. Instead he rips off a piece of pita bread and scoops out its center. Inside he places three falafel balls before slipping it into his pocket.

Oh Kadhim, do I have a surprise for you.

Soon after the warden leads everyone back in. Charlie stands rigidly in the corner, certain that someone will spy the bulge in his pocket. However, no one does, and instead the supplicants lie back and take a nap. A while later, a couple of stern looking policemen, in khaki uniforms and black berets, enter. They announce themselves to the secretary then plant themselves on the couch opposite Charlie. They stare at Charlie. Unnerved Charlie turns his gaze towards a poster of the Kaaba.

"Matthews," the secretary says.

Charlie jolts from his trance. The latest supplicant is leaving the warden's office.

"Get in there," he says in Arabic.

Charlie heads for the office, his gaze firmly on the floor.

Here we go.

Charlie enters the warden's office. Its mahogany chairs, plush rug and crystal lampshades are no doubt gifts from some of the very men who have been lounging in the anteroom. Behind the desk, the warden leans back with his fleshy hands over his protruding belly. Dressed in a sparkling white thobe, he exudes the aura of a man who knows that at this institution, at least, he's God.

"I have a question for you, Matthews," he says in Arabic.

Charlie knows better than to say anything.

"If a journalist were to ask you how you were treated in this prison what would you say?"

Charlie's mind races.

Journalist?

He assumes it's got to be a Westerner. If it were a Saudi, the warden wouldn't be worried. Charlie wonders which news organization they're from and who the hell had authorized the interview.

Who cares? Kadhim's going to go insane when I tell him.

"Well?" the warden says.

"I'd say that I've been treated exceptionally well."

"You really mean that?"

"Absolutely, sir."

The warden raises a manicured eyebrow.

"Just in case I have a document for you to sign."

He gestures to a piece of paper and turns it in Charlie's direction.

"It relates how humanely you were treated here; that you believe you would have been much worse off if you had been imprisoned in one of those terrible jails back in the United States."

The warden holds a gold pen out to Charlie.

"Go on then," he says.

Charlie takes the pen. He is about to scrawl his name when a thought strikes him. He looks up.

"I'm sorry, sir, but something doesn't make sense. If I'm not mistaken you said 'how humanely you were treated here.'"

"So?"

"Well I don't mean to correct you but surely you meant 'are'."

"No, Matthews, I choose my words carefully. Now go on, sign the document."

Charlie realizes why the policemen are out in the waiting room.

I'm being transferred to Al' Hair prison.

He scribbles his signature and hands the document back. Outside a familiar roar rises up from the courtyard.

Kadhim.

"If I may," Charlie says. "I'd prefer to stay here."

"Are you mad?"

"Perhaps, but I've come to like this place. I don't want to go to Al' Hair."

"Al' Hair. Why do you think you're going to Al' Hair?"

Outside a crackle sizzles through the air and the crowd lets out another full throated roar. Charlie's back spasms as if it's him not Kadhim who's tied to the post. The warden lifts himself out of his chair.

"It is my duty, Matthews, to inform you that the Deputy Prime Minister and Commander of the National Guard, His Royal Highness, Crown Prince Abdullah, has pardoned you and ordered your immediate deportation from the Kingdom."

Another crackle. Another roar. Tears flow down Charlie's cheeks as the crowd delights in Kadhim's torment.

"I'm sorry," Charlie says, "but I need to go. You see, my friend, Kadhim, he needs me."

The warden frowns.

"Don't you understand what I just said, Matthews? You are returning to the United States of America. Your stay in Saudi Arabia is over."

The warden shouts for the policemen. They come in and each take one of Charlie's arms. They lead him out of the office and down the corridor. The crackles and roars are now muted but it doesn't put a stop to Charlie's tears. They enter an elevator and descend to another corridor. They pass through a series of electronic doors until they come upon a parking lot where a police car is waiting. Out here the roars are louder. The courtyard is on the other side of a sixteen-foot wall. One of the policemen opens the passenger door and gestures at Charlie to get in. Charlie breaks free and sprints towards the wall.

"Kadhim," he shouts. "Kadhim."

The crackle and subsequent roar are now so close that Charlie might as well be part of the crowd.

"Charlie!" Kadhim cries out.

The policemen grab Charlie by the arms.

"Kadhim, Kadhim."

The policemen drag Charlie to their car and throw him in the backseat. The door slams shut. Charlie tries to open it. It's locked. He scrambles to look out the back window. The policemen get in and the police car drives out of the prison. It's not long before they are speeding through the vast expanse of desert towards Riyadh. Tears run down Charlie's cheeks. He feels like he has betrayed his only true friend in this world. It is only when they approach the airport on the very same road that he and Noor fled down nine years earlier that it truly sinks in.

I'm going home.

Yet rather than being elated, Charlie is petrified. As far as he's concerned he has nothing to go back to.

FOUR

IT HAS BEEN a few hours now. A couple of prayer calls have come and gone and a third can't be too far away. For all that time Charlie has been waiting in a room not too dissimilar to the one Abdullah once tortured him in. It contains nothing more than a Formica desk and a plastic chair. He hasn't been offered any food and stupidly ate the falafel balls in his pocket the moment he got here. The small bottle of Evian they gave him he drank long ago. He is beginning to wonder if this is nothing but a twisted joke on the Prince's part.

Perhaps they're going to leave me here to die.

The door opens and a Saudi official, carrying a Benetton shopping bag, strolls in accompanied by a rosy-cheeked white woman in a head scarf and a long sleeved shirt and pants. In her hand she holds a leather briefcase. She places it on the table and opens it.

"Mr. Matthews, my name is Janine Potts. I'm from the American embassy. This is Mr. Aziz from the Saudi Interior Ministry. We are here to facilitate your departure."

Charlie blinks as if he's just been dragged out of the hole.

"Would you mind standing by that wall, Mr. Matthews? I need to take a photo of you."

Charlie does as he's told. Janine takes a Polaroid out of

the briefcase and snaps a picture. The Polaroid spits out a photo. She waves it in the air and proceeds to cut out a portion of it. She extracts a document from the briefcase and glues the photo to it. She stamps it and hands it to Charlie.

"This is your temporary passport."

Charlie stares at his matted beard and gaunt appearance.

"Good look, isn't it?"

Janine takes an envelope out of the briefcase.

"This is for initial expenses," she says.

She hands it to Charlie. Inside he finds two one-hundred dollar bills. Janine sticks out her hand. The official frowns. Janine keeps it outstretched. Charlie grasps it for longer than is normally polite.

"I'm sorry," he says. "But you're the first woman I've met in almost nine years."

Janine smiles.

"Good luck, Mr. Matthews. I'm so glad you're going home."

Janine exits the room. The official tosses the Benetton bag at Charlie's feet.

"Put these on," he says.

Charlie strips off his grimy cotton shirt and pants. They lie on the floor like a discarded snakeskin. Naked, he reaches into the bag and pulls out a brand new shirt, some khaki pants, a leather belt with a clunky steel buckle, a pair of socks, some boxer shorts and a shoebox. He puts the clothes on. The pants are a couple of sizes too big and an inch too long. The belt offers little help. Even on its tightest notch it droops towards his groin. He undoes it.

"There is a problem?" the official says.

"The belt's not tight enough. It's okay, I don't need it."

"No. Wait."

The official opens the door.

"A knife," he says.

One of the policemen unclasps a penknife from his belt.

He hands it to the official who gives it to Charlie.

"Go on," he says. "Make a new hole."

Charlie uses the point of the blade to carve a new notch. He buckles the belt again and this time his pants stay up. Charlie opens the shoe box. Inside is a pair of brand new leather moccasins. He brings them up to his nose and inhales. They smell like a long lost friend.

"Hurry," the official says.

Charlie shoves on the shoes and follows him out the door. Along with the policemen, he escorts Charlie down the corridor. They come to a set of stairs. At the top is a door. Charlie hears a high-pitched whine and smells the saccharine scent of kerosene. The official pushes the door open. Charlie shields his eyes from the bright light. When they adjust he sees a Saudi Airlines 747 mere feet away. The official leads Charlie up a set of steps and onto the plane. A couple of male flight attendants stand by the door. They smile at Charlie. The gesture is so unusual it halts him in his tracks.

"Come on," the official says.

The official enters business class. Apart from a few American businessmen, it is filled with Saudi men in thobes and ghutras and Saudi women in niqabs and abayas. There is only one seat free. The official points at it.

"Goodbye, Mr. Matthews. Please don't come back."

The official leaves. Charlie sits down in his expansive seat. A flight attendant comes up to him.

"Would you like a drink, sir?" he asks in English.

"What do you have?" Charlie says in Arabic.

"Coke, Sprite, orange juice, coffee, tea, water."

Charlie takes a moment. The choice is overwhelming.

"A Coke, thank you," Charlie says.

The Coke duly arrives in an ice filled glass. Charlie lifts it to his lips and takes a sip. He moans. He doesn't think he's tasted anything so wonderful in his life. The airplane backs away and it's not long before they are trundling down the runway. Charlie takes another sip relishing the Coke's salty sweetness. The plane lifts off into the air. He looks out the window. Down below there is nothing but copper colored desert. He stares at it entranced. Despite everything he's been through there is a beauty to its barrenness. He thinks of Kadhim and wonders how he is doing without him.

Oh Lord, please do everything in your power to protect him.

"So what's your story?"

Next to him is a bull of a man with a thick neck and pecs so large they look as if they might pop off his shirt buttons.

"I'm sorry," Charlie says.

"Look like you got lost in the desert. Smell like it too."

Charlie hasn't even thought about the way he smells. In Buraydah they only get to shower on Fridays and he'd missed his opportunity today.

"I was in a Saudi prison," Charlie says.

"No shit. What for?"

"Drug smuggling."

"Idiot thing to do in a country like this, don't you think?"

"I didn't do it."

The man chuckles.

"That's what they all say."

Charlie ignores the man and reaches for his glass.

"I'm sorry, I meant no offence," the man says. "What was your sentence?"

"Two hundred and fifty lashes and life in prison."

The man whistles.

"Motherfuckers."

He holds out a hand.

"Thad McDaniels."

Charlie shakes it.

"Charlie Matthews."

"So how come you got out early?"

Charlie doesn't have an answer. It's the first time he's contemplated the question.

"I bet it was a P.R. thing," Thad says. "You know, given how most of the hijackers were Saudis."

Charlie ruminates on Thad's explanation. It makes sense. Certainly nothing else does. The intercom chimes and there is a sudden commotion in the cabin. Charlie looks around. Many of the Saudi women are discarding their abayas to reveal fabulously made up faces and bodies clad in slinky dresses and skin tight jeans. Thad holds out his glass of Coke.

"To no longer being in Saudi airspace," he says.

He clinks Charlie's glass. Thad takes out his cellphone. Charlie stares at it. It's as small as a pack of cigarettes. Thad notices and hands it to Charlie.

"It's a Nokia. Has a bunch of cool features. Stopwatch. Calculator. Games. Snake is my favorite. Oh yeah, and you can text on it too."

"Text?"

"You know send messages to other cellphones. Rumor is they're bringing out a device that'll let you get your emails too."

"What's email?"

"Shit, brother, how long did you say you were in that jail of yours?"

"Almost nine years."

"And you never learned about anything outside the prison walls?"

"The attack on the World Trade Center. That's about it."

"Well get ready to have your mind blown."

Thad takes Charlie on a journey that encompasses the internet, email, web browsers, instant messaging and AOL. There's the internet boom and the subsequent internet bust, technology that allows music and photos to be stored digitally, Dolly the sheep, the human genome project and an impeachment scandal for a two term president Charlie never even knew had been elected. There had been the Florida recount, Bush versus Gore. Bush had won or had been given the Presidency by the Supreme Court depending on your political point of view. Thad being a Republican naturally believes the former.

"So George Bush is President Bush's son?" Charlie says.

"Yeah, who else would he be?"

Charlie laughs.

"I don't know. I thought the father had somehow got himself elected again."

The flight attendants bring lunch and the history lesson is interrupted. It's wondrous. The bread rolls and butter alone bring tears to Charlie's eyes. The pasta and the steak are unimaginable, the cheesecake divine. Charlie downs a second Coke. His heart races and he visits the bathroom to relieve a gastro system in a state of shock. Charlie returns to his seat.

"Where were we?" Thad says.

"Y2K," Charlie says.

"Oh yeah, the biggest non-event in the history of mankind."

Thad admits he's not a cultured man, however, he's still able to give Charlie an overview of what's being going on in popular culture. There was a film about the Titanic which was the biggest movie of all time and starred a heartthrob called Leonardo di Caprio. There was a hugely popular sitcom called Friends, a TV drama called E.R. with a guy called George Clooney, except he's not in it anymore and is now a huge movie star and has just come out in a blockbuster called Ocean's Eleven which stars another movie star called Brad Pitt who Charlie vaguely remembers from a bit part in Thelma & Louise. There's a game console called the PlayStation, the Chicago Bulls won six N.B.A. titles with Michael Jordan and America had hosted the World Cup. Princess Diana had died, so had J.F.K. Jr. Yizhak Rabin had been assassinated. There had been wars - the Chechen war, the Yugoslav war, a genocide in Rwanda, and the emergence and now destruction of a fundamentalist group called the

Taliban in Afghanistan. And, of course, after a decade of increasingly lethal terrorist attacks there had been 9/11.

"It's like no day I've ever experienced," Thad says. "For a moment you wondered if the attacks were ever going to stop. And then the towers came down. Whoosh. One after another. It was chilling, man. Almost three thousand lost."

"And most of the hijackers were Saudis?"

"Yeah, fourteen or fifteen, I think."

"Yet nothing seems to have changed between America and Saudi Arabia?"

"Course it hasn't. They've got the oil and we need it. Besides the Saudis have been on their best behavior. Promising cooperation in the War on Terror."

"War on Terror?"

"That's what they're calling it. America's going to kick some ass. I'm telling you, Afghanistan's only first on the list. Others better fall in line or they'll be next."

"Like who?"

"Iraq."

"They were involved in 9/11?"

"Hell you gotta believe it."

By now, Charlie feels woozy from the inundation of facts, from the unfamiliar food still curdling in his stomach and from the sugar and caffeine crashing out of his system.

"Mind if I get some shut eye," he says.

"Hell no, go for it," Thad says.

Charlie closes his eyes. After what seems like only a few minutes, Thad shakes him awake.

"We're here buddy."

Charlie looks out the window and is shocked to see the wintry skyline of lower Manhattan. It is grey, pallid and awe inspiring even with the Twin Towers no longer standing tall at one end. He's been out over eight hours. Soon after the plane lands and they disembark. Charlie traipses along with the rest of the passengers down the lengthy concourse, amazed that nearly everyone seems to have a cellphone stuck to their ear.

If I had one, I wouldn't even know who to call.

They arrive in the immigration hall and come upon a long, twisting line. Three international flights have arrived ahead of them. Many of Charlie's fellow passengers grumble. It's been a little over two months since 9/11 but already the goodwill, that event engendered, has dissipated. When Charlie reaches the front of the line, he hands over his temporary passport. The officer swivels in her chair and types Charlie's information into her computer. She scrutinizes what comes up on her screen and stamps his passport and customs form.

"That's it?" he says.

"You're free to go."

Free.

It is still too weird a concept for Charlie to fully grasp.

Charlie wanders into the baggage claim area and walks past the throng of waiting passengers. The customs line is shorter and when he presents his custom form, the customs official barely looks at it. He carries on up a ramp towards a pair of automatic doors. They part and he wanders into the arrivals hall. All around him is a swirl of activity. Relatives lean over the railings waiting eagerly for their loved ones to come out. Suited drivers hold up handwritten signs. Digital displays flash adverts. He joins the stream of passengers heading for the exit. He steps outside and gets in line at the taxi rank. It's not long before he's at the front.

"Where to?" the dispatcher asks.

Charlie doesn't have a clue.

"Come on, buddy, we ain't got all day."

"Manhattan," Charlie says.

"Need to be more specific than that."

"Union Square. That'll do."

The dispatcher holds open the door and Charlie slides in. The cab driver is of South Asian descent. He speeds away and they are soon on the Van Wyck expressway inching towards Manhattan. Charlie stares out the window at all the unfamiliar cars around him. Cars have gotten rounder since he last saw them, S.U.V.s larger. He remembers the time his father picked him up on his return from Pakistan; the rage and desperation he felt, the way he jumped out of his father's car and stalked away.

If only I could get that moment back. My God, I'd approach it differently.

The cab reaches Manhattan and arrives at Union Square. The fare is eighty dollars. Charlie hands the driver one of his two one-hundred dollar bills.

"Keep the change," he says.

Charlie steps out into Manhattan's cold, loud embrace. Snow is falling. Cars and buses, their flashlights ablaze, race around the square as if they're vying for first place. Charlie turns his face upwards and closes his eyes. He luxuriates in the snowflakes that melt on his face.

"Hey, idiot. Get out of the way."

Charlie steps backwards and a burly man in a Mets cap barrels past. Charlie stares up at the clock tower. It is half-past nine in the morning. He knows he can hang out at a diner or coffee shop for most of the day, but he will need to find a place to sleep tonight. He now regrets giving the cab driver such a tip. He only has a hundred dollars left and he will be pushed to find a hotel room in Manhattan for that price. He spies a bank of telephones across the street. He racks his brain as to whom he might call. For a while nobody comes to mind but then it occurs to him.

She won't be happy to see me but I've no one else.

He spots a Starbucks and goes to get some change.

FIVE

CHARLIE SITS ACROSS from Natalie. Out the window, Central Park stretches into the distance, its trees and lawns dappled with snow. Natalie's expression is as frigid.

"I didn't expect to ever see you again," she says.

"I never expected to be freed," Charlie says.

"Your father was never the same man after you were arrested. He became obsessed. Spent endless hours lobbying government officials, staring at the computer worrying himself sick."

"I know I have a lot to apologize for."

"But an apology isn't going to give Anne and Elizabeth their father back, now is it?"

Charlie takes a sip of his water. Natalie had at least been polite enough to offer him a glass. He glances at the plethora of silver framed photos dedicated to his father and Natalie and the girls. There's not a single one of him.

"How did Dad die?" Charlie asks.

"Pancreatic cancer. It wasn't more than a couple of months from his diagnosis to the day he died. His doctors say there was nothing he could have done, that for the most part it's a genetic disease, but I think, well I'm sure you can hazard a guess as to my views on the subject."

Natalie sweeps her coiffured hair away from her forehead and stands.

"Let me go get the envelope."

Before Charlie can think to ask what's she's talking about, Natalie has left the room. He wonders if he should broach the subject of money when she returns. She certainly doesn't seem in the mood to give him any.

Then again what's the harm? You're unlikely to ever see her again.

Charlie rises from his chair. His back spasms. He winces. He has no clue how he'd have gotten through another week at Buraydah prison. Charlie wanders over to the grand piano. He picks up a photo of his father. He's at some Wall Street function wearing a tuxedo and smiling. Charlie knows he'll spend the rest of his life regretting that they never reconciled.

"Here you go," Natalie says.

Charlie turns. Natalie is holding out a Manila envelope.

"Inside's a key. It opens a safety deposit box at the Chase bank on Broadway and Thirty-Eighth."

"What's in it?"

"I don't know, your father never told me."

Charlie takes the Manila envelope. It suddenly seems inappropriate to ask Natalie for even a twenty. Natalie turns smartly about and leads Charlie out of the apartment, her heels click clacking on the marble floor. They arrive at the front door.

"One last thing," Natalie says. "On his death bed, Jeremy made me promise to look after you if you ever returned. At least until you got back on your feet."

"Look, Natalie, I really don't expect anything ..."

Tears spring in Natalie's eyes.

"I know you always saw me as a usurper, Charlie, but I loved your father very much, and I want to fulfill the promise I made. I've booked you a room at the Waldorf. I thought a couple of weeks would be an appropriate amount of time unless you disagree."

"Thank you, it'll be more than enough."

Natalie sticks out a hand.

"Well then I suppose this is it."

Charlie shakes her hand.

"I'm sorry for everything, Natalie. I truly am."

"Goodbye, Charlie."

Natalie shuts the door. Her high heeled shoes click clack back down the hallway. Charlie sighs. He presses the elevator button and rides it to the ground floor. He walks all the way to the Chase bank. By the time he gets there his teeth are chattering. Inside he luxuriates in the bank's warm embrace. At the counter, he presents the key and his temporary passport and an employee takes him down to a large room with a multitude of safety deposit boxes on either wall. At the far end, a woman in a fur coat gives him a furtive glance. He locates his box. He turns the key and pulls it out. He places the box on a waist high table in the middle of the room. Inside it are a white envelope and his father's Patek Phillipe watch. He winds the mechanism and it ticks. He puts it on his wrist and smiles. His father once told him that it was his proudest possession. He opens the envelope. Inside is a handwritten letter.

Dear Charlie:

By the time you read this I'll be long gone. My doctor gives me six months but when she says six months it's never with much conviction. I suspect if I get a couple more I'll be lucky. It is one of my greatest regrets that I'll never be able to lay eyes on you again or hold you in my arms. You are my little boy, my one and only son. If nothing else please know that I love you more than you can possibly imagine.

I apologize that my own efforts in securing your release have fallen so short. Please believe me I have tried with every fiber of my being. Yet despite my own failure, I have this innate sense that you aren't destined to live out the rest of your days in a Saudi prison. Fate will intervene. How I don't know but one day it will. I have set aside a million dollars for you. On the back of this letter I have written the number of the Morgan Stanley brokerage account where it resides. Don't worry, the taxes have been taken care of. It's yours. Go live your life.

I know that over the years we've had our run ins. When your mother died, I wasn't there for you in the way I should have been. It is another regret as are the many years when we didn't speak. I was angry at you, I thought you were throwing your life away when all you were trying to do was find its true purpose, and boy did you find it in Noor. It may sound like a cliché but as your last days approach you realize that love is all that matters. Everything else - work, status, money - it doesn't just pale in comparison, it doesn't bear comparison.

I am proud of you, Charlie. In fact, I don't believe it's possible for a father to be any prouder. You stood by your convictions, followed your heart and put your life on the line for those you love. You are, in short, a man. I am ashamed to say that when the C.I.A. first came to see me, I believed their lies about Noor and went along with their schemes. I thought it was the only way to save your life. However, on reflection, I soon realized that you weren't the type of man to deal drugs nor the type to fall in love with someone who did. I am glad Noor was too smart to fall into their trap, and I know from the once yearly phone call I receive from Mr. Gardener at Langley that she still hasn't.

I'm not a religious man but I pray that the two of you are able to reunite and when you do I just ask that you make a toast to your old man.

I love you, always,
Dad.

Charlie stares at the letter. His hands shake. The last part doesn't make any sense. Charlie wonders if it's nothing but the rantings and ravings of a sick and deluded mind.

Noor's dead.

These last nine years it has been a fact as unassailable as the laws of physics. Charlie grips the sides of the table to steady himself.

Think. How could it possibly make sense?

His mind races back nine years to the moment he was on his knees in the Prince's riding ring. The Prince is holding Malaya's head in his hand. Her eyes are agape, blood drips onto the sand from her severed neck.

"I wanted you to see this," the Prince says. "For this will not only be your fate but Noor's once my son is born. We caught her the moment she stepped off the plane in New York."

All these years Charlie has taken the Prince's word for it.

Why wouldn't I?

But now the situation has changed. He's being asked to choose whom he trusts more. The Prince or his father.

It's not even a contest.

He laughs. The woman in the fur coat glances warily in his direction. He doesn't stop. He finds it impossible to. The woman rams her deposit box back into its slot. She turns the key and scurries from the room. Charlie's laughter accompanies her all the way out onto the street.

PART II

escape

SIX

IVOR SURVEYS THE cave. The ammo boxes, the shredded mattresses, the curled mounds of shit near the back wall.

And these are the fuckers who took down the Twin Towers.

Ivor limps towards the entrance, his cane and false leg clacking along the cave's granite floor like an out of sync snare drummer. He reaches the entrance. Rick Townley waits in his brand new, orange North Face jacket and a University of Wisconsin beanie. His nose and cheeks are rosy pink, his nose a streaming mess. His intermittent coughing creates giant billows of frozen air. He couldn't look less like a field operative. To be fair, until three weeks ago, he was nothing more than an analyst on the Russian desk with a reputation for being a polyglot. Now, after Ivor's intervention, he's halfway towards mastering Pashto and standing at the very epicenter of the world's attention. Townley bends down so Ivor can curl his arm around his neck. Together they shuffle down the steep incline and emerge outside. Ivor withdraws his arm. He might have lost his right leg and balls back in Khartoum but still has his pride. He takes in the sweep of the bombed out plateau.

This must be what no man's land looked like in World War One.

A platoon of Rangers is scouring the pockmarked and

obliterated earth for intelligence.

Shame a battalion of them didn't arrive a week ago to cut off the mountain passes.

"Who knows if bin Laden's even there," the army brass had said.

Oh, he was here all right. Either that or all the captured A.Q. are having the same fucking hallucination.

At the edge of a massive bomb crater, Ivor spies a jihadi on his knees. His wrists are zip tied behind his back and he is babbling away in Arabic to a couple of C.I.A. officers who don't understand a lick of it.

"Tell him to slow down," one of them shouts.

The translator advises the man but it has no effect. The officer kicks the jihadi in the ribs and the jihadi tumbles onto his side. His utterances only become less intelligible.

"Come on," Ivor says to Townley.

They pick their way over. Ivor does his damnedest not to wince as his false leg jars into his stump.

"What's up with this one?" Ivor says.

"Motherfucker's selling us the same line of bullshit," one of the officers says.

He drives his foot into the man's right kidney. The man groans.

"Perhaps that's because he's telling the truth," Ivor says.

The officer grunts. No one here, and certainly no one back in D.C., wants to admit that they've let the entire A.Q. leadership slip through their fingers.

"Fuck him. He's all yours," the officer says.

He and his friend stalk away like a couple of fraternity brothers on a college campus.

"Help me down," Ivor tells Townley.

Townley grips Ivor's arm and Ivor drops onto his solitary knee. Ivor withdraws a flask and offers it to the jihadi. The man gives him a wary look.

"It's okay," Ivor says in Arabic. "It's only water."

The man nods and Ivor lifts the flask up to his lips. The man takes a series of gulps. Ivor stares at him. He's no different from all the rest, his cheeks sunken, his eyes wild, his beard mottled with dirt, his future fucked. The man coughs and Ivor withdraws the flask.

"I'm looking for someone," Ivor says.

"I have already told your friends," the man says. "Bin Laden left days ago. Zawahiri too. To where, I have no clue."

"No, I'm interested in Tariq Khan."

The man's expression falters. Up until now the information he's given he knows is common knowledge.

"I know of no such person," the man says.

"Sure you do," Ivor says. "Afghan. Has only one arm. His sister's married to a Saudi Prince."

"Oh yes, now I recall."

He jerks his head towards the crater.

"He died when they dropped the big bomb. Like so many others."

Ivor thrusts his hand down the man's pants. He grabs a hold of his balls and twists them like he's throttling a chicken. The man squeals. Ivor withdraws his bowie knife with his other hand and slips it down there also.

"This is your last chance to tell me the truth," Ivor says.

The man stares at Ivor wild eyed. Ivor presses the blade up against his balls. The man twists his gaze towards the snow covered peaks behind them.

"I saw him heading towards Pakistan."

"When?"

"Some days ago."

"With the others?"

"No, by himself."

Ivor withdraws his knife. He wipes the blood off on the man's pants and looks up at Townley. To the kid's credit, he looks unfazed by the incident.

You're learning quickly.

"Let's go," he says.

Townley extends a hand and hoists Ivor onto his feet.

"Where now?" Townley says.

"Islamabad."

SEVEN

THE BEDSIDE RADIO clicks on and the newsreader's voice wafts in Noor's direction. The lead story, as it has been for almost a month now, concerns the war in Afghanistan and specifically the failure to track down Osama bin Laden in the mountains of Tora Bora. Noor can't help but be struck by the fact that three months ago the average American couldn't pick out Afghanistan on a map but now they're familiar with such places as Jalalabad and Mazir-Sharif.

Noor switches on her lamp and her gaze settles on the photo of Charlie and Baba. It takes pride of place on her bedside table. Elma had gotten it from Rod, the journalist she'd once had such high hopes of marrying. Charlie is seated on a rug outside their mud hut to the left of Baba. He is grinning in that confident, easy way that Noor found so irritating at the time, his right hand outstretched as he makes a point. Baba, dressed so proudly in his threadbare blazer, is stroking his chin while pensively glancing in the direction of Noor who's out of frame and who, he knows, is furious. At that moment in time Noor had never wanted to lay eyes on Charlie again so long as she lived. However, now she'd give almost anything to see him. Elma has made plain that that's never going to happen. Her sources at the State Department have been emphatic. The Saudis will never release Charlie especially now that the Prince is a member of the Saudi government. Noor refuses to give up hope.

One day it will happen even if we have to wait until I'm eighty and you're eighty-three.

She kisses her middle finger and, as is her routine, places it on Baba and then Charlie.

"I love you," she says.

Noor swings her legs out of bed and pads across her room. She enters the hallway and opens the door across from hers. Her gaze is drawn to the *N'Sync* poster on the far wall. She's still not sure why she allowed Charlotte to put it up. Is it really appropriate for an eight-year-old? Then again is it really appropriate that Charlotte be reading *Harry Potter* or going for a sleepover at Kelly's house where *The Sisterhood of the Traveling Pants* is going to be the main attraction?

These are certainly not concerns Mamaan ever had.

Noor will never forget the day she discovered her unborn child was a girl. When she had first arrived in North Carolina, Elma had given her money for rent and expenses, but Noor soon discovered that everything but the most routine medical care was outside of her budget. The local hospital told her about a free clinic in Asheville so she took the two-hour bus ride there and sat in a waiting room with thirty other uninsured women. It hadn't been until the end of the day that they had been able to see her. The gynecologist performed an ultrasound and smiled.

"I'm happy to tell you your baby's healthy," the gynecologist said. "Would you like to know its gender?"

"I already know, thank you," Noor said.

"Have you chosen a name?"

"Charlie."

"That's cute for a girl."

Noor frowned.

"Except I'm having a boy."

"No, Miss Naipaul, you're having a girl."

The gynecologist swiveled the monitor around. At twenty-six weeks there was no doubting her child's sex and Noor burst into tears.

Noor gazes at Charlotte lying curled up in the fetal position and a surge of parental love flows through her. Charlotte's long, black hair drapes over her pillow and her eyelids quiver as if she's in the midst of an intense dream. Noor hates to wake her. Noor gently shakes her shoulder. Charlotte's eyes open.

"Is it six already?" she groans.

"Actually it's a little past."

"Got it."

Charlotte slumps out of bed and plods to the bathroom. Noor follows in her wake. There they wash themselves and brush their teeth before heading into the living room. The only light comes from the twinkling Christmas tree in the corner. Outside it's still pitch dark. Charlotte goes to the closet. She returns with two small rugs and places them on the floor in the direction of Mecca. They stand before them and raise their hands to their ears.

"Allah-u Akbar," Noor says.

They clasp their hands over their chests and perform two rakahs. Afterwards Noor remains on her knees and asks Allah to keep them safe and to bring Charlie back to her. Noor opens her eyes. Charlotte is kneeling beside her.

"Oatmeal or French toast?" Charlotte says.

"It's cold out. Let's go with oatmeal."

"You got it."

Noor smiles and heads down the corridor to the bathroom. She turns on the shower and undresses. She stares at her naked body in the mirror. It is still slender and lean, due, in no small part, to the five mile runs she does three times a week. She closes her eyes and attempts to remember the night she and Charlie spent together in Riyadh. The way he touched her, the way he kissed her, the way he moved inside her. Her hand wanders, her body tingles and she lets out a soft moan.

"You want orange or grapefruit juice?" Charlotte shouts from the kitchen.

Noor's eyes flash open.

"Orange," Noor shouts back.

"Coming up."

Noor leans against the sink and shakes her head.

Some other time.

Noor showers and gets dressed. When she arrives in the kitchen, a steaming bowl of oatmeal awaits her, along with a tall glass of orange juice.

"You're a superstar," Noor says.

Charlotte grins. Noor sits across from her daughter at their tiny kitchen table. Charlotte attacks her own bowl as if she were an orphan in Oliver Twist.

"So you're really okay with me being Mary in the town pageant?" Charlotte says.

"Of course."

"I just wonder if I'm being hypocritical, that's all."

Hypocritical. Where does she get such words?

"It's not hypocritical," Noor says. "Mary is considered the most righteous woman in Islam. The only woman in fact to have a surah named after her."

"And she was a virgin?"

"Absolutely. We just don't believe Jesus was the son of God. Instead he's one of our greatest prophets."

Charlotte lets her spoon slide back into her bowl.

"What?" Noor says.

"Nothing."

"No, go on, tell me."

"I'm just wondering if I'll ever be able to tell people I'm a Muslim."

Noor takes Charlotte's hand in hers.

"I know it's tough, darling."

"Allah says it's wrong to lie."

"Yes, but He also says you should never throw yourself with your own hands into destruction."

"And if I ever told people we were Muslim we'd be destroyed?"

"I'm never going to let anything happen to you. Ever. But for now that's the way it has to be."

"Tommy Paterson said that Muslims are devil worshippers and that his Dad's got proof."

"Come on, didn't Tommy once tell you that the moon was made of ice and only came out at night so the sun wouldn't melt it?"

Charlotte giggles.

"And from what I hear his father isn't the sharpest tool in the shed either."

"I was so mad I wanted to punch him in the face."

"But you didn't because you're a good Muslim."

"Yet no one knows that."

"Allah does and, trust me, He's the only one that matters."

Charlotte forces a smile and picks up her spoon. Together they finish their breakfast in silence.

"I'll take care of the dishes," Noor says. "You go get dressed."

Charlotte hastens away and Noor carries their two bowls over to the sink. She stares out into their gloomy garden. She gasps. A man is standing inside the thicket of trees that surround their home. Noor holds her breath. He doesn't move but rather continues his silent vigil.

They've found us.

Noor backs away from the window and sprints down the hallway. In her bedroom Charlotte is singing *Bye, Bye, Bye* out of tune. Noor grabs her loaded pistol from her bedside drawer and races back to the kitchen. The man's still there.

Noor unlocks the back door and eases it open. The freezing air bites into her exposed skin. She raises her gun.

"Who are you?" she shouts.

He doesn't reply. She edges across the lawn, her boots crunching in the snow. Noor arrives at the tree line. She forces herself to slow her breathing and aims at his heart.

"I'm not afraid to shoot, you know."

The man mocks her with silence. Noor continues on. Ten feet away she realizes the man is nothing more than a large branch that must have fallen in the night. Its appendages are perfectly proportioned to represent the form of a human being. Noor lowers her gun and breathes easier.

"You know I would've taken you out."

She kicks the branch and it topples to the ground.

We're still safe.

"Mommy. Mommy. Are you out there?"

Noor sticks the gun in the back of her pants and pulls her sweater over it. She heads for the house. Charlotte is standing on the back porch smothered in a puffy jacket, hat and gloves.

"What were you doing?"

"Just thought I'd take a quick walk."

Charlotte frowns.

"You know you're really weird sometimes."

Noor laughs.

"I'll take that as a compliment."

Noor goes to her room and puts on her jacket. She slips the 9mm into the zippered compartment of her purse. Charlotte is waiting for her in the hallway. They head outside past Jimmy's Cadillac and tramp down the driveway. It may be close to freezing but unless it's pouring with rain or blowing a blizzard they always walk. They amble down the hill towards town. Charlotte is never one to be at a loss for words and today she transitions effortlessly between why she believes the skiing's better at Appalachian rather than Sugar

Mountain, why she thinks the students should wear uniforms and what she is going to read to Betty over the holidays.

"I thought I'd start with Anne of Green Gables. Remember how much Betty said she loved it when she was a kid."

Noor forces a smile. It's as if Betty's life has come full circle as it nears its end.

They come around the bend and upon Main Street. It looks like something out of a Frank Capra movie. At its nearest end, on opposite sides of the street, the snow dappled Presbyterian and Episcopal churches eyeball each other while beyond lie a series of mainly two story brick buildings. There are two stop lights, numerous stores filled with idiosyncratic items for the tourists who come in droves at the weekends, an ice cream and fudge store, a smattering of restaurants, a coffee shop and a couple of realtors selling high priced second homes to the banker set from Charlotte. Holiday wreaths adorn old fashioned lampposts and as ever, on days like these, Noor and Charlotte walk down salted sidewalks, the snow packed against the sides of the buildings. On most days Noor and Charlotte would continue on to the gas station at the end of the street. It's unique since its store doesn't just sell chips and soda but also European wines and fine cheeses. It's also the one place in town that sells the New York Times and every morning Noor buys a copy. With Charlotte kicking her heels, Noor will cast her eye over the front page and then flip through the relevant sections and, like a lottery ticket buyer whose numbers don't line up, she will experience momentary disappointment before reminding herself that she was silly to even hope in the first place.

Noor glances at her watch. Her foray into the woods has put them behind schedule.

I'll go at morning recess.

They head down an alley towards the school and enter through its front doors into a cocoon of warm air.

"Love you, Mommy," Charlotte says.

"Love you too darling," Noor says.

A year ago, Charlotte would have given Noor a huge hug and kiss but nowadays she rushes off to her classroom without even a wave. It's a cliché, Noor knows, that children grow up before you know it, but with Charlotte, Noor is more desperate than most parents for her child to stay young. She knows that the older Charlotte gets and the further afield she travels the more danger she'll be in.

There will come a point when I won't be able to protect her anymore.

Despite the claustrophobic heat, Noor shivers. She shoves the unwanted thoughts to the back of her mind and heads for the teacher's lounge. It's packed with teachers who are almost as giddy as the children that winter break is upon them.

"Morning," she says.

"Morning, Indira," their voices ring out.

Noor retrieves the usual assortment of notices that the principal loves to pepper them with and turns to find Jeff Howarth lurking with a steaming mug in his hand.

"I made you coffee, Indira. Cream, no sugar. Just the way you like it."

"That's very thoughtful of you, Jeff. Thank you."

Noor takes the mug and Jeff blushes. Noor looks to make her exit. She learned long ago not to encourage Jeff. However, before she can, Janet Evans barrels over, her prodigious girth blocking Noor's path. She is swathed in a bright green cotton dress that could clothe an elephant if called upon.

"So I heard about the incident," she says.

"What incident?" Jeff says.

"Indira was assaulted."

A couple of the teachers gasp. Jeff looks stricken.

"Now that's not altogether true," Noor says.

"Just like you, Indira, to play things down," Janet says.

"What happened?" Cindy Shepherd says.

Cindy, a pretty mother of two boisterous toddlers, is Noor's best friend amongst the staff. She looks hurt that Janet knows something she doesn't.

"Really," Noor sighs, "it was nothing. I was just running back into town yesterday afternoon when a punk in a pickup threw a Slurpee at me."

"According to Gavin, they nailed you in the back," Janet says.

"Why would they do such an awful thing?" Cindy says.

"Why do you think? They think she's a damn Muslim."

It's comments like these that remind Noor why she loathes Janet so much.

"But that's ridiculous," Jeff says, "Indira's a Hindu."

"But how would they know?" Janet says.

"You're right," Noor says. "Brown people really do all look alike, don't they?"

Janet burns bright red.

"You need to press charges," Cindy says.

"Sadly I didn't get their license plate."

Noor smiles to cover the fact that almost everything she has just said is a lie. To begin with she had been terrified when the pickup had screeched to a halt and reversed in her direction. She was convinced that the Prince's men had finally found her. She had no gun on her, she never did when she was out running, so she scrambled for the woods at the side of the road. Somehow, some way, she had to get to Charlotte before they did. However, before she could reach the tree line, she was struck in the back. She went sprawling and felt an icy cold penetrate her flesh.

So this is what it feels like to be shot, she thought.

She crawled forward on her hands and knees expecting them to deliver a coup-de-grace to the back of head.

"Go back to where you came from, you fucking sand nigger," a man bellowed.

The pickup screeched away and she reached around to discover her back was covered in blue gunk. A Slurpee cup lay nearby. She laughed with relief and trudged into town. There she ran into Gavin Spencer, the youngest member of the town's police force. Her splattered running top was too hard to explain away. Incensed, Gavin was determined to track the men down, however, Noor gave him little to go on despite having registered the pickup's license plate. The last thing she wanted was for the men to be arrested and for there to be any mention of it in the local paper.

Don't create a stir.

It has been her motto ever since she arrived here.

"Sometimes the ignorance in these parts makes me so mad," Jeff says.

"I'm just glad you're all right," Cindy says.

"You're not going to get rid of me that easily," Noor says.

Everyone laughs, Janet Evans perhaps a little too hard. Noor heads to her classroom and arranges paper and crayons on each of the six circular desks. She estimates her morning project will eat up the first hour and a half of the day. After that she will read the class the opening chapter of Stuart Little. She hopes they will be as entranced as she was when Baba read it to her underneath the apricot tree in their garden in Kabul. At the time, she couldn't imagine a more exciting place than New York City, yet now, when she remembers her actual time there, she can only shudder. She wonders whatever happened to the murder investigation of Stephen Erickson.

It's surely a cold case by now.

The first of her first graders traipses in. Noor doesn't even have to turn around to know it's Matthew Grimes. Matthew is always first, his father an ex Marine who views punctuality as one of life's great virtues. Noor knows Matthew is a huge disappointment to his father. He is a sweet, bespectacled child with a vivid imagination. In the school yard he can always be found with his two best friends Susie White and Tammy Judson recreating elaborate fantasies while the other boys alternate between chasing each other around and beating each other up.

"Morning, Matthew," she says.

Noor hears sniffling and turns to discover tears streaming down Matthew's freckled cheeks. She rushes over to him.

"Matthew, what's the problem?"

Matthew is too overcome to get a word out. Noor hugs him to her chest until his sobs die down.

"Daddy's been called up."

For once Noor doesn't know what to say. She imagines for some boys the idea of their father going off to kill evil terrorists would be an exciting development, but in Matthew's view it portends terrible things. Noor can't help but think that Matthew has a more mature outlook than most Americans. For a while after 9/11, America resembled a nervous woman walking home at night. However, now, after the recent successes in Afghanistan, a false bravado has come to the fore and the President is acting like a gunslinger out West.

"I don't want him to go," Matthew says.

"Of course you don't, but he won't be gone forever. He'll come back."

"How can you be so sure? What if one of the bad people kills him?"

How do you answer such a question from a six-year-old?

"Do you love, your dad?" Noor says.

"Lots."

"And do your brother and sisters and mom love him too?"

"Sure do."

"Then that's all he'll need because that love will create a force field around him that will keep him safe."

"That really true?"

"You bet."

Matthew smiles and Noor ruffles his hair. Other students scuttle in. John Wolf, a roly poly bear of a boy with a hearty laugh. Nina Stockman, a pretty blonde with a bossy disposition. Next comes, Teddy Christie, a budding paleontologist who can name two hundred and fifty-nine different dinosaurs, and then Ally Perkins, the class tomboy, who has eleven ferrets at home and accompanies her father on hunting trips throughout the season. The first of the two school bells rings and the dribble of students turns into a flood. By the time the second bell rings every one of Noor's thirty students is sitting attentively at their desk. After they stand and recite the pledge of allegiance, Noor asks each of them for a suggestion as to what they could do to help their parents during the holiday.

"Gut my Dad's deer," Ally says.

A host of groans rise up.

"Not a bad idea, Ally," Noor says. "How about you, Hank?"

"I could open my sister's presents," he says.

"I don't know if that's really helping her."

"But that way she can get to them quicker."

"Perhaps, but how about something else."

Hank screws his face up as if he were solving Pythagoras' theorem.

"I could wipe my butt so my mom don't have to."

The kids roar with laughter. Noor puts up a hand and everyone quiets.

"I think your mom would really appreciate that, Hank," she says.

Noor elicits an answer from every child and has them write it down in the form of a letter to their parents before drawing a picture of it. It takes longer than Noor thought and by the time the recess bell rings most of them have only just finished. The children bundle up in their jackets and rush outside. Noor puts on her own and follows in their wake. However, instead of continuing on into the schoolyard, she slips out the front door. She hustles down the alley and turns down Main Street towards the gas station. She passes Sonny's Grill just as Bert Donahue steps out. Bert wears his usual rumpled suit. It goes perfectly with his rumpled grey hair and rumpled personality.

"Indira, does the principal know you're playing hooky? I wouldn't want to see you get detention."

"And shouldn't you be seeing patients, Bert? I wouldn't want to see you get your license revoked."

"Some days I wish the damn fools would do just that."

"You don't mean that."

"I'm too damn old to be dealing with this town's aches and pains."

"So what's going on in there?"

"It's Friday. The regular meeting of the old codgers' club."

Noor glances inside Sonny's Grill and spies Harrison Morgan, Joe Paley and Ted Harcourt sitting around a table deep in conversation.

"Solving the world's problems, I see."

"Oh, there's no listening to those idiots. I mean Harrison has always been far out on a rightward limb but Joe and Ted, it's astonishing, they think the sun shines out of the President's you know what, and well you know where I stand when it comes to George W."

"Hence your early departure."

"If I had to listen to another word."

Noor smiles. Bert likes to portray himself as the town's sole liberal but what he really is, is the town's premier contrarian. 'If everyone in town voted Democrat,' Betty once said, 'Bert would be a Republican.'

"Are you going to check up on Betty today?" Noor says.

"I'm going by right now. How's she doing?"

"You know Betty, as feisty as ever."

"You just saying that?"

"No, really, when I saw her last night she was up and about. It was almost as if she was back to her old self."

Bert shakes his head.

"Those new fangled cancer drugs she's on," he says, "they are fiendishly deceptive. They trick you, make you think you're on the road to recovery, but they can only mask things for so long before the inevitable occurs."

"You don't think she's got long?"

"I'd be surprised if dear old Betty makes it to two thousand and two."

Noor swallows. For a while now she has been trying to ignore the reality of Betty's situation, but for Bert, of all people, to put it in such stark terms is chilling.

"I'm sorry, Indira ..."

"No, I need to know, if for no other reason than to prepare Charlotte."

"Your little girl's going to be devastated."

"Betty might as well be her grandmother."

"And loves her more than any of her grandchildren that's for sure. Hell, her own sons, much as they care for her in her dying days."

"They have careers, Bert, you know that. It's tough when you don't live close."

Bert grunts again. His opinion of James Jr. and Martin couldn't be much lower. 'A cold blooded lawyer and a Hollywood flake,' is how he usually refers to them. Noor glances at her watch and realizes she has less than five minutes until the end of recess.

"Look Bert, I've got to —"

"No, no, I understand."

Bert wraps his arms around Indira and holds her close. He smells as ever of Old Spice and coffee.

"Did I ever tell you, you were the best damn thing to ever

happen to this town?"

"A thousand times, Bert."

Indira kisses him on the cheek and breaks free.

"Don't get too worked up about the world," she calls out. "Things are never as bad as they seem."

"With that bastard Cheney pulling the strings—"

"Enough, Bert. Now go take care of Betty."

Noor crosses the street and double times it to the gas station. She hustles into the store.

"Morning, Fred," she says to the bearded cashier.

"Oh, darn," he says. "I thought you weren't coming in today, Indira."

"You sold out?"

"All those banker types are up for the holidays. Snatched every last New York Times, the Wall Street Journals too."

"It's fine. I'll get one in Boone later. Look I'm sorry, I got to run. I'll see you tomorrow."

"Don't you worry, I'll set one aside especially for you."

"You better."

Noor scurries out of the store and arrives at the school just as the bell rings. The kids come rushing in and she is swept along the corridor and back to her class. By now their excitement is almost at a fever pitch. It is only two more hours before winter break is upon them. She gathers them around her and reads *Stuart Little*. The boys, especially, squirm and glance out the window looking for their parents. When Noor decides they can barely take it any longer she makes her announcement.

"Before you go off on your Christmas break, there's one last thing. Your presents."

The children's eyes open wide.

"You mean you have one for each of us?" Nina Stockman says.

"I do, but there's a wrinkle. You're going to have to solve a clue to find it."

Noor hands each of them a folded clue and soon the classroom is a mad cornucopia of children running here and there, screaming out in delight when they eventually discover their hidden present. By the time they're all done it's almost time to go.

"Just promise," she says, "to be helpful and kind to your parents this holiday, and I'll see you all in three weeks' time."

"We promise."

The bell rings.

"Merry Christmas," she shouts.

"Merry Christmas," they yell back.

The children sprint from the room. Noor stands at the window and watches as they stream into the arms of their parents. She remembers an earlier time when she looked out another classroom window and saw an ominous black S.U.V. waiting for her with Tariq's cohorts inside. She shivers.

Tariq.

She hasn't thought about him in some time. She wonders where he is and whether he still works for the Prince.

"Sounds like your lot had a blast?"

Noor turns to see Charlotte standing in the doorway. Noor smiles.

"I'm guessing you didn't."

Charlotte rolls her eyes. Nothing more needs to be said about Janet Evans' teaching style.

"Well think about it this way, you only have one more semester before you're in the fourth grade."

"Ugh, that's an eon away."

Only when you're eight years old.

Noor puts on her jacket and grabs her bag. The two of them retrace the route they took that morning. It begins snowing and Charlotte castigates Noor for not taking Jimmy's Cadillac.

"The fresh air will do you good," Noor says.

"Why? It's not like it's any different than the air indoors."

"Well, no, I suppose not technically."

"Then what's so fresh about it?"

"Okay, how about this. The exercise will do you good. It gets your heart beating, circulates the oxygen around your body quicker."

"Then that's what people should say."

"I will make a note to do so from now on."

"It's like Mrs. Evans in class today. She said it was 'hot as hell' and opened a window, but I'm pretty sure that hell's a lot hotter than our classroom, I mean people burn in it to begin with, and anyway how would she know how hot hell is? It's not like she's been there or anyone else has for that matter. Least not anyone who's come back to tell the tale."

"I hope you didn't say all that to her?"

Charlotte fishes in her bag and pulls out a teacher-parent notice.

"I'm sorry but I couldn't help myself."

Noor tries her damnedest to give her daughter a disapproving stare but ends up laughing. She shoves the notice in her pocket.

"You're too damn smart, you know that?"

"And why do people say that? It makes no sense —"

"Oh stop it!"

Charlotte giggles and takes off running.

"Last one home is a rotten egg."

Noor sprints after her daughter. She lets Charlotte get to their front door a second before she does. Charlotte whoops and raises her arms in triumph. Inside they wash and pray. Afterwards they eat a quick sandwich. Noor changes into her running gear while Charlotte puts on her basketball outfit. Ensconced in warm jackets, they get in Jimmy's whale of a Cadillac. As ever it takes three turns of the key before the engine sputters into life. They trundle down Main Street before joining the highway that skirts the edge of town and head down the hill towards Boone. On either side of the highway the steep, pine forested slopes are covered with gleaming snow.

"When we fled from Kabul we travelled through a landscape just like this," Noor says.

Charlotte removes her nose from *The Giver,* her latest book, and glances out the window.

"I'm guessing there weren't billboards in Afghanistan."

"No, nor churches, shacks selling boiled peanuts or The Tweetsie Railroad. But if you erase all those then it was just like this."

Charlotte rests her forehead on her window. Her breath fogs up the glass.

"Were you scared, Mommy?"

"It's been so long I can't really remember but I guess I must've been."

"And sad?"

"Terribly. Mamaan had just died."

"Were you crying?"

"Some of the time I'm sure I was."

Liar. Everyone else was while you took it upon yourself to be strong.

"If you died I don't think I'd ever stop," Charlotte says.

"Well I'm not going to. Not for a long time at least."

"And you won't leave me either?"

"Never."

"Phew, well that's a relief."

Noor catches Charlotte's gaze in the rearview mirror. Charlotte grins and returns to her book. Noor castigates herself for telling Charlotte another lie.

You can't guarantee that. Only Allah knows the time and place of your death.

It is Noor's greatest fear, one that has kept her up countless nights.

What'll happen if I'm in a fatal car accident or diagnosed with a terminal disease?

For a few years Noor had comforted herself with the thought that Betty could step in. However, with Betty not long for this world, that's no longer an option.

I need to think of someone. I can't leave Charlotte to the wolves.

Before Noor knows it, she finds herself pulling into the rec center parking lot, the drive down the hill and through Boone a barely remembered blur.

"Come on, Mommy," Charlotte says. "We're late."

Noor grabs her purse and Charlotte shoulders her basketball bag. They hustle inside. Charlotte spots one of her teammates and they take off towards the basketball court. Noor remembers that she was going to stop at the newsstand on the way. She thinks about slipping out. She decides against it.

You can get it on the way home.

Noor passes the gym just as a young man with a buzz cut and extensive tattoos on his arms comes out. He halts.

"Folks like you shouldn't be allowed in here," he says.

Walk on.

Noor eyeballs the young man.

"Well luckily the great thing about this country is that we are."

"That it's great has nothing to do with you goddamn Muslims."

Noor knows what she needs to do. She needs to tell him he's mistaken, that she's a Hindu and timidly drop her gaze to the floor. Yet, for some reason, she finds herself unable.

"I wouldn't be so sure," she says.

The man laughs.

"Tell me one goddamn thing Muslims have contributed to America."

"Well let's see, in the tenth century a Muslim named Al-Khwarizmi invented algebra and without algebra modern mathematics and science wouldn't exist and without either of those well that cellphone in your hand would certainly not work and nor would most other things you value in your home including that TV set you sit in front of every night and from which I assume you derive your Neanderthal views."

The man reddens. He puffs his chest out and steps towards Noor.

"What the fuck did you say?"

Noor unzips the compartment in her bag in which her gun rests. The man catches sight of it. He freezes.

"You got a permit for that?"

"You better believe I do, and considering your hostile manner and the fact that all of this is being caught on camera, I find it hard to believe that the D.A. will prosecute me for shooting a steroid junkie like yourself."

The man glances at the camera in the ceiling.

"You're all going to hell."

He pushes past Noor and storms outside. Noor continues on to the basketball court. She sits in the bleachers and watches Charlotte's coach put Charlotte and her teammates through a dribbling drill. She keeps glancing at the double doors half expecting the man to return with a cop. Noor doesn't have a concealed weapons permit. The background check was too way extensive for her to risk it.

How could you be so stupid? If you're arrested your whole story will unravel.

Noor looks about and spies Charlotte's basketball bag near a court side bench. She navigates her way down the bleachers past the smattering of parents and hustles over to Charlotte's bag. She kneels down and slips the 9mm into one of Charlotte's zippered compartments. She shoves one of Charlotte's spare basketball vests on top of it and zippers it closed. She returns to her former position and waits.

What came over you?

Noor isn't sure. After all everything she has done these last eight-and-a-half years has been in the service of staying under the radar.

You don't make waves.

Two years ago, for instance, the school had won an award from the state of North Carolina and the local paper sent a journalist over who insisted on taking a photo of the proud faculty. Immediately Noor feigned a stomach ache and made her escape. Janet Evans was rather pleased, Cindy later told her, that Noor hadn't been featured in the paper but Noor was even more so.

Don't create a stir. That's your motto. Yet this afternoon you took it upon yourself to create one. A massive one.

The double doors creak open and Noor swings her head in their direction. To her relief it turns out to be a teammate of Charlotte's and her father.

Perhaps I'm tired of being invisible.

Perhaps you are, a second voice inside of her replies, *but this is about Charlotte, not you. It's always been.*

But what kind of role model am I if what I'm teaching her is to cower and submit.

Trust me she would be doing a lot more cowering and submitting in Saudi Arabia.

Noor stops arguing her case. She knows she's beaten. She watches Charlotte and her teammates do a lay up drill. When it's Charlotte turn, Charlotte furrows her brow and drives in and shoots a basket. Charlotte has luckily inherited her mother's tall, lean figure rather than the short, pudgy one of her father. Charlotte sinks it.

"Nice shot, Charlotte," the coach shouts out.

Charlotte grins. As soon as she gets to the end of the re-bound line, she and a teammate break into animated conversation. Noor knows there isn't a chance in hell that Charlotte would be doing this in Saudi Arabia even if the Prince was a rational man. No, she's at the age when she would be split from any contact with the men outside her immediate family and discussions about whom she would marry would already have already begun.

Charlie sacrificed his freedom so Charlotte could be free to do things like this. The least you can do is sacrifice your ego.

For the rest of the practice, Noor sits uneasily in the bleachers, counting down the minutes until practice is over. The coach gathers the girls around for one final word and Noor once more navigates her way down the bleachers so she can snatch her daughter's basketball bag before Charlotte can get to it. Charlotte races over to her.

"Can I stay a little longer and shoot hoops with Stacy?"

"I wish you could, my love, but we've got to get going. Betty's expecting us."

Charlotte rushes back to give a couple of friends a hug, and she and Noor make their way out of the rec center. At the front entrance Noor does a quick survey of the parking lot and hustles Charlotte to their car. She turns the ignition. Once, twice, three times. The engine roars and she speeds away before Charlotte's even put on her seatbelt.

"Whoa, slow down, Mommy."

Noor glances in her rearview mirror to see if the idiot is following them. It's not easy. Since they arrived it has begun to snow even harder and the vehicles behind are tough to make out in the blaze of headlights. When Noor first came to town she would look in her mirrors constantly, convinced that the Prince's men had somehow tracked her down. Every S.U.V. with tinted windows seemed a threat, every car that stayed behind her for more than a couple of miles she would let pass. It's why she got Betty to teach her to shoot and, once she outgrew Betty's limited instruction, why she became a regular at the local shooting range. Yet this afternoon she doesn't spy anyone and soon they are heading back up the highway towards Blowing Rock.

Noor glances in her rearview mirror. Charlotte is deep into her book. When Noor had first arrived her skin color and subsequently her daughter's had been somewhat of a curiosity to the locals. After all Watauga County was ninety-seven percent white and its remaining denizens were mostly black or Native American. But now, after 9/11, their color represents something sinister. Not to Betty or Bert or the teachers or anyone who knows them well, which Noor must admit means nearly everyone in Blowing Rock. However, Noor has noticed, that too often when she journeys into Boone, strangers will give her a second glance. After so many years of feeling secure, Noor has begun worrying for her daughter's safety.

We're vulnerable again.

They drive along Main Street and past their tiny home and continue all the way up to the very top of the hill where they park in front of Betty's house. It is a magnificent white wooden affair with tall bay windows, a wrap around porch and a lawn out front that falls sharply away. On most days you can look out over tens of miles of blue and purple tinged mountains. It's as if Betty lives at the very top of the world. However, right now, the Blue Ridge Mountains are obscured by thick clouds and swirling snow.

"You really want to run in this?" Charlotte says.

"It's not so bad," Noor says.

Another lie. It's going to be miserable.

However, Noor knows she needs to ease the tension within her soul. They head inside through the front hall and the living room with its gargantuan Christmas tree. In previous years there would be stacks of wrapped Christmas presents underneath it. Betty couldn't just give you one present. She had to give you at least ten. However, this year they are few and far between. Betty's illness had nixed any shopping outings. They enter the kitchen and find Martha, Betty's caregiver, slicing potatoes.

"Is Betty awake?" Noor says.

"She just hollered asking where the hell the two of you were," Martha says.

"Guess I better go see her," Charlotte says.

Charlotte sprints from the room.

"Tell her I'll be right there after my run," Noor shouts after Charlotte

Noor looks back at Martha.

"You okay?" she asks.

"Go. I think I can just about handle the two of them."

Noor leaves the warm confines of Betty's house and starts down the hill. It's not long before she is back on Main Street. She passes a couple of parents. They shout out greetings and Noor holds up a hand in acknowledgement. She passes the gas station and turns up the road to Grandfather Mountain. She comes to the stone walled entrance to Bass Lake and strides down its steep drive to the car park below. There she joins the path around the lake. The snow drives into her face. She peers out across the frozen expanse of ice towards the other side of the lake. On most days there's at least someone walking their dog. However, no one is out today.

No one, but you, would be such an idiot.

Noor forges on to the lake's earthen dam. The wind slams into her, and like a pilot caught in turbulence, she fights to maintain a steady course. Once past, Noor turns away from the path and crosses a bridge that spans a small stream. She enters a wood filled with tall, denuded trees. The wind dies down and the snow flurries drop away. Noor forces herself up the gradual incline. Two miles in she comes to a clearing in which a wooden apple barn stands. Every time she sees it she can't help but shiver. Betty had once told her that a man had hung himself in it one winter and his desiccated body wasn't found till the following spring. The snow once more has the opportunity to lash into her. She knows she has two options. To the left is a short trail that will take her back to the lake. To the right is another that edges ever higher until it finally reaches Moses Cones' mansion at the very top of the hill. It's an extra four miles.

Screw it.

Noor takes the second path and powers on. She is now in an almost meditative trance. The trees whip by and her feet kick up a trail of fallen leaves. Once more the trees fall away. Ahead the usually imperious manor of Moses Cone, the one-time textile magnate, with its sweeping verandah and high windows stands like a huddled vagrant desperate for relief from the relentless deluge. Noor quickens her pace. She realizes she has miscalculated. She has half an hour of light left and still has a good three miles to go. On the other side of the manor, the trail becomes enveloped in trees. Noor stretches her legs out and descends to the road below. She runs back into town and makes the turn down Main Street. The snow has chased away the last shoppers and the side-walks glow like golden blankets under the luminous street lamps.

"Indira," someone shouts behind her.

Noor jolts out of her runner's trance and looks back. A man is running towards her with his right arm raised. She thinks about bolting away only to decide that a crazed killer is unlikely to have used her first name. The man gets close enough that she can make him out. It's Fred, the clerk from the gas station.

"I thought that was you," he says.

Fred pants so hard he might as well have done the same nine mile run as Noor.

"When I was cleaning up I found this," he says.

He hands Noor a snow drenched copy of the New York Times.

"For some reason, it was muddled up with some unsold copies of the Charlotte Observer."

"You're a savior."

"I know how much you like reading it."

Noor wraps her arms around Fred's sizable girth and kisses his bearded cheek.

"You're a true friend, Fred."

Fred blushes and before she embarrasses him any further, Noor turns tail and carries on up the hill, the newspaper rolled up in her right hand like a baton. The last half mile is ugly. The pause has halted Noor's momentum and her legs suddenly feel as if they are lathed out of wood. Noor staggers through Betty's front door and heads for the kitchen. She places the New York Times on the counter and grabs herself a glass. She goes over to the sink and downs three glasses of water. A wave of warmth floods her body. She's exhausted and never felt so good. Martha enters from the laundry room carrying a basket of folded clothes.

"I was about to file a missing person's report."

Noor grins. She glances upstairs.

"Those two still at it?"

"Like a pair of thieves."

Noor struggles up the stairs. She arrives at the doorway to Betty's bedroom to find Charlotte lying next to Betty chatting away. Betty's once plump figure looks particularly shriveled tonight, her curly gray hair now a shock of white. Charlotte knows that Betty is ill but she has no clue that she's going to be gone so soon.

Oh, how am I going to break it to her?

Betty spots Noor. Noor smiles.

"Charlotte tells me she's going to be an astronaut one day. And not any old astronaut but one that travels to Mars."

"The moon's so boring," Charlotte says. "There's nothing there."

"Mars is a long way away," Noor says.

"Do you think Christopher Columbus said that when he went searching for America?"

"I think he was searching for India."

"Well he found America."

"And no I don't think he did, but his mother sure did."

Charlotte groans and slides off the bed.

"Can I watch TV?"

"Just a little and then we're off home."

Charlotte races from the room only to run back in and give Betty a kiss on the cheek.

"I love you," she says.

Charlotte rushes away. Noor takes her spot on the bed. Betty is still glowing from the unexpected kiss.

"That girl's going to achieve whatever she puts her mind to. My only regret is I won't be around to witness it."

"Don't be morbid," Noor says.

"You know, as well as I do, that I'm not long for this world. I'm just thankful that God's allowed me these last eight years."

"Now you're being sentimental."

"I'm allowed to be. I'm old."

"And forgetting how great all those other years were."

"I'm not saying they weren't. They were fabulous. It's just with Charlotte, I have this incredible hope that things might turn out all right for humanity. Believe me, when you're staring death in the eye that's a blessing like no other."

"Well I thank God every day that I found you."

"I sure was a mess the day you met me."

"You had every right to be. Jimmy had just died."

"Sobbing at the fruit and vegetable section of the Food Lion, those teenage cashiers gawking at me like I'd escaped from the local nut house."

"Well to be fair you have always been a little nutty."

"Give me one example."

"Your driving lessons."

"All right, I admit they weren't by the book."

"By the book! You made me drive down the Parkway my very first lesson."

"And by the end you had mastered the basics."

"We ended up in a ditch."

"You took your eyes off the road."

"Because you lit up in the car."

"I'm sorry, Indira, but you've always been such a puritan when it comes to cigarettes and alcohol."

"And how about those shooting lessons here on the front lawn?"

"A free citizen should be entitled to fire a gun on their own property."

"Not if stray bullets have a chance of hitting someone down the hill."

"They didn't hit anyone."

"One when right through Bert Donahue's toilet window."

"Serves the damn man right for sitting on it so long. Besides if you hadn't missed the target—"

"It was my first lesson."

"Well all I can say is thank God you've improved."

"A little."

"Oh, Indira, why do you always have to be so damn modest? I doubt there's a better shot in Watauga County."

"I think Gareth Perkins might have something to say about that."

"I'll lay a thousand-dollar bet that you could beat that hill billy in a one on one."

Noor laughs.

"Oh, it'll be wonderful," Betty says. "The whole town will come out to watch. You've got to do it. Just make sure to tell me about it when you visit my grave."

"There you go again."

"Oh come, Indira, if there's one thing we don't do it's lie to each other. This cancer's got me good. You know it, Bert knows it and the good Lord sure as hell does."

Noor attempts a smile but fails to muster one. Betty's right. They don't lie to each other. In fact, Betty is the only person Noor's ever entrusted with her true story.

"I don't know where I'd be without you," Noor says.

"Nonsense all I did was help give you a leg up."

"You paid for my teaching degree, gave me Jimmy's car, kept my secrets and allowed me to pour my heart out endless nights—"

"And you gave me purpose. Trust me, I would've shriveled up in this gargantuan house without you and Charlotte's presence."

Noor wipes away a tear.

"Oh, stop it," Betty says. "You can have a good old cry when I'm gone but not a moment before. Now help me up."

Betty uses all her remaining strength to sit up straight. Noor puffs up her pillow and places it behind her back to make her comfortable.

"That good?"

Betty catches her breath and smiles.

"Much better."

Betty takes Noor's hands in hers.

"Now there's something I want to talk to you about and I want you to keep your mouth shut till I've said my piece."

"If this is another attempt—"

"Just listen to me, will you?"

Noor purses her lips.

"Believe it or not, this isn't about you, it's about Charlotte. She needs a man in her life."

"You proposing she be a child bride—"

"Oh, don't be absurd, what I'm saying is that every girl needs the guidance of a father figure and up till now all she's had is a gaggle of women clucking around her."

"I'm surprised she's managed to survive at all."

"Don't be obtuse."

"And don't be old fashioned. That's the kind of argument I'd expect from an uneducated mullah, not you."

Betty's withered face creases.

"I'm sorry, Betty, I didn't mean that, but don't think I haven't gone back and forth on this ad nauseam. Wouldn't it be better to find a good man, even one I don't love, so if anything were to happen to me at least Charlotte would be taken care of. But what I came to realize is that the greatest gift I can give her, that you've given her, is the conviction that she must always stay true to who she is, and if I gave up on Charlie I might as well throw that lesson out the window."

"But he's not coming back, Indira. He never will."

"I don't care. I'll love him till the day I die, just like you loved Jimmy, and I'm never going to betray that."

"Well at least I can go to my grave knowing I tried."

"You've more than tried. This has been a four-year long campaign."

"The same length as the civil war."

"And what I'm Ulysses Grant and you're Robert E. Lee?"

Betty laughs.

"I damn well hope not. Now one last thing, before he died, Jimmy put most of our wealth and the house in a trust for the boys. I loved the man to death but he was of a certain generation who believed such decisions were the husband's prerogative. That said there's always been an account that has been solely under my control, and I've instructed Mr. Aldridge, my attorney, that the money be put in a trust for Charlotte with you and him its trustees."

Noor' eyes water.

"Oh, Betty—"

"What did I say about tears. Now there is enough in there to pay for Charlotte's college and, if managed properly, for a modest down payment on a house as well. That little girl's my hope for the future. All I ask is that you make sure she gets there so she can effect it."

"I promise I will."

Betty pats Noor's hand.

"Good. Now be a dear, and help me back down."

Noor pulls Betty's pillow away and with a hand on her back lowers her until she is in a prostrate position. Noor plumps the pillow and places it underneath Betty's head. Noor lies down beside Betty and stares into her rheumy eyes.

"I don't want to lose you. I've lost so many people I was close to. Mamaan, Baba, Charlie …"

"And every time you've dusted yourself and kept on."

"It's so exhausting."

"It's not easy, I'll grant you that, but life is but a series of phases. For goodness sake look at us. Jimmy was only three weeks passed when I ran into you."

"So what's my next phase?"

"Only the Lord knows, but I have a sense that it's going to be glorious. Now come give me a hug."

Noor nestles her head on Betty's bony chest. Betty strokes Noor's hair as if she were a child.

"I know it's a terrible thing to say, but I love you more than either of my sons. It's the truth."

"And I love you."

"You better."

Noor clings to Betty and soon Betty's breathing moderates. Noor knows she should get Charlotte home but for a while she clings to Betty. Finally, she extricates herself and slips away. Downstairs in the living room Charlotte is asleep in front of the TV. Martha enters from the kitchen.

"I'm sorry," Noor says, "I didn't mean to keep you up."

"No, I understand. It was the same with my mom. You want to eke out every last moment you have with them."

Noor lifts Charlotte's mumbling form off the couch and carries her to Jimmy's car. Martha follows in her wake. She holds out the New York Times.

"I assume you want this," she says.

Noor grabs the now crinkly newspaper.

"Don't know what you see in it," Martha says. "It's just full of liberal nonsense."

"You've spent way too long around Betty. You know that?"

Martha laughs. Noor gets in the car and drives away. Back home, she carries Charlotte to her bed and gazes at her daughter's peaceful face.

"Don't head off to Mars too soon."

Noor kisses Charlotte's forehead. She returns to Jimmy's car and retrieves the newspaper, her purse and Charlotte's basketball bag. She takes out the gun and places it in her bedside drawer. She heads to the bathroom and showers and once clad in a set of plaid pajamas she wanders into the living room. She takes in the Christmas tree, the cheap furniture and old appliances, the second hand computer they bought at a yard sale the previous summer. They have A.O.L. and the ability to search but Noor has never once looked up Charlie's name. She had read an article that the government could trace your searches and she always feared that the Saudis might be able to track her down if she made even one innocuous search. Noor gets out her prayer rug and prays. By the time she finishes she is almost drifting off.

Noor struggles to her feet and heads down the corridor. She pokes her head into Charlotte's room. Charlotte sucks on her thumb in the identical way she did when she was a baby. Noor closes the door and retreats to her bedroom. She gets in her bed and takes in the photo of Charlie and Baba.

"Night guys."

She switches off the lamp only to turn it on again.

The Times.

Noor slides out of bed. The newspaper lies in the front hall next to Charlotte's basketball bag. She carries it back to bed and scans the front page headlines. None of them pertain to Charlie.

They never do.

With a practiced ease, she flips to the World section. She drags her gaze over its first page, then its second and finally its third. Right at the bottom there's a headline.

'American Prisoner Released By Saudis.'

Noor's heart skips a beat. She closes her eyes and reopens them certain that what she just saw was a hallucination. The headline hasn't changed. She continues reading.

'RIYADH — An American prisoner was repatriated to the United States yesterday after receiving a royal pardon from Crown Prince Abdullah. Charlie Matthews, 34, was convicted on drug smuggling charges nine years ago, and at the time was sentenced, amidst much outcry in the United States, to a life sentence and two hundred and fifty lashes. It is thought that his early release is one of a number of measures aimed at improving Saudi Arabia's image in the United States.'

Noor stares at the newspaper unable to fashion a thought. Eventually one pushes its way through.

I need to find him. Right away.

EIGHT

CHARLIE LETS THE warm water cascade down his back. He's been in the shower for at least half an hour. He wonders if The Waldorf has any way of monitoring its guests' usage and if an irate manager is marching down the corridor towards his room right this second. Yet he isn't worried about being thrown out. He's already decided to leave.

Yesterday afternoon, Charlie had felt like the king of New York. At Morgan Stanley, an unctuous, young banker had ushered him into a conference room and pitched him all sorts of investment products. Charlie didn't ask a single question. Instead he beamed as the same words repeated over and over in his head.

Noor is alive. Noor is alive.

Charlie allowed the banker to shift a quarter of his portfolio into a set of funds whose names sounded like a collection of Greek Gods and then asked for a thousand dollars in cash and a temporary checkbook. He had glided back to The Waldorf oblivious to the cold. After checking in he had taken a detour to Sir Harry's, the bar right off the main lobby. There he had ordered a Jack Daniels and toasted Noor. After one glass he was tipsy, after two he was drunk and by the time he had downed his third, the tables around him were spinning quicker than the horses on the Bryant Park carousel. He has no recollection of how he got to his room. Two hours ago he had woken up on the floor with a splitting headache that was way worse than any lashing he had received at Buraydah Prison. He had crawled to the phone and begged room service to bring up a bottle of Advil and a selection of toiletries. At the time he had castigated himself for having gotten so drunk, but now he considers it a blessing.

It was the fastest way to make me face reality.

The reality is that Charlie has no way of locating Noor. After all, if the combined talents of the C.I.A. and the Saudi General Intelligence Directorate haven't been able to track her down, how the hell will he? No, the only way they might reunite is if Noor comes looking for him, and Charlie knows that's a recipe for disaster.

Right now I'm a big fucking hook and the Prince will reel Noor in the moment she bites.

Charlie steps out of the shower and leans against the counter. He stares at his long hair and ragged beard. In the hotel bar he had seen a C.N.N. report on John Walker Lindh, the American Taliban, and right now a stranger would be hard pressed to tell the difference between them. He takes a pair of scissors and snips away at its scraggly tufts. He lathers his face and uses every one of the ten disposable razors room service delivered to rid himself of his facial hair. He stares at his gaunt, leathery and now bloodied face.

"She wouldn't recognize you anyway," he says. "Hell, I hardly recognize you."

He brushes his sorry teeth and administers the first spray of deodorant to his armpits in over nine years. He pads back into his room. The only clothes he has to wear are the ones he was handed in Riyadh. At J.F.K. airport he will rectify that state of affairs. He puts them on and sinks to his knees. He prays the same prayer he recited every morning in Buraydah then asks God to give him the strength to walk away and never look back. He hasn't decided where he'll go but it will be out west. There he will travel along the coast until he finds a small town where he can rent a one bedroom and reacquaint himself with American life.

Who knows, perhaps I'll even learn to surf.

Charlie wanders over to the window. Down below on Park Avenue, yellow cabs have emerged from their pre-dawn hibernation, their blasting horns a riposte to anyone that's still asleep.

It's time to go.

Charlie makes his way to the door. The phone rings. He turns and stares at it. It rings a second time. He can't help but be drawn to the writing desk. He picks up the receiver.

"Hello."

"Charlie?" a woman says.

Charlie recognizes the voice but can't place it.

"Yes."

"Are you familiar with the Alice In Wonderland statue in Central Park?"

"Of course."

"I'll meet you there in an hour."

The woman hangs up just as Charlie realizes who she is.

***

CHARLIE LEANS AGAINST one of the statue's bronze toadstools and hugs himself. Why he hadn't bought any clothes yesterday he'll never know. At this time in the morning the park is almost deserted. The morning joggers have returned to their apartments while the nannies and stay-at-home moms are yet to arrive with their children and three hundred dollar strollers. Charlie stares down the flight of steps to the boating pond beyond. As a child his mother would bring him here on summer days and as she lounged on one of the benches with a book, he would kneel at the water's edge and guide his motorized gunboat between the model sailing boats, their elderly owners snarling at him if he passed too close to theirs. There are no boats on the grey waters of the pond today and only one elderly man. He wears a greatcoat and is scanning the apartment buildings on Fifth Avenue with a pair of binoculars.

"Charlie."

Charlie turns to find Elma standing there. Her face is fuller than when she lived in Peshawar, her gaze less piercing. She wears a long red woolen jacket, stylish grey pants and a pair of black leather boots. It is a far cry from the last time he saw her in Ivor's bed, a bed sheet held tight to her naked body. Charlie detects a certain shock in her eyes.

"I lost some weight since you last saw me," he says.

Elma jolts out of her trance.

"Were you followed?" she says.

A middle aged couple in burly jackets and Chicago Bears baseball caps meander around the statue. The husband takes out a camera and snaps some photos.

"I don't know," Charlie says.

The wife rubs the forehead of the Mad Hatter.

"Morning," she says.

The hairs on Charlie's forearms rise. Her accent sounds more New Jersey than Midwest.

"Let's walk," Elma says.

They head down the steps and make their way past the elderly man.

"What are you doing here?" Charlie says.

"Noor asked me to find you."

"You spoke to her?"

"We've been in contact. She wants me to take you to her."

Charlie's heart quickens.

"How can I trust you?" he says. "You betrayed us."

"It's the biggest regret of my life. I'm eternally sorry."

Charlie detects tears in Elma's eyes. He steals himself. If there's one thing he's always suspected about Elma Kuyt it's that she's a superlative actress.

"Noor came to me when she arrived in America," Elma says. "I helped her escape and set up a new life."

"Where?"

"I can't say. Not here."

"And her son?"

"Please, Charlie, I'll tell you more at the appropriate time."

Charlie feels a weight press down on his chest.

Of course.

He shivers and leans over as if he were a runner catching his breath.

"She's found somebody, hasn't she?" he says.

"No. She's waited all these years for you."

Charlie stares up at Elma. Tears now glisten in his own eyes. His tears turn to sobs. Elma takes him by the arm and guides him over to a bench. Elma puts an arm around his bony shoulders and the agony of the previous nine years pours out of him. The middle-aged couple give him a weird look and move on. The elderly man is oblivious. After a while Charlie quiets.

"You know when Noor first arrived in New York," Elma says, "she came to this very spot. It's one of the reason I chose it. She was scared, alone, she could feel the net closing in on her, yet she resolved to never give up. Not on life and not on you. Trust me, Charlie, I haven't been an ally of yours. On a number of occasions I've counseled her to find a new man but she's always been steadfast. 'I'm going to wait for him, Elma, even if I have to wait until I'm eighty and he's eighty-three.'"

"She's always been stubborn."

"She certainly has."

Charlie sits up straight. The elderly man's binoculars are twirling in an arc. Above the tree line Charlie catches sight of a grey hawk circling in the air. The hawk lands on the stone ledge of an apartment building.

"That's Pale Male," Elma says. "He's been nesting there for over a decade."

"With the same mate?"

"No, unlike Noor, I don't think he believes in true love."

Charlie chuckles. The elderly man hobbles away, his vigil complete.

"I can't see her, Elma. It's too dangerous. You know that as well as I do."

"Don't worry, I have a plan. I promise. It's full proof."

Elma hands Charlie a slip of paper.

"This is where we'll meet. At three o'clock this afternoon."

Charlie registers the address.

"Now tell me," she says, "did you buy those utterly inadequate clothes yourself or did the Saudis give them to you?"

NINE

CHARLIE UNDOES HIS Benetton shirt and drops it on the floor. He sits on the bed and takes off his leather moccasins, now sodden from the slushy Manhattan sidewalks. He turns them over and stares at their scuffed heels.

Could a tracking device really be implanted in one of them?

Elma had definitely thought it plausible. She also viewed his clunky belt buckle as highly suspect. He's tempted to investigate but Elma had advised him not to.

"Don't let them know we're onto them."

Charlie undoes his belt and stands. His pants slide to the floor. Next come his boxer shorts and socks. He glances at his naked body in the mirror and is reminded of photos he'd seen back in high school of American P.O.W.s who'd been liberated from Japanese war camps. Charlie looks away. There's no time now for either self-disgust or self-pity. He bends down and picks up a Macy's shopping bag. He upends it and clothes spill onto the bed. He selects a pair of Christmas tree boxer shorts, a pair of blue jeans, a white collared shirt, a beige woolen sweater, a red Patagonia waterproof jacket and a pair of tan Timberland boots. He puts them on and grabs a small dark green backpack off the floor. In one of its pockets is an additional twenty-five thousand dollars he withdrew earlier from Morgan Stanley. He packs the remainder of his clothes into the bag as well as his toiletries. He lifts it up and a spasm shoots up his back. He waits for the pain to subside.

Fuck, I'm a mess.

With the backpack on he takes a last look at the room and the clothes he's left behind. If there really is a tracking device in any of them, he hopes the Saudis will think he's taking a rest.

Charlie exits his room and glances up and down the corridor. No one's there. He hustles towards the elevators and presses the down button. An elevator arrives and its doors open to reveal a middle-aged woman in a long fur coat.

Could she be one of them?

He steps in beside her and stares straight ahead. The elevator descends. It stops on the ninth floor for a couple with a raucous toddler and on the fifth floor for an Arabic looking man in a sharp suit. Charlie's stomach turns. The man catches Charlie's gaze and nods at him. Charlie focuses on the panel. The elevator arrives in the lobby and Charlie bolts out. Rather than heading towards the main entrance and Park Avenue, Charlie heads deeper into the hotel until he comes to the elevators to its residential towers. He presses the down button and looks back. None of the occupants of his elevator are coming his direction.

Good.

The elevator dings and its doors open. Charlie steps inside and hits the button for the garage.

"Would you be so kind as to hold the elevator?" a man calls out in a British accent.

Charlie spies a bespectacled man in a beige trench coat striding towards him. The doors close. The man sticks a foot in and they spring open.

Damn.

The man steps in beside Charlie.

"Sorry about that," Charlie says.

The man musters the barest of smiles. The doors close once more.

Don't Brits call elevators lifts?

The man stares ahead, his back ramrod straight as if he were on a parade ground. The elevator descends one story to the covered garage. Charlie steps out and hurries past a line of waiting cabs and limos. He arrives at the exit to 49th Street. He glances over his shoulder. The man in the trench coat is staring after him.

Shit.

Charlie darts around the corner. A woman is getting out of a cab. Charlie barges down the sidewalk and slips inside it before she has time to close the door. He slams it shut.

"Union Square," he says.

The Bangladeshi driver accelerates into traffic and crosses Park Avenue just before the light turns red. Charlie lays his backpack on the seat beside him and swivels around to see if anyone is following them. It's impossible to tell. A pack of yellow cabs seems to be in pursuit. The cab turns down Fifth Avenue towards the Empire State Building. Charlie takes a couple of twenty dollar bills from his bag and hands them to the driver.

"Drop me as close to the subway entrance as you can."

"You got it, boss."

The driver presses down on the accelerator. Charlie sits coiled in the backseat. Up ahead he glimpses the spiked apex of the Empire State Building. They pass by the New York Public Library with its two marbled lions, past Madison Square Park and the Flatiron Building, which his mother always insisted was her favorite building in the whole of New York. All the way down Fifth Avenue, American flags hang from every building, competing in these patriotic times for attention with the numerous Christmas displays.

Almost there.

The cab takes a left on 14th Street and approaches the heaving expanse of Union Square. Charlie spies the green domed entrance to the subway.

"Closest I can get you is right here," the cabbie says.

"Perfect."

The cab lurches to a halt. Charlie grabs his backpack and jumps out. He darts across 14th Street and through the crowds to the subway entrance. Charlie descends the stairs two at a time. In the vast, archaic ticket hall he maneuvers through the seething mass of humanity. At the turnstile he takes out a ticket he bought earlier and swipes it. He breaks into a run for the southbound N. Over the hum of the crowd and the incongruent melodies of a couple of buskers, he hears a train approaching. He makes it to the gangway and sees the train on the platform below. He bounds down a second set of stairs and dives into the nearest carriage. The doors close only to burst open again for a stringy haired college student. The doors close. The student glances in Charlie's direction and looks away.

Fuck. Could he be?

Charlie grabs a hold of a steel bar and stares at his wild-eyed reflection as the train rattles into a darkened tunnel. They stop at 8th Street and Prince Street. At neither stop does the student get out. Rather he has found a seat and has his head bent all the way back. The train continues on. Its brakes screech. The white tiled walls of Canal Street station burst into view. The doors clunk open.

Wait. Wait. Wait.

Charlie glances at the student. He's still staring at the ceiling.

Now.

Charlie leaps from the train. He sprints for the exit. The doors close and the train continues on. At the turn he looks back. The student is making his way down the platform.

You got to be kidding.

Charlie races for the stairs. He bounds up them skirting a saxophone playing busker and bursts out into the chaos and pungent smells of Chinatown.

Don't stop.

Charlie sprints across Lafayette Street. A cab horn blares. He dives into a souvenir shop selling all manner of Chinese knickknacks and throws his backpack to the ground. He wrestles his red jacket off and turns it inside out. He puts it back on, its black inner layer now on the outside. An old Chinese woman approaches him.

"Can I help you?" she says.

"Just looking," Charlie says.

Charlie stares out the window. He sees the student emerge from the station. The student turns in a circle. Charlie steps back. He waits and looks again. The student has his back to him. Charlie sees a pack of tourists about to pass. He slips out of the store and mingles amongst them until he comes to the second entrance to Canal Street Station. He leaps down its stairs and takes off for the northbound platform. When he gets there he finds a small crowd waiting for the train. He makes his way to the far end of the platform.

Come on. Come on.

He looks back expecting the student to emerge at any moment. The train arrives. He slips into the furthest most carriage. No one else boards. The train speeds north. Every minute or so it stops at a station and Charlie watches those getting on. No one seems suspicious. They pass Union Square, 23rd Street, 28th Street and 34th Street. Charlie thinks of getting off at 42nd Street. He glances at his father's watch. Twenty to three.

You still have time.

He decides to wait one last stop. The train pulls into 49th Street and he steps off immersing himself in the throng heading for Times Square. When he emerges it feels oddly familiar. The same neon signs flash the names of the same multinational brands while the same crowds of tourists crane their necks and take photos. He works his way south hoping, in the unlikely event that someone is still following him, to get lost in the crowd. He looks over his shoulder. On a jumbo screen below a gargantuan Budweiser bottle, Donald Rumsfeld is giving a news conference. Everywhere American flags are in evidence, from the scaffolding over a new Toys R Us to the vast neon flag shining bright over the scrolling NASDAQ ticker. Beneath the ticker, a group of earnest twenty-somethings stand in a line. Dressed in black, they wear paper face masks and have placards hanging over their chests that read 'Our grief is not a cry for war.' Charlie can't help but think that their plea might have come a little too late.

He cuts down 46th Street and heads past the Rodgers Theatre. An ambulance comes wailing past. He cuts down the canyon that's 8th Avenue with its electronic goods and smut stores. He keeps up a brisk pace. He can feel his heart beating out his chest. He glances at a clock in a store front window. Two minutes past three.

Shit, I'm late.

He sprints, his backpack bouncing against his back. He cuts down 39th Street. A yellow cab is parked at the far corner. The passenger door flies open. He dives in and slams the door shut behind him.

"Let's go," Elma says to the driver.

The cab turns onto Ninth Avenue and veers right. It swings around the ramp for the Lincoln Tunnel and soon they are within its eerie confines. Charlie turns to Elma.

"Were you followed?" he says.

"If I was, I lost them," she says. "You?"

"The same."

Elma smiles.

"Then the hard part's over."

Charlie slumps back in his seat.

It's only taken nine years.

TEN

"WHERE'D YOU LIKE me to drop you?" the cab driver asks.

"The gas station's fine, thanks," Charlie says.

The cab pulls up under the stone walled eave. Charlie fishes in his backpack.

"How much did we say again?"

"Two hundred dollars."

Charlie hands the driver three one hundred dollar bills. The driver beams.

"That's mighty kind of you."

The driver jumps out and opens Charlie's door. Charlie steps out into the biting cold.

"You sure this is okay?" the driver says. "I'd be glad to take you to your final destination."

"No, this is perfect. I need the exercise."

Charlie sticks out a hand.

"You have a safe journey home, Bob. Merry Christmas."

Bob shakes Charlie's hand.

"Merry Christmas."

Bob drives away. Charlie watches his green taxi until it disappears around the bend. Not being dropped off at Noor's house had been the final precaution he and Elma had agreed upon. It came at the end of a litany of others. Their cab from

New York had deposited them at the United terminal at Newark airport. There they had gone down to arrivals and taken another cab to Newark Penn Station where they had paid cash for two tickets to Boston and one to Charlotte. They boarded the Boston train only for Charlie to slip off just before it departed and make his way to the Charlotte train. That had sped him south and at six this morning he had stolen off it just before it departed High Point. No one else had gotten off. Any tail the Saudis had placed on hi, he knew he'd long since shaken. Yet nevertheless he had told Bob to drop him here.

You can never be too cautious.

Charlie stares up Main Street. It's two days before Christmas yet there is a barely a car driving down it. He spies a couple of old timers entering a cafe advertising ham and biscuits, and a bundled up woman walking her chocolate Labrador past the twinkling Christmas tree outside the town's modest town hall, but that's it. Charlie can't imagine a more tranquil place for Noor to have put down roots.

It's the kind of town Aamir Khan would have dreamed of living in.

Charlie shivers. He doesn't know when he last felt so excited and yet so apprehensive. Despite being in first class, he'd hardly slept. Rather he had spent the entire journey imagining his and Noor's reunion.

"You walk up Main Street," Elma had told him, "right past a couple of churches and up the hill until you see a white cottage with a green front door at the end of a short driveway."

Charlie imagines the cottage can't be much more than half a mile away yet he finds himself seized by such anxiety it might as well be a hundred.

There's no rush.

Charlie enters the warm confines of the gas station's expansive store. A bell rings to announce his arrival.

"Morning," the bearded clerk says.

"Morning," Charlie says.

Charlie edges over to the wine section and peruses a selection of Pinot Noirs, before moving on. He arrives at a card rack and spins it around. He pulls out a card. On it a couple of T. Rexes are perched on tiny outcrop as Noah's Ark sails off into the distance. 'Oh crap! Was that today?' one says to the other. Charlie chuckles. The door bell rings.

"Morning, Indira."

"Morning, Fred."

Charlie instantly recognizes Noor's voice.

"Don't worry I have your New York Times under lock and key," Fred says.

Noor laughs.

"I feel like I've just walked into a Swiss bank."

"If only I made that kind of money."

"Trust me you'd be miserable."

Charlie turns around. Noor is leaning against the counter with her back to him. She is wearing a black puffy jacket, a bright red beanie, jeans and a pair of green Wellington boots. A brown leather purse hangs from her shoulder.

"Can I get you anything else?" Fred says.

"A small French roast would be lovely."

Fred pumps coffee from a large thermos into a paper cup. Noor flips through the paper.

"They're saying bin Laden's gotten away," Fred says. "Probably in Pakistan by now."

Fred returns with Noor's coffee.

"One thing you can say about the guy, he's one slippery bastard."

"They'll find him one day," Noor says. "Don't worry."

"From your lips to God's ears."

"How much do I owe you?"

"Two dollars."

Noor hands him a couple of dollar bills.

"See you tomorrow," Fred says.

"You better believe it."

Noor never turns in his direction. Instead she heads straight for the door. Charlie stares after her.

"Don't think you're the first," Fred says.

Charlie jolts out of his stupor.

"Excuse me."

"To be knocked off your feet by that girl. Hell, every man in town was the day she rolled in. Many of us asked her out, but she turned every single of one us down. The rich and good looking ones as briskly as more unfortunate souls such as myself. Rumor has it her husband died and she's vowed to stay true to him till the day she dies. So you buying that?"

"Yeah, if that's okay."

Fred smiles.

"Don't believe there's a law against it."

Charlie goes up to the counter and hands the card over. He glances out the door. A pickup with a dead stag hanging off the back has pulled up next to one of the pumps.

"Larson's one of my favorites too," Fred says. "The way his mind works. Genius."

Fred scans the card.

"That'll be three dollars eight-three cents."

Charlie hands Fred a hundred-dollar bill. Fred opens the till. Charlie looks towards the door.

"Damn, I'm out of twenties," Fred says. "Gonna have to make your change out of smaller bills."

"Just keep it."

"You crazy?"

"Merry Christmas."

Charlie races out of the store. He circles the pickup truck and looks up and down Main Street. Noor is already a third of the way down it. He sprints after her.

"Noor. Noor. Wait."

The coffee cup drops from Noor's hand. Charlie staggers on up to her.

"Noor, it's me."

Noor turns and stares at Charlie. Charlie's heart shudders. She is as beautiful as he remembers her if not more so.

"I wasn't expecting you so soon," she says.

"Have I come at a bad time?"

"A bad time! Charlie, I've been waiting nine years for you."

Charlie places his hand against her cheek. She closes her eyes. Her whole body shakes.

"I can't believe it's you," she says.

"Indira!"

Noor jerks away. Across the street a heavy set woman in a quilted jacket is staring at them.

"Morning, Janet," Noor says.

"Enjoying your vacation?"

"Very much, thank you."

"So I see."

Janet turns her gaze towards Charlie.

"I'm Kadhim," Charlie says. "Indira's first cousin. On her mother's side."

"I'm sorry, Janet," Noor says, "but we need to get going. I have to pick Charlotte up from Mary Chappell's. She had a sleepover with Kelly."

"Well it's been a pleasure meeting you, Kadhim. Are you staying long?"

"Hoping to. Certainly through Christmas."

Noor's gloved hand slips into Charlie's. It feels wondrous.

"Let's go," she hisses.

Hand in hand, they carry on up Main Street.

"Who is she?" he says.

"A colleague of mine as well as the town gossip."

"Shit."

"It's fine. You'll see, nothing stays secret in Blowing Rock for long."

"Except your identity, Indira."

Noor laughs. Charlie's heart soars. Not even a choir of angels could sound so heavenly.

"So why Kadhim?" she says.

"He was friend of mine in prison. A good friend."

Noor's hand tightens.

"Is he still there?"

"Not for much longer, thank God."

Noor whimpers.

"It was terrible, wasn't it?"

"I survived. Just like you did. Now what I want to know is who's Charlotte?"

Noor halts in front of a stone church with a gambreled slate roof. Inside a choir is practicing *O Holy Night*.

"Elma didn't tell you?" Noor says.

"She told me almost nothing."

"Charlotte's my daughter."

Charlie's stomach drops.

"With whom?"

"The Prince, of course."

"But …"

Noor smiles.

"I know. Trust me, that was my reaction too."

Charlie laughs.

"Of course, she had to be. It's perfect."

"Now come on. We keep standing out here much longer, we'll be on the front page of The Blowing Rocket."

Noor takes Charlie's hand in hers and they make their way up the hill. Noor keeps up a steady pace and Charlie soon finds himself out of breath. He slows.

"We're almost there," she says.

They come upon a driveway. At the bottom is a white one story house. Noor unlocks the green door and pushes it open. They step inside and their lips meet. Noor reaches out a hand and slams the door shut behind them.

ELEVEN

NOOR STUDIES THE patchwork of scars across Charlie's back. They are garish pink and raised up as if a multitude of worms have burrowed underneath his skin. When they had made love, Charlie had been desperate for Noor not to see them, however, her hands had soon found them and she had run her fingers up and down their ridges like a visitor to some war torn land. At the time she had burst into tears, the enormity of the pain Charlie had suffered almost too much to bear.

"It's my fault," she had said.

He had taken her face in his hands.

"Never," he had said and he had kissed her with an un-expected ferocity that she had matched.

Afterwards they had lain facing each other and stared into each other's eyes. For nine years Noor had had a photo of twenty-five-year old Charlie next to her and she had spent countless hours lost in his deep blue eyes. Yet the ones that stared back at her were milky grey as if the Saudi sun had bleached the color out of them. Deep crow's feet arced away from his eyes. His skin was as brown as shoe polish and as gnarled as old leather. His cheeks were hollowed out and his lips pale and flaky. If Charlie hadn't called out her name on

Main Street, she doesn't know if she would've recognized him.

Oh my love, what did they do to you?

She catches a sob in her throat.

Stop it.

She knows she can't let him see her this way.

It's my turn to be strong.

Charlie stirs. He flips over onto his back and smiles. Her heart breaks into a thousand pieces once again.

"Hey you," he says.

"Hi."

"How long have I been out?"

"Five, nearly six hours."

"Jesus. I don't know the last time I slept so soundly."

"Well get used to it."

"Think I just might."

Charlie sits up and looks towards the door.

"Is Charlotte here?" he whispers.

"No. I asked Kelly's mother if she could keep her a little longer. They all went off to Boone to see Harry Potter."

"He a friend of hers?"

Noor laughs.

"No, a teenage wizard."

Charlie frowns.

"Don't worry, Charlotte will be thrilled to tell you all about him."

"When will she be back?"

"A couple of hours at most."

"So what do you want to do?"

"I don't know. Fancy a walk?"

"Sure."

"Really?"

"Noor, when have I ever lied to you?"

"How about the day you came by my school and claimed to be a certain Mr. Skeppar?"

"I lied to your principal not to you. And for good reason, I had to see you."

Noor tries to think of another instance but fails.

He's right. It's one of the reasons I love him so much.

"We should get going," she says, "before we lose the light."

He leans in and kisses her. Noor closes her eyes. She could remain like this forever.

"I love you," he says.

"And I you."

Charlie slides off the bed. Noor notices him seize up and try not to wince. He retrieves his clothes and puts them on.

"Ready," he says.

They head for the door. In the hallway Noor grabs her jacket and purse. Outside Charlie eyes Jimmy's old Cadillac.

"Cool ride."

"Betty, a friend of mine, gave it to me," she says. "It was her husband's."

Noor turns the ignition. As ever it takes three attempts before the car starts. She reverses out of the driveway, her mind so overwhelmed, that she nearly reverses into a black S.U.V. idling outside her gates. Noor does a U-turn and they head through town and on to Bass Lake. She pulls into the parking lot. She thinks about bringing her purse but then discounts the idea.

We won't be long.

She places it behind Charlie's seat and they get out. Noor locks the car. The lake is completely iced over and shimmers in the late afternoon light. In the distance a wild turkey gobbles.

"It's beautiful," Charlie says.

"I run here all the time."

"I forgot that about you, that you like to run."

"Three times a week, sometimes more. It clears my mind."

"In prison I had this routine. Push-ups, sit-ups, that kind of thing. Then I'd pray."

"You pray?"

"Not to any one in particular. Well I suppose God. Not a Christian one or a Muslim one or anything like that."

"Well I'm glad He gave you solace."

"How do you know He wasn't a she?"

Noor smiles.

"Given how contrarian you are, I'm sure She was."

"Every day I prayed to God to keep you safe."

Noor spreads her arms wide like a runner crossing the finishing line.

"Well here I am, so it must have worked."

Charlie laughs. Noor takes his hand.

"Now come on, let's go. The light at this time of year fades fast."

They head along the pathway for a while in silence. Nothing feels more natural.

"For eight years I thought you were dead," Charlie says.

Noor stares at him in horror.

"It's okay. In a bizarre way, I think it helped. It stopped me clinging to some false hope that I might see you again. Allowed me to make the most of my situation, however…"

Charlie's voice trails away.

"However what?" Noor says.

Charlie winces.

"However hellish it was."

Tears form in Noor's eyes.

"I want to thank you, Charlie—"

"It's not necessary."

"Not for saving me as much, but for saving Charlotte."

"You saved her as much as I did, Noor."

"Damn it, Charlie, would you just accept my thanks?"

Charlie turns towards Noor. By now they have made it halfway around the lake and are standing on the earthen dam.

"In prison, I was always trying to thank Kadhim for the favors he did me, which were many, and Kadhim would always reply, 'that's what friends do for each other, Charlie.' He was right. Thanks are in some ways immaterial."

Noor shakes her head.

"You know you're as stubborn as ever."

"That's rich coming from the stubbornest person I've ever known."

"Well just wait till you meet Charlotte. She's even worse."

"Then I guess that will make us three peas in a pod."

Noor smiles. She doesn't know if she has ever heard sweeter words.

"Let's go back," she says. "I can't wait for you to meet her."

Charlie takes her hand only to freeze. He peers across the lake. Noor follows his gaze past the island in its middle and towards the parking lot on the other side.

"What is it?" she says.

"You see that black Chevy?"

Apart from Jimmy's Cadillac it's the only other vehicle in the parking lot.

"It was outside your house," he says.

Charlie searches the paths on either side of the lake. He points.

"There," he says.

A dark skinned man, in a Yankees baseball cap, strides along it, one hand inside his leather jacket. Noor trembles.

A gun!

Noor spots a hooded man keeping a similar pace on the other side of the lake.

"There too," she says.

"They're looking to cut us off," Charlie says.

"Quick. This way."

With Noor in the lead, they sprint across the earthen dam. Across the way, the man in the baseball cap starts sprinting too. They reach the end of the earthen dam. Noor barrels down the path to the right. They cross the wooden bridge and plunge into the wood. They follow the twisting and turning path up the hill, the light so dim that they can barely see the turns before they are almost upon them.

"They must have followed you from New York," Noor says.

"It makes no sense. I took every precaution."

"Charlie, two armed men are chasing us."

"I get it, but I would've surely seen them."

"Not if you have a tracking device on you."

"I don't. I—"

Charlie halts in his tracks. Noor looks back. Even in the murky light, Noor can see he's paled.

"What?"

"A few weeks back, I had this rotten tooth. They let me see a dentist, even put me under to extract it."

"You think the tracking device is in your mouth?"

"Either that or somewhere else in my body."

"So we can run all we want—"

"And they'll never lose us."

Charlie stares down the path. Noor hears shoes crunching through the snow. Charlie grips Noor by the shoulders.

"Hide. I'll lead them away from you."

"No, I'm not abandoning you again."

"You got to, otherwise you and Charlotte stand no chance."

Noor tries to process everything he's said.

Think. Think. Think. There has to be another way.

The footfalls get ever louder.

"My gun," she says. "It's in the car."

"Good. You'll be able to protect yourself."

"No, listen. Keep going. At the apple barn take the path to the right. Then further up go left. Four miles up, at the top of the hill there's a white mansion. I'll meet you there."

"Noor, no—"

"Unless you promise, Charlie, I'm staying right here with you."

Charlie looks back down the path. The man's so close they can hear his labored breathing.

"Okay," he says. "Now go, hide."

Charlie sprints off. In no time he is enveloped by the gloom. Noor notices a fallen tree close by. She scrambles over it and cowers. The man's footsteps get ever closer. Then she sees him, his hood trailing behind him, a gun in one hand, some device in his other. Even in the dim light, she can discern that his skin complexion's much like hers and Charlotte's.

He's either Saudi or Pakistani.

He barrels past leaving the sickly sweet smell of his after-shave in his wake. Noor waits for the second man to appear. He doesn't. She crawls underneath the fallen tree and creeps up to the path. Up hill she can hear twigs snap as the first man gets ever further away. However, down below, she hears nothing. She realizes the other man must have gone back to their car.

He's going to cut Charlie off.

Noor charges down the hill. She reaches the bridge and tramples across it. Bass Lake comes into view. In the dark it looks like a vast black parking lot. Noor sprints across the dam. She makes the turn. Her right foot slips on some ice and she tumbles to the ground. Her right hip screams in pain. She scrambles to her feet and hobbles on. She peers ahead. The Chevy's gone. She races up to her Cadillac and flings open the driver's side door. She leans back and grabs her purse. She unzips it and grabs her pistol. She turns the key. The engine sputters. She tries again. It sputters again. She tries a third time but, unlike on every other occasion, it doesn't roar to life. Noor tries again and again. The engine only gets weaker. Noor punches the steering wheel.

You can still make it.

Noor yanks the door open and races up the steep drive-way. Halfway up she turns down another wooded path. Noor runs like she has run only once before in her life; the day Tariq's cohorts chased her through Kacha Gari camp. As she does, questions come flying at her.

Who are these men? Are they the only ones? And if not have the others already located Charlotte?

Her throat constricts. She feels the urge to vomit but forces herself to keep going.

It's okay. They can't know she's at Mary's. Not yet.

Three quarters of the way up the hill her lungs burn like someone's poured battery acid into them.

Don't stop.

Noor stumbles forward like a drunk who's been kicked out of a bar. The trees thin and fall away. Cone Manor comes into view. Its lights are off, its exterior dim and ghostly. Noor slows. She holds her gun out and creeps forward until she comes to the end of the manor's wrap around porch. She peers through the railing. She forces herself not to gasp. The man in the baseball cap is standing at the far end with his back to her. She points her gun at him. He's only thirty yards away. She knows she could kill him with one shot.

Where the hell are you, Charlie?

The man's radio squawks.

"Almost here," the other man says in Arabic. "I'm bringing him up to the house right now."

Noor bites down on her lip.

"How about the Princess?" the baseball capped man says.

"He's going to take us to her."

The man turns around and Noor ducks. His shoes clunk along the wooden boards. The man heads down the steps. Noor pokes her head around the side. In the distance, she makes out two figures heading towards the manor. The one in front has his hands tied behind his back.

Charlie.

The baseball capped man strolls towards them.

Noor edges around the back of Cone Manor. She comes upon the parking lot. The Chevy is parked no more than ten yards from her position. She hears the men approaching. Noor crouches behind a fence.

"Where's her son?" the man in the baseball cap says in Arabic.

"Excuse me."

It takes a moment for Noor to realize the second voice is Charlie's.

"The Prince's child?" the man says.

A surge of relief passes through Noor. Charlotte's safe.

For now.

"I don't know," Charlie says. "She said she was going to pick her up on the way to Wendy's."

"Her?"

There is a pregnant silence.

"Why did you say her?"

"I didn't mean to," Charlie says. "My Arabic's not so good."

"It sounds perfect to me."

The man cocks his gun.

"She never had a son," Charlie says. "She had a daughter."

The hooded one laughs.

"The Prince's going to be in for a hell of a surprise."

The men come into view, the baseball capped one in front of Charlie, the hooded one behind him.

"And she said she'd meet you at this Wendy's?" the hooded man says.

"Yes. At ten. With her daughter. On the dot."

He's giving me time to escape.

"You're positive?"

"You think she's going to leave without me again?"

They reach the S.U.V. The hooded man nods at his partner and opens the backdoor. Charlie bends down to get in. The baseball capped man raises his gun and points it at the back of Charlie's head.

"Wait!" Noor screams.

Noor shoves her gun into the back of her pants and stands. She walks towards them. Charlie gives her a desperate look. The baseball capped man glances at his partner.

"You got her?"

The partner aims his gun at Noor.

"I got her."

The baseball capped man holsters his gun and takes out some plastic cuffs. He approaches Noor. Noor's heart beats out of her chest. She glances at the hooded man. His grip on his gun is careless, his stance lackadaisical.

Another man with no respect for women.

She looks away. The baseball capped man is close enough that she can smell his aftershave.

Now.

Noor reaches for her gun and arcs it in the hooded man's direction. They fire at the same time. The hooded man misses while Noor's three shots strike his heart. Noor swivels towards the baseball capped man. He is reaching for his gun. Noor fires three more shots and the man crumples to the ground. She glances at Charlie. He looks almost as shocked as the men.

"Check to make sure he's dead," she says.

She turns her attention to the baseball capped man. He lies on his back in the snow, his face creased with pain as he wheezes air into his lungs.

"He's dead," Charlie calls out.

The baseball capped man tries to raise his gun only for it to fall from his hand. Noor takes it and kneels beside him.

"How many more of you are there?" she says.

The man shakes his head. Noor places the tip of her gun

against his temple.

"Tell me."

She knows it's an empty threat. The man's expression becomes increasingly vacant.

"La aloha ill Allah," the man rasps.

It is the phrase dying Muslims say in order to aid their entry into paradise. The man's body relaxes as if the frozen ground beneath him has transformed into an eiderdown. Noor senses a presence beside her and turns to see Charlie standing there, his hands still cuffed behind his back. She wraps her arms around him and hugs him close. For a while they stand there swaying, their warm breath on the nape of each other's neck.

"It's my fault," he says. "I should never have come."

"Don't. It's going to be okay."

However, Noor knows it isn't. Everything has changed. *Once more we're being hunted.*

"You think we should call the police?" she says.

"No. They can't help us."

Noor knows Charlie's right. If anything it would just deliver them into their enemies' hands.

"Then we need to get rid of them," Noor says.

Noor strides over to the Chevy. She throws open the trunk. She gasps. Someone has duck taped a blue tarpaulin over the entirety of its surface. On one side is a tall orange bucket containing a flashlight, a hammer, a set of shears and a pickaxe. On the other is an aluminum jerry can and a shovel. Charlie comes up behind her and stares at the interior of the trunk. He can't help but shiver at his aborted fate. Noor grabs the shears.

"Turn around," she says.

Noor snips off Charlie's plastic cuffs. Charlie goes over to the hooded man. He lies slumped against the back wheel of the Chevy. Charlie pats him down and extracts a cellphone, a wallet, a Zippo lighter and a set of keys.

"Can you take his legs?" he says.

Noor comes over and grabs ahold of the man's ankles. Charlie bear hugs him.

"On three. One, two, three."

They lift up the man and stagger around the side of the Chevy. Charlie heaves the man's torso into the trunk. Noor swings the legs in. They complete the same exercise with the baseball capped man. Noor goes to close the trunk.

"Wait," Charlie says. "The casings."

He hands her the flashlight. She turns it on and passes its beam over the snow. The casings glint like nuggets of gold. Noor bends over and picks them up. Charlie appears with the orange bucket and the shovel, and scoops up as much of the blood drenched snow as he can. Charlie places the bucket in the trunk and slams it shut. They climb into the Chevy.

"You and Charlotte need to get out of town and drive south," Charlie says.

"And you?"

"I'll get rid of the bodies and head north. Try and draw the rest of these bastards away from you."

"No. You're not leaving me again, Charlie."

"It's our only option."

"Not if we get it out."

"And how are we going to do that?"

Noor takes out her cellphone and dials a number. After three rings someone picks up.

"Bert. It's Indira. I'm sorry to call you so late, but is there any way I could meet you at your clinic?"

TWELVE

"I'M ONLY DOING this because this girl's so dear to me," Bert Donahue says.

"I understand," Charlie says.

Bert, in his checkered sweater, crosses his arms like a golfer waiting for his partner to tee off.

"Well, go on, strip down to your underwear and lie on the table."

Charlie takes off his clothes and lays them on a chair. He notices specks of blood on the back of his jeans. He hopes to God that Bert doesn't. He lies down on the examination table. Bert whistles.

"Damn, your back's worse than a runaway slave's."

Bert runs his fingers down it.

"I doubt they'd be dumb enough to put one in your front but ... ah, there it is. You see, Indira? That incision mark. The sucker's right under the subcutaneous tissue."

Bert presses down and Charlie's back spasms. Charlie fights the urge to cry out.

"Can you get it out?" Noor says.

"Sure. I just need to know this boy isn't involved in any of this terrorist crap?"

"I promise," Noor says. "In fact quite the opposite."

Bert grunts. It's all the assurance he needs.

"You think it has anything to do with my back spasms?" Charlie says.

"Sure," Bert says. "It's most likely pressing up against a nerve. Now lie still. I'm going to inject a local anesthetic."

A syringe pierces his skin and a numbing feeling ripples across his lower back. Charlie thinks back to the insanity of the night. After he had separated from Noor, he had staggered on, his depleted body like a car sputtering on fumes. It hadn't been long before the hooded man had come up behind him. Charlie had closed his eyes expecting to be shot. He was at peace. At least the tracking device would die along with him. Instead the man had cuffed him and ordered him up the hill in English. Charlie replied in Arabic and when the man had carried on the conversation in that language, Charlie knew he was Saudi. It all made sense. They hadn't released him to appease America. They had released him because they hoped he'd lead them to Noor and Charlotte.

And like an idiot I did.

"Okay, Charlie, do you feel that?" Bert says.

"No."

"Then I guess I can begin."

The Saudi agent had asked Charlie where Noor was.

"Don't lie," he had said. "We saw her with you."

After asking him a couple more times, the Saudi agent had spun Charlie around and delivered a crunching hook with the butt of his pistol. Charlie had toppled to the ground and the tip of the agent's pistol had ground into his skull.

"This is your last chance," the man had said.

Charlie had doubted it. Right then they needed him alive. He had thought about continuing the silent treatment but then it had occurred to him that he could lead them away from Noor and give her more time to escape.

"We split up," he had said. "We were going to meet at Wendy's later."

"Who's Wendy?"

"It's a fast food restaurant in Boone."

"When?"

"Ten o'clock."

Charlie had estimated it was around five o'clock. It would give Noor five hours to get away.

"Stand up," the man had said.

Charlie had struggled to his feet. The man had shoved him forward and they had continued their forced march up to the manor. Every step of the way Charlie had prayed that Noor had abandoned him and when the baseball capped agent had appeared and there was no sign of her, he had assumed she had. When she had screamed out, Charlie couldn't work out what she was up to. He had feared it was some forlorn attempt to make up for him saving her back in Saudi Arabia. Instead Noor had drawn her gun and within seconds both of the Saudi agents were crumpled on the ground. He had stared at her in disbelief. Of all the things he had imagined Noor had become in their years apart, the very last was a modern day Annie Oakley.

Bert lets out another of his trademark whistles.

"Goddamn, will you look at this thing? You could track a goddamn shark with it."

Charlie twists around to look.

"Not you. Lie still."

Charlie returns to his prone position.

"It's state of the art," Noor says.

Bert edges around the examination table and hands Charlie a bloody circuit board the size of a quarter. It is attached by a couple of wires to a unit the size of a matchbox. Charlie assumes it contains the battery and transmitter.

"They could have tracked me from miles away," Charlie says.

"More like a thousand miles," Bert says. "Now give me a couple of minutes to sew you up."

Charlie realizes that back in New York the British man in the elevator and the college student on the subway were most likely not working for the Prince. Instead the Saudi agents had stayed back and watched him scuttle about New York like a rat in a maze.

Noor crouches next to him. Their faces are only inches apart.

"I'm sorry," Charlie says.

"How were you to know?"

"I'm going to do everything I can to protect you and Charlotte. I promise."

"I know you will. You always have."

Bert coughs.

"You're done, young man."

Noor holds out her hand.

"Give it to me. I'll destroy it."

"No," Charlie says. "I have a better idea."

Noor frowns. Charlie gives her a look and sits up.

"Bert, I can't thank you enough," he says.

"Like I said, there's nothing I wouldn't do for this young lady. Now let me get you some supplies."

Charlie puts on his clothes. Bert hands him some gauze, tape and a container of pills.

"Dress it once a day and take a couple of these every eight hours. May not hurt right now but once the anesthetic's worn off, it's going to throb like hell."

Bert walks them to the front of his doctor's office.

"I'm guessing this is goodbye," he says to Noor.

"Unfortunately it is," Noor says.

"This town's gonna be a hell of a lot worse off without you."

"And I'll be a hell of a lot worse off without it."

Noor wraps her arms around Bert and they hug. Bert turns to Charlie. They shake hands.

"Look after them," Bert says.

"I promise."

Charlie opens the door, and he and Noor step outside. It has begun to snow again. They head for the black Chevy.

"One last thing," Bert calls out.

They turn back.

"I'm assuming your real name's not Indira," he says.

"No, it isn't. It's Noor."

Bert smiles.

"It's beautiful."

Charlie opens the passenger door. Noor climbs in. Charlie gets in the other side. He turns on the windshield wipers to clear the window. Charlie drives away, big fat flakes of snow smudging the windshield like wet confetti. Noor doesn't take her eyes off a waving Bert until he disappears out of view.

"Do you know where the nearest Greyhound station is?" Charlie asks.

"Boone. Why?"

Charlie takes the tracking device from her.

"This needs a new home."

Noor glances at the trunk.

"And the bodies?"

"I'll dispose of them at the same time."

"You'll need my help."

"No, you need to be with Charlotte."

Noor nods. She knows he's right.

"Then you should drop me off here," she says.

Charlie rolls to a stop at a lamp lit intersection. The two of them sit there, the only sound the hum of the engine and the rhythmic clunk of the windshield wipers.

"How will I find you?" he says.

"Betty Johnson. She lives at One Treetop Lane. Anyone in town will be able to give you directions."

"I'll be back in a few hours."

"You better be."

Noor rests her forehead against his.

"I love you," she says.

"I love you too,"

Noor gets out. Charlie watches her trudge up the hill until she is swallowed by the swirling snow. He drives on down the windy road and spots a sign for Boone. He turns onto the highway and soon Blowing Rock is behind him and he is heading down a four lane road that meanders down the mountain valley like an icy river. At this time of night there are still a fair number of cars and he follows the backlights of the pickup ahead of him until he reaches Boone's main drag. He spies a McDonalds and on cue his stomach growls. He turns into its drive-through lane only to realize his mistake.

You insane?

Charlie backs up and barely avoids running into a car. The car honks its horn. Charlie waves an apology and pulls into a parking spot. He undoes his seatbelt and jumps into the backseat. A couple of overnight bags lie on it. He unzips them and pulls out all the clothes they contain. He throws them over the dead Saudis until the trunk looks like he's on his way to do a drop off at the local Salvation Army. He gets out and locks the Chevy. Inside a few families are dining in the restaurant as well as a group of teenagers and a couple of policemen. One catches his eye and it takes all Charlie's resolve not to turn tail. The policeman returns to conversing with his partner and Charlie reaches the counter. He stares up at the menu. The amount of food that comes with each meal continues to astound him. He orders a Big Mac, fries and a Coke from an acned teenager. He hands him a hundred-dollar bill.

"You wouldn't know where the Greyhound bus station is, would you?" he says.

"Sure," the kid says. "Keep heading into town and you'll see a Citgo on the left. It's not so much of a station though. More a stop."

"Thanks."

The kid hands Charlie his change and his order. Charlie returns to his car and continues on to the Citgo. He pulls up across the street. Six people with bags at their feet are huddled under the gas station's awning. Charlie wolfs down his burger and fries, and sucks down his Coke. Ten minutes later a bus rumbles in. Charlie grabs the tracking device and jogs across the road. A couple of red eyed passengers disembark. The six waiting passengers hustle up the bus' stairs eager for its warm embrace. Charlie climbs on board. The driver looks as frazzled as the passengers who just exited.

"My girlfriend got off a while back," Charlie says. "Thinks she left her purse on board. Mind if I take a look?"

"Hurry up," the driver says. "I'm already behind schedule."

Charlie works his way down the aisle past a soldier in combat uniform and a couple of sleeping college kids. He finds an empty row and gets down on his knees. He pushes up the seat cushion and squeezes the tracking device between it and a metal support. He struggles to his feet and makes his way back down the aisle.

"No luck," he says. "Where's the bus headed?"

"Atlanta," the driver says.

"Well hopefully someone will turn it in."

The driver rolls his eyes. Charlie steps off and the door hisses shut. He gets back in the Chevy and drives back towards Blowing Rock. Halfway up he spots a road that disappears into a mass of trees. He turns up it. The higher he goes the thicker the whirling snow gets. Two miles up he spots a dirt track. He switches off his lights and turns down it. To his relief the blinding snow disappears. The tree cover is so thick that he might as well be heading through a tunnel. He trundles down the track peering for any signs of human dwellings. He sees nothing but the track suddenly fall away. He slams on the brakes and the Chevy shudders to a halt.

Charlie grabs the Saudis' flashlight. He clambers out.

"Holy shit."

A couple of feet beyond the front tires is a vertical drop. Charlie wafts his flashlight beam into a forty-foot deep ravine. It is filled with old washing machines, tires, television sets, broken cabinetry, even the hulk of a rusting car.

It's perfect.

Charlie returns to the Chevy and opens the trunk. He tosses the clothes to one side. The two men stare up at him. Charlie grabs ahold of the hooded man's jacket and yanks him out of the trunk. The man lands with a thump. He hauls him to the edge of the ravine and shoves him into the dark yonder. There are a couple of thuds and an almighty crunch. Charlie points his flashlight below. The man has ended up with his back against a washing machine as if he is waiting for the spin cycle to finish.

Charlie returns to the Chevy. It's not long before the baseball capped man has joined his colleague. Charlie grabs the can of gasoline, the pick axe, a T-shirt and the hammer from the trunk. He clambers down the side of the ravine using the hammer like an ice pick. By the time he reaches the bottom he's panting so hard he hasn't a clue how he is going to climb back up. Charlie catches his breath and goes in search of a tire. He lifts it onto its side and alternately rolls and heaves it across the mangled trash. He takes multiple breaks. It feels as if he is doing the whole exercise twenty thousand feet up the side of a mountain. Finally, he reaches the hooded man and hoists the man's legs through the tire. He yanks on them until the tire's wrapped around the man's waist.

One more and you're done.

He stumbles over to the other man and galvanizes himself for the ordeal ahead. This time it takes far longer. Bert's drugs are beginning to wear off and his back feels like it's been branded with a red hot poker. Charlie retrieves the can of gasoline and pours its contents over each of the men leaving a few final dregs for the T-shirt. He takes out the Zippo and lights the T-shirt. He tosses it onto the hooded man and the Zippo onto his friend. They are soon engulfed in flames. The tires throw off thick plumes of black smoke that funnel up into the tree canopy. Charlie watches mesmerized. He can't help but be reminded of the Highway of Death back in Iraq. Eventually the flames die out leaving the men's bodies blackened and shriveled. Charlie takes the hammer and approaches the first corpse. The man's eyes are hollowed out sockets, his lips gone, his teeth arced in a gruesome smile. Charlie swings the hammer and the man's teeth shatter as easily as if they were made of glass. The other corpse's teeth offer little more resistance. Charlie takes the axe and proceeds to dismember each of the men. It's harder than he thought, like chopping through a large rump of meat.

You can't stop now, he tells himself.

He hacks on until each of the men is nothing more than six constituent parts. Charlie hides the pair of heads inside the bowels of the washing machine, the two pairs of legs and the torsos in the trunk of the rusting car. The four arms he shoves inside a Seventies era fridge. With the bottom of his shirt, he wipes down the handle of the jerry can, the shears, and the pick axe. He tosses them away and with the hammer and flashlight in hand, he edges his way back up the ravine. It is a slow, painstaking exercise and by the time he gets to the top his arms and legs feel like jelly. He lies on his back and stares up at the trees. Through their barren branches he can make out a pale blue sky. Though it hardly seems possible, it's close to dawn.

Charlie struggles to his feet. He gathers all the clothes, the bags and the tarpaulin and throws them into the ravine. He decides to keep the hammer and flashlight. They may come in useful. He wonders when the men will be found. It will happen eventually perhaps by some teenagers up to no good or a hunter's dog. Whoever finds them, he suspects the sheriff will have a hell of a time trying to figure out who the men are and what really happened. It'll become a part of the local folklore, the work of some monster in the woods.

Kids will never venture out here again, least not unless they're drunk.

Charlie returns to the Chevy. He turns the ignition and allows the warm air to defrost his frozen body. Something buzzes beside him. In the cup holder one of the men's phones is vibrating. He picks it up and stares at the display. He recognizes the country code. Ninety-Two. Pakistan. Charlie finds himself unable to resist. He answers it.

"Hello," he says in Arabic.

"What's going on?" a man replies in Arabic. "Have you got them yet?"

"Who is this?"

"The Prince, who do you think it is?"

Charlie doesn't say a word.

"Saeed? Hello? Is that you?"

Charlie presses end. It's final confirmation.

It was a trap all along.

Charlie puts the Chevy into reverse and twists around to look out the back window. Down the way he spies a set of headlights approaching.

Shit.

A pickup is bouncing down the track towards him.

THIRTEEN

NOOR GAZES OUT Betty's kitchen window at the pale blue sky and the mountains beyond. They stretch into the distance like a white blanket tossed on a bed. The storm has passed.

If only I could say the same for my life.

Noor takes a sip from her sixth cup of tea.

Where the hell is he?

After she had arrived at Betty's house, (she hadn't dare return to her own), Noor had called Mary Chappell. Never had the sound of her daughter playing sounded so sweet. Mary had said she was quite happy for Charlotte to stay another night and in the background Charlotte had begged Noor to say yes. Noor had been tempted to let her. She was less likely to be found there than at Betty's.

But at least here I can protect her, she had thought.

So Noor had driven Betty's Lexus over to Mary's place. When she had arrived Charlotte had pouted before Mary had assured her that there would be plenty more opportunities for sleepovers over the Christmas break.

"Can we, Mommy?" Charlotte had begged. "Please."

"Of course," Noor had said as she watched Charlotte give Kelly a hug.

"See you around, Ginny," Charlotte had said.

"Later, Hermione," Kelly had shouted back.

Noor had to force a smile. It was exceedingly unlikely the girls would ever see each other again. Her smile had remained fixed all the way to Betty's house as Charlotte had relived the best moments from the movie. The reason Kelly was Ginny, she had proclaimed, was because just like the character in the books, Kelly had a crush on Harry Potter. She, of course, didn't and hence that was why she was Hermione. For the most part, in Charlotte's world, boys were morons.

Noor had only half-listened. Her mind was elsewhere. Fixated, as it is now, with how Charlie was doing; with whether the shots at Cone Manor had been reported and whether the police had gone to investigate; with whether there were any other Saudi agents in Blowing Rock; with where they would go; with what she would tell Charlotte and how Charlotte would react; with Betty and how she was going to say goodbye.

When they had rolled up to Betty's house, Charlotte had asked why they were spending the night there. Noor had told her that Martha needed help in the morning and Charlotte hadn't bat an eyelid. They had stayed there so many times before that Charlotte had pajamas and clothes in a closet upstairs. Inside, Martha had informed her that Betty was already asleep and Charlotte had dutifully headed upstairs while Noor had gone down into the basement and raided Betty's gun cupboard for fresh bullets. She had reloaded her magazine and went back up to the kitchen to brew her first cup of tea. There she had played over in her mind the encounter with the Saudi agents. Two things stood out. First the agents had never mentioned any others or received a call from anyone else.

Surely if there were more in the area they would've informed them of Charlie's capture.

Secondly, they had no idea Charlotte was a girl. It meant they had done little to no investigating.

We are safe for now, she had thought. *We still have time to get away.*

For a while this had calmed her. However, as the hours had eked by, her fears had returned and she had become increasingly concerned that Charlie was dead. After all it made sense if the Saudis had placed a tracker inside his body that they'd have one in the Chevy too.

Perhaps a new set of agents have hunted him down. Perhaps they're on their way to Betty's house right now.

Noor had gone to Charlotte's room and held her daughter's hand as she slept. For a brief moment she'd wondered if the two of them should flee in no more than the clothes they were wearing. Yet somehow she had managed to calm herself.

No, go make yourself some more tea and wait for him.

And wait for him she had.

Noor rises, ready to pour herself a seventh cup, when she hears a car drive up. She takes her gun from her purse and creeps into the front hallway. She looks out the window and sees the black Chevy idling outside. She holds her breath. The driver's door swings open and Charlie steps out. A wave of relief washes over her. Noor yanks open the front door and races outside. She flings her arms around Charlie. He reeks of smoke.

"It's done," he says.

"Did you come across anyone else?" she asks.

"Just at the end. A couple of hunters, but luckily they were more interested in getting to their stand than asking questions."

Noor could weep with relief.

"There was one thing," he says.

She lets go and looks into his weary eyes.

"The Prince called one of the men's phones."

"What?"

"He wanted to know if they'd got you and Charlotte yet."

Noor shivers.

"The funny thing is his number was a Pakistani one," Charlie says.

"What's he doing there?"

"I thought you might know."

"I haven't a clue."

Charlie sways and Noor reaches out a hand to steady him.

"Come on," she says. "You need to get some sleep."

"No, we need to get going."

"Not before you sleep."

Noor guides Charlie inside and upstairs to Chris' room. It's stuck in a time warp with faded movie posters on the wall from when Chris was a teenager. Charlie lies down on the bedspread and his eyes close as soon as his head touches the pillow. Noor senses an overwhelming exhaustion come over her. She places her gun on the bedside table and lies down beside Charlie. She puts her arms around him and the next thing she knows someone is shaking her. Noor scrambles for her gun.

"Mommy."

Noor sees Charlotte standing at the side of the bed.

"Who's that man?"

Noor forces herself up off the bed her mind a blur.

"Who is it, Mommy?"

"It's Charlie."

"The Charlie?"

Noor nods and Charlotte's eyes widen.

"Is he coming to live with us?"

Noor knows she can't lie to her daughter anymore.

"We're going to leave with him," she says.

"Today? On Christmas Eve?"

Noor glances at the bedside clock and is shocked to see it is already eleven o'clock.

"You should go and pack a bag."

"For how long?"

"I don't know."

Tears spring in Charlotte's eyes.

"We're going to miss Betty's last Christmas, aren't we?"

"Charlotte—"

"You're the meanest person I know."

"Charlotte—"

Charlotte races from the room. Her fleeing footsteps pound down the corridor and her bedroom door slams shut. Noor places her head in her hands and breathes deeply.

How can one's life fall apart so fast?

"She'll get over it, I promise."

Noor looks up. Betty is standing in the doorway in her robe.

"You should be in bed," Noor says.

"With all this excitement in the house, are you crazy?"

Betty shuffles over and stares down at Charlie.

"So that's Charlie"

"The one and only."

"Did he get here last night?"

"Yesterday morning."

Betty's nose wrinkles.

"Something's happened, hasn't it?"

"They've found us."

"And where are they?"

"Dead. At least two of them are."

Betty's eyes widen.

"The rest, we don't know when they're coming."

Betty plunks herself down next to Noor.

"I don't want to leave you," Noor says.

"Why? I'm about to leave you."

"I should be here with you at the end."

"Don't worry, I'll have Bert and Martha. The boys if they have the gumption to get here in time. Most importantly, I'll have my memories. Of you and that beautiful, little girl.

Tears stream down Noor's cheeks.

"Come on, Noor, don't be sad. What you, me and Charlotte had was a blessing. Something so unexpected and wonderful that I was spoilt it went on this long."

Noor wraps her arms around Betty and hugs her frail body to hers. Charlie stirs. His eyes flicker open.

"We haven't been introduced," Betty says. "I'm Betty."

Betty sticks out her hand. Charlie sits up and shakes it.

"Charlie."

"After hearing so many tales about you, young man, it's truly an honor to meet you in the flesh."

Charlie glances at Noor's tear stained cheeks.

"I'm sorry we have to meet under these circumstances."

"Me too, but in life I've always thought it important that you play the hand you're dealt and not the one you wished you'd been."

"I'm guessing you're a dab hand at poker."

Betty chuckles.

"Bridge. In the old days Jimmy and I used to clean up at the country club."

"That's the thing about bridge, you're only as strong as your partner."

"In which case, you and Noor are going to do just fine."

Charlie smiles. Noor only wants to cry more. She knows that Betty and Charlie would have been fast friends.

"Anyway enough chit-chat, you three need to be on your way," Betty says. "Now you, young man could benefit from having a shower and a change of clothes. Chris has plenty in the closet to choose from."

Charlie swings his legs off the bed and stands.

"Betty, I'm so glad we got to meet," he says.

"Me too," Betty says. "You were the last piece in the puzzle."

Charlie heads out of the room. Betty turns to Noor and takes her tear stained cheeks in her hands.

"And you, young lady need to get it together. You have a very precious girl to think of."

"She's going to hate me forever."

"No, she won't. She hasn't got it in her. Now go, get ready. I'll go talk to Charlotte."

Noor grabs her gun and heads to the bedroom she uses when staying at Betty's. She changes into a fresh set of clothes and packs an overnight bag. She slips her gun into the side pocket. Charlie pokes his head in, a towel around his waist, his dirty clothes in his hands.

"You good?" he says.

She bites her lip.

No.

"Yes," she says.

"I'll be down in a couple of minutes."

"Okay."

Charlie carries on to Chris' room and Noor heads downstairs. In the kitchen, Martha is at the sink washing dishes.

"Everything okay up there?"

"Yes, fine."

Martha cocks an eyebrow but doesn't push the point. She places the final plate in the drying rack.

"Right, I'm off to Food Lion," she says.

Martha heads for the garage.

"Martha," Noor says.

Martha turns.

"Thanks."

"Whatever for?"

"I don't know. Everything."

Martha shakes her head. As far as she's concerned the whole house has gone mad.

"Don't let her do anything stupid while I'm away."

"I won't."

Martha opens the door to the garage. It slams shut behind her. Noor springs into action. She makes three sets of turkey sandwiches and wraps them in tinfoil. She grabs some Cokes from the fridge and shoves them and the sandwiches into the overnight bag. On the kitchen counter she spies her purse. She grabs it. Inside she spies her cellphone, its green light flashing away. Only now does it strike her.

You idiot.

She fumbles open its back cover and yanks out the battery. She chucks both of them in the trash

"All set?"

Noor turns to find Charlie in the doorway. He is wearing jeans and a woolen sweater that Betty bought for Chris last Christmas.

"Where's Charlotte?" Noor says.

"With Betty at the front door."

Noor grabs her overnight bag and her purse, and together they make their way to the front hall. Betty is sitting in the grand old chair that for years they would toss their jackets and scarves on when they came in from the cold. Charlotte is facing her, a pink knapsack at her feet. Noor puts a hand on Charlie's arm. Betty whispers to Charlotte and Charlotte nods as if agreeing with her every word. Betty envelops Charlotte in her arms. Betty looks their way and smiles. 'It's fine,' she's saying. 'I've taken care of it.'

As you so often have.

"Charlie, would you be so kind as to take Charlotte to the car," Betty says.

"Of course," Charlie says.

"I love you, Charlotte," Betty says.

"I love you too," Charlotte cries.

Charlie opens the front door. Cold air rushes in. Charlie picks up Charlotte's knapsack and takes her arm. They head for the car only for Charlotte to rush back and give Betty one final hug.

"Never compromise," Betty says. "You hear me, never."

"I promise."

Charlotte stumbles away. Charlie opens the Chevy's back door. Charlotte slips into the backseat. Noor notices Betty shudder when it closes. With a shaking hand, Betty reaches into the pocket of her robe and pulls out a white envelope.

"Here," she says.

Noor opens it. Inside is ten thousand dollars in one hundred dollar bills.

"Jimmy always thought it important to have cash on hand in case of an emergency."

"You didn't have to—"

"Oh stop it, what am I going to do with it? Fly to Vegas?"

Noor laughs through her tears.

"Now go."

Noor finds she can't move.

"The last thing I want is for you to set a bad example to your daughter."

Noor bends down and kisses Betty on both cheeks. She takes a step back and for the first time she notices tears in Betty's eyes.

"I love you, Betty."

"And I you, Noor. More than you can possibly imagine."

Noor grabs her purse and bag and walks outside. Halfway to the Chevy, the front door slams shut and this time it's her turn to shudder. Noor looks back. Betty's gone. Noor climbs into the passenger seat and Charlie drives away. Noor turns around. Charlotte is huddled in a ball, her forehead resting against the window. She refuses to look Noor's way. They drive down the hill, past their home, along Main Street past the churches and the stores, the school and the gas station. They come to a red light.

"I think we should go south," Charlie says. "Stay one step ahead until we figure out something permanent."

Noor nods. It makes sense.

"Then you should turn right."

The light turns green and Charlie does exactly that. They drive down the mountain in silence. Noor is loathe to discuss anything that might upset Charlotte more. From time to time, Charlie reaches out his hand and takes hers in his. It's a sweet gesture, however, it is of little comfort. As far as Noor's concerned the world is collapsing around them. Halfway down, as they pass through Lenoir, she gets out a sandwich and a Coke and offers them to Charlotte. Charlotte contorts her body so Noor can see even less of her face. Noor offers one to Charlie and he takes it. Around Hickory, Charlotte falls asleep and soon after so does Noor. When she wakens she finds they are well past the South Carolina state line and close to Columbia.

"We should find a motel for the night," she says.

"I was thinking we should at least get to Georgia," Charlie says.

"No, we've put more than enough distance between us and Blowing Rock."

Charlie doesn't argue and exits the freeway. A half mile down the road they come upon a Mom and Pop motel with a flashing vacancy sign. Charlie pops into its wood-paneled office and emerges some time later with a key. He hands it to Noor.

"You open up. I'll get Charlotte."

Noor gets out. The air is warm and moist. It's as if they're in another continent not the next door state. She heads down the barracks like building until she comes to room eight. She unlocks the door and turns on the light. Inside are a couple of queen sized beds with stained floral bedspreads and an assortment of chipped and mismatched furniture. The room reeks of tobacco. Charlie appears behind her with Charlotte cradled in his arms.

"Where do you want her?"

"The second bed's probably best."

"You got it."

Charlie pulls back the covers before gently laying Charlotte down. Noor can't help but marvel at the care he takes. She realizes that Charlie will protect Charlotte as if she were his own and right then she realizes what she must do.

It's the only hope we have.

Charlie pulls the covers over Charlotte.

"I was thinking of going across the road to the liquor store," he says. "You want anything?"

"Just water."

Charlie heads out and Noor kneels beside her sleeping daughter. She wonders how often Mamaan did this with her without her knowing. She strokes Charlotte's hair and traces the contours of her face with her fingers.

Will she end up looking more like me or the Prince?

Noor drinks her daughter in like a convicted felon savoring a twenty-five-year old Scotch the night before he must report to prison. There is a gentle knock on the door and she turns to find Charlie standing in the doorway. He has a six pack of Budweiser in one hand and a large bottle of Evian in the other.

"Care to join me," he says.

"I'd love to."

Noor and Charlie sit down on the bench outside their room. He hands her the Evian and unscrews the cap of a Budweiser. He takes a long swig. Noor finds herself transported back ten years to his garden in Peshawar; the two of them sitting on the highest bough in the grand old oak tree.

In those days we thought we'd conquer the world.

"I'll go looking for a car in the morning," he says. "The sooner we dump the Chevy the better."

Noor stares at the liquor store across the road. A couple of black men, silhouetted by a bright blue Pepsi vending machine, sit on its stoop drinking forties. One laughs as if his buddy is telling him the funniest story known to man. She ponders postponing the inevitable.

What would be the harm in waiting a week?

Yet she knows she can't. A week would soon turn into a month and a month would turn into a year, and every day she postpones her decision she will be putting Charlotte in ever greater danger.

"I need to go back," she says.

"You can never go back, Noor."

"Not to Blowing Rock. To Pakistan."

Charlie swivels in her direction. Noor refuses to look at him. If she does, she doesn't know if she'll have the willpower to finish what she has to say.

"The Prince is never going to quit, Charlie."

"Maybe not, but that doesn't mean we can't stay one step ahead of him."

"We didn't this time."

"That was my fault."

"And the next time it could be mine or Charlotte's even. No, one day, whether it be six months or ten years from now, his men will track us down."

"And traveling to Pakistan will solve what?"

"I'm going to kill him."

Over at the liquor store, the two men struggle to their feet and with an arm around the other's shoulder they stagger off down the road.

"This is crazy," Charlie says.

Noor faces him.

"No crazier than you going to Saudi Arabia to save me?"

"Do you have a plan?"

"At least I'll be able to blend in better than you ever did."

"And how exactly are you going to kill him?"

"After last night do you have any doubts about my expertise with a gun?"

"The Prince is probably one of the best protected men in Pakistan."

"I'll find a way, just like you did."

"And get away."

"That too."

Charlie downs the rest of his Budweiser.

"Charlie, I'm not going to have Charlotte spend the rest of her life looking over her shoulder."

"What? You'd prefer her to spend it mourning her mother instead."

"Yes. That would be infinitely more preferable."

Charlie opens a second bottle.

"We don't even know what he's doing there."

"You need to trust me, Charlie, I'll find a way."

Charlie takes a swig and stares across the street. She knows what he's thinking.

"No, it's got to be me."

"Why?"

"Because it'll be easier for me to get there. Because I'm her mother. It's my responsibility to save her life."

Just as it was my mother's to save mine.

"And me and Charlotte?" he says.

Noor knows his resistance is broken.

"Just keep her safe."

"Till you return."

Noor smiles. Charlie Matthews may have been dealt a rough hand in life but he remains an optimist.

"Exactly."

Charlie leans his forehead against hers.

"Goddamn it, Noor, if I didn't love you so much—"

"But you do."

He kisses her. She kisses him back and for a moment all their troubles are forgotten.

FOURTEEN

AT DAWN CHARLIE walks over to the liquor store and buys himself a coffee, a donut and a dog eared map of the United States. He sits on the stoop and ponders where they should go. His gaze is drawn west. He zeroes in on Los Angeles.

A city vast enough to get lost in.

He traces the route down through Georgia and Alabama and all the way along the southern edge of the United States through Mississippi, Louisiana, Texas, New Mexico, Arizona until he finally reaches California. By now Charlie assumes that a second contingent of the Prince's men will have arrived in Blowing Rock. He wonders if an A.P.B. has already gone out on a thirty-something white male traveling with a South Asian woman and an eight-year-old girl.

I need to dump the car.

He studies the map and reconsiders his route. He has to assume the Chevy will be found eventually and when it is the Saudis will be informed.

I need to fake them out.

He casts his gaze down the East Coast and decides they'll take the 95 to Jacksonville as if their final destination is Miami. There he'll buy a used car before heading west on the 10. He hears a door slam and looks across at the motel. Noor and Charlotte are heading from their room for the Chevy. Charlotte's cheeks are wet with tears.

Time to go.

He crosses the street.

"All good?" he says.

Noor nods. Despite her best efforts her own eyes brim with tears. He bends down till he's at eye level with Charlotte.

"I promise it's all going to work out," he says.

Charlotte gives him a withering glance and gets in.

"She'll come around," Noor says.

Charlie drives as slow as he can into Columbia trying desperately to postpone what everyone in the car knows is inevitable. The Greyhound bus station has the look of a used car dealership that's fallen on hard times. Milling about is a mainly African American clientele interspersed with the odd service member in uniform. Charlie parks at the side of the road. He grips the wheel and looks in the rearview mirror at Noor. Every muscle on her face is strained.

"You have the money?"

"In my bag."

"Keep it close."

"I will."

He swallows.

"Anything else?" he says.

Noor shakes her head. They had discussed everything last night. When she was successful, for they refused to countenance there being an if, Noor would place a marriage announcement in the New York Times for an Olive Dean and Michael Daniels with the name of a church. There they would reunite at noon a week after the announcement.

Charlotte flings her arms around her mother.

"Don't go," she weeps. "Please."

Noor strokes her trembling daughter's hair and whispers in her ear. Charlotte's sobs only grow louder. Noor looks at Charlie. Despite her tears, there is a firmness in her gaze.

"I love you," she says. "Both of you. More than you'll ever know."

She extricates herself from Charlotte's grip.

"No," Charlotte screams.

Charlotte clutches at her mother.

"Charlie, please," Noor says.

Charlie leans over and grabs a hold of Charlotte. Charlotte kicks and screams. Charlie pins Charlotte's arms to her side. Noor grasps her bag and opens the door. She gets out and looks back.

"Merry Christmas," she says.

Charlie is taken aback. He had forgotten it was today. Noor slams the door shut. Charlie lets go of Charlotte. Charlotte rushes at the door with the ferocity of a crazed Rottweiler. Charlie punches the accelerator and the Chevy takes off down the street. Charlotte wrestles with the door handle and attempts to lower the window. Neither will budge. Charlie had had the foresight to turn on the child safety and window locks the night before. Charlie glances in his side mirror. Noor is standing as immobile as a statue. All he wants to do is turn around and tell her that her plan is doomed to failure and that it's better to spend however much time God gives them together than for her to go on this Quixotic mission. He doesn't however. He knows she'd never come.

Out the corner of his eye, he spies Charlotte launch herself at him. She grabs ahold of his hair and scratches at his face.

"Stop the car," she screams. "Stop it now."

Charlie tries to push her away but her grip is too strong. A horn blasts and he turns to see they've swerved across the dividing line and are heading straight at a tanker truck. He corrects the wheel. The truck roars past. Charlie pulls over onto the verge and twists around.

"Do you want to die?" he shouts. "That what you want?"

Charlotte collapses into her seat, her fighting spirit gone.

She sobs uncontrollably. Through the rear window Charlie spots a police car speeding towards them, its siren wailing.

Oh God, no.

He awaits the inevitable only for the police car to fly past. He takes a deep breath and looks at Charlotte huddled in the back.

"I'm sorry," he says. "I really am."

He pulls away and heads for the freeway.

PART III

extinguish

FIFTEEN

CHARLIE LOOKS UP from perusing the classified section of the Florida Times Union. Charlotte sits across from him with her arms crossed. She glares at the stack of pancakes in front of her as if they're a bunch of turncoats.

"Come on, Charlotte, you've got to eat something."

Charlotte's gaze remains fixed on the pancakes. Charlie's getting worried. It's one thing for her not to say a word these last twenty-four hours but it's another not to eat. He returns to the used car section and identifies a nearby dealership. 'Jerry's Cars - America's Greatest Used Car Seller,' its ad proclaims. Alongside a selection of cars that are all 'once in a lifetime opportunities' is a photo of Jerry with his slicked back hair, perma-tan and stars and stripes tie. Charlie spears the last sausage link into his mouth and folds up the paper.

"You coming?" he says.

Charlotte doesn't say a word. Charlie counts the number of pancakes in her stack, seven, and lays a twenty-dollar bill on the check. He slides out of the booth.

"I'll be waiting by the car."

He wanders outside to the Chevy. With his back to the restaurant, he opens the newspaper and glances in the side mirror. Charlotte is still staring at the pancakes.

Come on. You can do it.

Charlotte looks in his direction.

Come on.

Charlie hears the squawk of a police radio and a Jacksonville police car pulls into the spot next to the Chevy. Charlie edges away from the S.U.V. in an attempt to divorce himself from any association with the vehicle. A couple of burly cops with buzz cuts step out. Any moment now Charlie expects them to draw their weapons and for a cavalcade of other cops to come screeching into the lot. No weapons are drawn. No police cars appear. Instead the cops swagger past him. Charlie sighs with relief and looks back towards the restaurant. Charlotte's no longer in the booth.

Shit.

He hurries for the door and yanks it open. Inside the hostess is leading the cops to a booth. Charlie looks up and down the restaurant. There's a family of four with a couple of syrup smeared toddlers, an elderly couple nursing two mugs of coffee, and a trucker digging into a mountainous breakfast, but no sign of Charlotte. Charlie wants to shout out her name but daren't draw the cops' attention. Time slows. His heart beats so hard he's sure everyone must be able to hear it. He hustles over to their booth and looks under the table praying Charlotte's pulled a prank on him. She isn't there either.

"Charlotte," he shouts.

The cops look up from their menus. Charlie hears a door slam and spins around. Charlotte trudges out of the ladies' restroom.

Thank you God.

Charlotte traipses past him and heads for the exit. He glances at the pile of pancakes and counts them. There are only five left. He breathes easier.

At least she won't starve today.

Back in the Chevy, they head along a four lane street dotted with auto repair shops, fast food joints and strip malls.

Jerry's Cars is hard to miss. On a forty-foot flag pole flies an enormous American flag. American flag bunting is strung throughout the lot and next to a billboard that proclaims 'No Credit, No Problem' is another with 'Jerry's Bill of Rights'. Charlie parks across the street.

"Come on," he says to Charlotte.

He gets out of the car and waits. He knows her modus operandi by now. In a couple of minutes, she will respond. Charlie is still at a loss as to how to treat her. To begin with he'd given Charlotte her space. She was inconsolable. He knew there was nothing he could do. However, last night, once they were ensconced in their motel room, he had tried to reach out to her and all he had achieved was a fresh round of tears. Charlotte had proceeded to lock herself in the bathroom and when, after ten minutes, she hadn't responded to his pleas, he'd broken down the door only to find her sitting on the toilet. This morning he'd had to spot the owner a couple of hundred dollars to pay for the damage.

Noor's wrong. I should have gone to Pakistan. I'm useless at this.

The back door opens and Charlotte slumps out. He holds out a hand and she pulls hers away as if his is diseased. He waits for a gap in the traffic and shepherds her across the road. Before they've even stepped onto the lot, a grinning Jerry is bounding out of his office as if he and Charlie are long lost brothers.

"Jerry Stansfeld," he says gripping Charlie's hand.

"Mike Daniels," Charlie says.

"And what might your name be, pretty one?"

Charlotte gives Jerry an icy glare. Jerry laughs.

"Your little girl woke up on the wrong side of bed, did she?"

"I'm not his little girl," Charlotte says. "And before you ask I'm not his daughter either."

Jerry frowns. Charlie is as much shocked by the fact that Charlotte's finally spoken as the situation she's put him in.

"Her mother and I, we're an item," Charlie says. "Fact we're heading to Miami to meet up with her and I need a car to get us there."

Charlie prays that Charlotte doesn't contradict his story. She doesn't and Jerry's smile returns.

"How much are you looking to spend?" Jerry says.

"Five thousand dollars at most. I want something reliable, nothing flashy.

"Well have I got just the car for you. The most reliable, bestselling car in this sweet land of ours in fact."

He guides them over to a white Toyota Corolla. Charlie knows immediately that it'll blend in perfectly.

"For three and a half I'll take it," he says.

"I can't take less than four and a half."

"Four and a quarter."

"Deal."

Jerry's smile broadens. He hasn't made an easier sale in twenty years.

"Now how'll you be paying?"

"Cash."

Jerry looks like he's won the jackpot.

"I'll go get the paperwork and get you on your way."

Jerry hurries for his office.

Not quite on our way.

First they're going to drive the Chevy to the airport and leave it in long term parking. After that they'll take a cab back to Jerry's and collect the car. From there on it's just a question of staying one step ahead of whomever is on their trail.

SIXTEEN

ABDULLAH STEPS OFF the plane. Waiting for him in the gangway is a private investigator named Trent Barnes.

"Welcome back to the United States," Barnes says.

Creased and weathered from his years as an F.B.I field agent, Barnes sports a sharp suit and a gleaming set of teeth.

Perfect teeth. A curious American obsession. That and now the capture of Osama bin Laden.

Abdullah remembers too well the last time he arrived at J.F.K. from Saudi Arabia. He had been with Ivor Gardener and it had been the beginning not only of his fruitless search for Princess Noor but also of his downfall at the General Investigation Directorate. At the time, he had no idea that the Prince, a man so radical that the Interior Ministry had him under surveillance, would moderate and become one of the Crown Prince's favorites. Over the next nine years the Prince would rise ever higher in the echelons of the Saudi government and the higher he rose the worse it became for Abdullah. The Prince blamed Abdullah for letting his fourth wife slip away, and slip away she had. One day she was moments from walking into an ambush in downtown Manhattan, the next she had vanished never to be seen nor heard from again despite the numerous contacts Abdullah had in the U.S.

government and the millions of dollars they had shelled out to private investigative firms. After a year, Abdullah had found himself back in Riyadh, shunted off to an office without a window, his remit the investigation of crimes involving migrant workers. It was a backwater far from the action, the cases almost always involving some miserable wretch from South Asia or the Philippines. More often than not the suspects were innocent but that didn't matter. Their Saudi employers had accused them of a crime and that meant they were guilty. Abdullah helped manufacture the evidence and justice was swift. If they were lucky they'd get off with a lashing and a deportation. If they weren't they found their heads separated from their bodies. If Abdullah was your average Saudi, he would hardly have come into the office without any fear of dismissal. However, he loved his job, at least his old job, and hated the Prince for the demise of his career, Princess Noor even more. To be outwitted by a woman hardly felt credible. He stewed hoping for a chance at redemption. After eight years it looked as if it would never come and he was on the verge of handing in his resignation when 9/11 had occurred.

Hold on, he had told himself. *They might need you again. There is sure to be upheaval in the Kingdom.*

Sure enough, two days ago, someone had called, but it wasn't whom he expected. It had been the Prince, now one of the Kingdom's illustrious Deputy Foreign Ministers. He told Abdullah he had a problem and he hoped Abdullah might be able to fix it. His tone was direct but affable as if he were blameless for Abdullah's derailed career. The Prince explained how the Foreign Minister had become obsessed with releasing Charlie Matthews as a way of assuaging American public opinion, and once the Prince realized he had no hope of derailing a royal pardon, he came around to the idea that it could be an opportunity. Why not place a device in him and track his movements? The Prince had sent two

agents to the United States. Initially everything had gone
better than even the Prince could have hoped. Charlie
Matthews had soon left New York in the company of a
woman named Elma Kuyt, a U.N. employee who'd lived in
Peshawar at the same time as Princess Noor. Abdullah knew
exactly who she was. Back in 1992, he and Ivor Gardener had
considered her a possible ally of Princess Noor's only to drop
her as a suspect. Oh, how he wishes he hadn't. At a discreet
distance, the two agents had followed Matthews to the town
of Blowing Rock. There the agents had checked in with the
Prince and told him that they had been spotted Matthews in
the Princess' company. The Prince had given the order to
abduct her and his son, and they'd said they would call again
once they had them and had disposed of Matthews. Yet they
never did. Finally, the Prince had called them. Someone had
answered speaking fluent Arabic only to quickly hang up. The
Prince had his people in Islamabad try and trace the agents'
phones but by then they'd gone dead.

"I need your help, Abdullah," the Prince had said.

It had taken every ounce of self control for Abdullah not
to tell the Prince to go fuck himself.

"Of course," Abdullah had replied. "I'll do anything in
my power to assist you."

To be fair, Abdullah most likely would have come if the
devil had asked. He was back in the hunt. There was no place
he more liked to be.

Barnes whisks Abdullah through immigration. He was
once one of the F.B.I.'s top investigators but nowadays works
for five times his previous salary for a firm that likes to
describe itself as the world's premier risk mitigator. Abdullah
knows that's gobbledygook. It's basically a private detective
agency, except in its case it's a global one with over a thousand agents, all hired from the world's top police agencies. Its
reach is almost as great as the F.B.I.'s while it doesn't have
any Congressional oversight to worry about.

A younger agent meets them in the arrivals hall of Terminal One and leads them to a station wagon idling at the curb. A police officer is minding it for them. They get in and Barnes begins his briefing. No piece of information is more stunning than that regarding the Prince's offspring.

"The Prince's child is a girl," Barnes says. "Her name's Charlotte Naipaul."

Abdullah protests that that can't be true. He still remembers seeing the gynecologist's report all those years back. Barnes hands Abdullah a photo of Charlotte from her latest yearbook.

She's beautiful. Just like her mother.

Yet she also has a definite look of the Prince.

His nose, his penetrating eyes.

"Have you informed the Prince?" Abdullah asks.

"No," Barnes says, "I thought you'd want to."

Yes, I definitely do.

How satisfying it will be to inform the Prince that he has another girl to add to his menagerie of daughters.

The man is truly cursed. He's the Henry VIII of Saudi Arabia.

"Anything on the agents?" Abdullah asks.

"Nothing."

"And Princess Noor and the girl?"

"They're on the run with Matthews."

Abdullah raises an eyebrow.

"We found footage from a camera in Blowing Rock that positively identifies the three of them in the S.U.V.—"

"That, let me guess, belonged to the two agents."

"That's correct."

"And are you still able to track him?"

"A couple of hours ago one of my agents found the device underneath the seat of a Greyhound coach down in Atlanta."

"So they've vanished into thin air and the Prince's agents are dead."

"That's what we assume."

Abdullah isn't surprised. He remembers Ivor Gardener telling him a few years ago how Matthews had confronted the Prince back in Peshawar after Princess Noor had been abducted. As the Americans like to say, the man has balls. Abdullah suspects Matthews was the person the Prince spoke to and that it was he who killed the Prince's agents. The Warden of Buraydah prison had attested to his flawless Arabic.

"Have you put out an alert on the agents' car?" Abdullah says.

"Yes, but nothing yet."

"And Elma Kuyt?"

"Her phones are tapped. An eight- man surveillance team on her at all times."

Abdullah can only imagine the daily rate Barnes' company must be charging.

"What did Princess Noor do in this Blowing Rock?"

"She was a teacher."

Of course, the apple never falls far from the tree.

"Where do you think they've gone?" Barnes asks.

"You live in a vast country, Mr. Barnes. It'd be foolish to speculate."

"So what next?"

"We start hunting."

And this time I'm going to track them down.

Abdullah stares at the Manhattan skyline, so brutally shorn of its tallest landmarks, and contents himself with the notion that he'll soon be in the Prince's good graces and back in his old position at the General Investigative Directorate.

SEVENTEEN

NOOR LEANS OVER the railing at J.F.K.'s Terminal Four and scans the arriving passengers. Around her throngs of straining relatives wait while slouched limo drivers hold up name cards. Every thirty seconds or so a group of passengers will emerge from around the corner. If one of them is a relation screams will erupt and their relatives will break from the waiting pack and race up to them. Noor wonders if she and Charlotte will ever have such a reunion.

Dear God, I hope so.

A good portion of the relatives are Pakistani. Two hours ago a Pakistani International Airlines flight from Karachi touched down. Noor fits right in. She is wearing a veil and a traditional shalwar kameez she bought yesterday in a shop in Jackson Heights after her visit to the jeweler in Brooklyn.

"He won't be cheap," Charlie had told her in South Carolina, "but he'll get you a passport."

Except he hadn't. When Noor had enquired discreetly whether she could use the jeweler's services, he had come round the counter with all the intent of a linebacker trying to get to an opposing teams' quarterback.

"Get out," he had shouted. "I've no idea what you're talking about."

In this post 9/11 world not only was the U.S. government paranoid, the illegal passport makers were too, terrified
no doubt that they were in the crosshairs of an F.B.I. sting
operation. Afterwards as Noor had stood on the sidewalk in
the freezing cold, she had thought of contacting Elma.

*Perhaps she'll be able to find a way to sneak me into Afghanistan.
From there I can journey on to Pakistan.*

However, Noor soon discarded the idea. Elma was surely
compromised. No, she'd have to find another solution. That
night, she had stayed in a grotty hotel in the shadow of the
Williamsburg Bridge. None of the guests seemed to be using
it to sleep. Loud music and laughter, the occasional scream
and the odd bout of vigorous fucking had kept her up and as
she lay there she had felt bereft. She even began to wonder if
she had left Charlie and Charlotte too hastily. But then, over
all the racket, she had heard the roar of an airplane and it
came to her. Maybe there was a way after all.

An hour after the P.I.A. flight had landed, the first Pakistani passengers had emerged. These were the Pakistani-
Americans and they clenched their dark blue American
passports like they were tickets to the most exclusive party in
town. The Pakistani passengers with visas had begun to
dribble out a few minutes ago. They looked relieved to have
survived immigration and their eyes darted about as if they
were fully aware that people with their skin color and dress
were now seen as potential enemies in this land.

Come on. There has to be a woman like me.

The dribble turns into a flurry yet the exiting passengers
offer Noor little joy. They are primarily men and elderly
couples here to visit their émigré children. The women, that
are her age, are accompanied by husbands who seem as
predisposed as the Prince to letting their wives carry their
own passports. Another twenty minutes pass. The proportion
of Pakistani passengers dwindles. Noor decides she will have
to come back tomorrow.

And then she sees her. A young Pakistani woman with long black hair, an olive complexion and a slim, pretty face. She is, by no means, Noor's doppelgänger but she's of a type. The woman pulls a suitcase while carrying a leather purse over her shoulder. Noor waits for a screaming horde of relations to rush up to her but they never materialize. Instead the woman heads for the exit. With her own bag in hand, Noor follows her. The woman stops. Noor pretends to be engrossed by the arrivals board. The woman heads for the restroom. Noor hurries after her. She pushes open the restroom door and looks around. The woman's suitcase is standing outside a stall. To her chagrin, the purse isn't sitting on top of it. Noor enters the next door stall and sits down. Soon enough the woman flushes her toilet and opens her door. Noor counts to ten and flushes her own. She exits and spots the woman redoing her lipstick in the mirror, her purse beside her. Noor takes the sink next to hers and washes her hands. She glances down. The purse is open and nestled amidst a cellphone, a host of travel documents and a leather wallet is a green Pakistani passport. Noor catches the woman's eye in the mirror.

"I'm sorry but I think we've met."

The woman's frown turns into an embarrassed smile.

"I'm Bushra Kiani," Noor says.

"Samina Qari," the woman says in heavily accented English. "I humbly apologize but I do not recall where."

"Karachi perhaps."

"I do not think so. I have spent little time there."

"Then perhaps New York."

"At N.Y.U.?"

"That must be it."

"Perhaps it was at the Pakistani Students Association."

"That's it. I'm friends with Abdul."

To Noor's relief, Samina's face lights up. Abdul had been the most common name she could think of.

"Abdul Qazi," Samina says.

"Who else?"

"Oh, do tell me, how is he?"

"You know Abdul ..."

Samina laughs.

"Always the joker."

"He never changes."

Samina puts her lipstick back in her purse.

Now or never.

"It was lovely seeing you again," Noor says.

"Oh yes, you too."

Noor wraps her arms around Samina and gives her a prolonged hug. Her left hand delves inside Samina's purse and extracts the passport. She slips it up her sleeve and releases Samina. Samina has reddened considerably.

"I can't wait to tell Abdul we ran into each other," Noor says.

Samina forces a smile.

"Khuda hafiz," Samina says.

"Yes, khuda hafiz."

Samina zips her purse closed and makes her escape. Noor stares after her.

Who have I become?

Noor allows the passport to drop into her shaking hand. She opens it to the identification page and studies Samina's photo. If anyone takes a quick glance she should be able to pull it off. If they give it a more studied examination she suspects she'll be in a heap of trouble.

The restroom door clatters open. The passport drops from Noor's hands. Noor expects to see Samina charging in. Instead it is a harried mother with a toddler in a stroller.

Come on, get it together.

Noor picks up the passport. She hurries out of the restroom and through the arrivals hall. She steps through a set of automatic doors and out onto the concourse. She spies

Samina getting into a cab. Noor waits until Samina's taxi is lost amidst the flow of other vehicles. She wonders when Samina will discover her passport's gone. She hopes not until she's at least at her destination. And what then? Maybe she will call Abdul Qazi and ask him about Bushra Kiani. Baffled he'll tell her he knows no such woman, and at this point Samina Qari will panic. She will call the police and report the theft because by now it's too late to call the Pakistani Consulate. They will take down her details but her report will be just one of many that day.

You might just get away with this.

Noor hurries inside and takes the elevator to the departures hall. She looks up at the board. The return flight to Karachi leaves in two hours. Noor walks up to the agent at the Pakistani International Airlines ticket counter.

"My name is Samina Qari. I just arrived from Karachi only to learn that my father has been involved in a car crash."

"Oh ma'am, I'm sorry to hear that."

"I need to get home right away."

"Of course."

The agent hits a couple of keys.

"I see you have a return ticket in the system," he says.

"Will it cost much to change it?"

"Given your unfortunate situation nothing at all. Now, if I could have your passport, please."

Noor hands it over. The agent turns to the identification page and glances up at her. Noor pinches the bridge of her nose and pretends to sniffle. The agent types in her details and hands back the passport.

"Would you prefer an aisle or window seat, Miss Qari?"

"A window seat, please."

Noor realizes she's done it.

Oh my God. I'm really going back.

EIGHTEEN

"JERRY STANSFELD," THE beaming salesman says. "How can I help you fellas?"

More perfect American teeth, Abdullah thinks.

Barnes flashes a badge with the practiced air of an ex F.B.I. agent.

"Agent Evans. This is my partner, Agent Gibney, and this is Agent Mahmoud."

The salesman's smile disappears, however, the twinkle never leaves his eyes.

This will be a story he'll tell till the day he dies.

Barnes hands Jerry a photo of Charlie.

"We've reason to believe this man came by your lot."

"Sure did. Him and a young girl. This a kidnapping? Because, I gotta admit, I found it mighty odd that a white fella would be with a little brown girl."

The salesman flashes his teeth in Abdullah's direction.

"No offense meant," he says.

"None taken," Abdullah says.

"Did he purchase a car from you?" Barnes says.

"Matter of fact he did. A white Toyota Corolla. Said he was off to meet the girl's mother in Miami. If you give me a minute, I'll get you a copy of the title transfer."

Jerry hustles across the sales lot towards his office. Abdullah feels the tips of his fingers tingle. His quarry is dripping copious amounts of blood.

The first spill had been a day ago at Jacksonville Airport. In Matthews' defense, before 9/11 parking a stolen car in a long term parking lot would have been a clever move. However, it isn't any longer. Stolen vehicles at airport parking facilities are of particular interest to the F.B.I. nowadays and the Chevy had soon flashed up on a watch list. The F.B.I. had notified Barnes, and last night Abdullah and Barnes' team had flown down on a private jet and claimed the vehicle on behalf of the Saudi embassy. In the trunk they had found specks of blood. It only confirmed that the Saudi agents were dead. To Matthews' credit their bodies still hadn't been discovered and, as far as Abdullah is concerned, it would probably be best if they weren't. Initially Abdullah had figured that Matthews, Princess Noor and the girl had boarded a flight using fake passports. Barnes had a local F.B.I. contact pull surveillance footage of the terminal but there was no sign of them. Abdullah requested surveillance footage of the concourse and soon spotted Matthews and the girl getting into a cab. Barnes tracked down the taxi driver and that had led them to this used car dealership. The only question that remained was why Princess Noor wasn't with them.

Why did they split up?

It makes no sense to Abdullah. After all these years apart why would Matthews and Princess Noor abandon each other so quickly? And why, more pertinently, would Princess Noor abandon her daughter?

Perhaps she's hoping to draw us away from her? But then why didn't she leave a trail for us to follow?

He wonders if they feared they would be spotted if they travelled as a group.

Perhaps they intend to meet up again in Miami or somewhere else. But then why wouldn't Princess Noor stay with her daughter? Why's

Matthews with her instead?

Abdullah knows something's not right. He just can't put his finger on it.

The door to the office swings open and Jerry comes barreling towards them waving a piece of paper in his hand as if it were a winning lottery ticket.

Don't worry, once you track Matthews down he'll tell you where Princess Noor is. After all you got him to reveal where she was once before. Why should it be any different this time?

NINETEEN

CHARLIE GLANCES IN the rearview mirror. Charlotte is curled up with her head resting against the window. She sips on a Coke and reads *Harry Potter and the Sorcerer's Stone* under the halo of the backseat light. Charlie had bought it for her along with the three other books in the series at a Barnes and Noble outside of Baton Rouge. It had been the start of their second day on the road and he didn't know if he could stand another of her sitting in the back like a zoned out mental patient. When she had brought them up to the register he had asked her if they were popular, and she and the cashier had looked at him as if he were from a different planet. Since then all she had done was read, eat and sleep. If she hadn't spoken at Jerry's Cars he might even be worried that her mother's departure had struck her dumb.

Today they had driven along the lush Gulf Coast, past the skyscrapers and belching refineries of Houston and on into the vast, flat emptiness of Texas. Now it's pitch black and their main company are the trucks that lumber along in the right lane in packs. His headlights illuminate the undeviating freeway ahead before they too are swallowed up by the dark. With the star speckled sky above, it feels like they're heading straight for a black hole.

Charlie hears the book slap shut. By the time he glances in the mirror Charlotte's already into the second book.

"How was it?" he says.

Charlotte sucks on her straw.

"Must be really good if you want to find out what happens in the second."

"I've read them all already."

She speaks.

"Well then they must be more than really good. What they about?"

Charlotte turns the page.

"A boy called Harry Potter I'm assuming," Charlie says.

Charlie's gaze flicks back to the mirror. He detects a roll of the eyes.

Derision. I'll take that anytime over her self-imposed silence.

"You know when I was in Saudi Arabia, in prison I mean, we didn't have any books to read outside of the Quran. It's funny, I was never a voracious reader in my previous life. Don't get me wrong, I read but not like your mom or grandpa. Fact it was only when I'd been in prison for a while that I realized how much I missed books. 'If only I could get my hands on one good novel,' I'd say to myself.'"

"Which would it have been?"

"Oh, I don't know, it was such a forlorn hope I never thought to think of one."

Charlie's eyes travel to the mirror. Charlotte's own have returned to her book.

Come on, keep her talking.

"Papillon perhaps though I guess it's not technically a novel. It's a true story. I read it out in Pakistan."

"What's it about?"

"It's about this guy, Henri. He's wrongly convicted of murder in France and sentenced to spend the rest of his life in this island prison off the coast of South America. Anyway it's a brutal place and so he decides to escape and escape he does, God knows how many times, yet each time they eventually catch him and throw him back in the hole."

"The hole?"

"Basically this dark, tiny cell which you stay in all by yourself."

"Were you ever in it?"

"A few times."

"What's it like?"

"You lose all sense of time and at some point begin to think you're never going to get out."

"Sounds just like Azkaban Prison. Sirius Black nearly went demented."

Charlie hasn't a clue what Charlotte's talking about, yet he resists the temptation to glance in the rearview mirror.

"So what happens at the end of your book?" she asks.

"Oh, well he escapes one final time and manages to flee to a country where they can never ever get him."

"A bit like us."

"Yeah, exactly. Just like us."

Though we aren't safe yet. Not even close.

"But not Mom."

"No, but I suppose the moral of the story is that you can never give up in this life, just like your mom never has, and if you do that then everything will eventually turn out all right."

"You really believe that?"

I don't know what I believe.

"Your mom's a survivor, Charlotte. Don't worry, we're going to see her again, sooner than later, I promise."

Charlie glances in the rearview mirror. Charlotte's brow furrows as she ponders his words. She picks up her book and delves back into its magical world. Charlie decides not to push it. The important thing is he's made progress. Up ahead his headlights illuminate a sign for a place called Fort Stockton. He indicates. It's time to call it a day and tuck his precious cargo into bed.

TWENTY

"WELCOME HOME, MISS Qari."

The Pakistani immigration officer hands back Samina Qari's passport. Noor can barely believe it. Noor passes through a set of automatic doors and on the other side is assaulted by the familiar sights and smells of a country that she thought she'd never see again. The arrivals hall reverberates with the din of a thousand voices and is as humid as a tropical forest. It reeks of body odor. Ten years ago Noor wouldn't have noticed but now she finds it both familiar and overwhelming. Taxi drivers cry out that they'll give her the best ride for the best price, porters in sweat stained shalwar kameez beg to take her bag. Noor ignores them and, with her purse tight to her chest and a firm grip on her suitcase, she barrels through the crowd until she arrives at an elevator bank. She takes a groaning elevator up to the departures hall and wheels her bag towards a bureau de change.

Noor has the ten thousand dollars Betty gave her as well as an extra five from Charlie. A third of it is rolled up inside a sock that lies at the bottom of her suitcase, a third is in her purse, and a third is in a money belt beneath her kameez. Noor takes three hundred dollars out of her purse and stands in line behind a Chinese businessman and a Pakistani woman with a scarf draped casually over her hair. Noor glances up at the departures board. A flight for Peshawar leaves in an hour and a half.

Perfect.

The customer at the window walks away and the woman approaches the booth. The clerk asks for the woman's passport and she slips it under the window. The clerk takes an inordinate amount of time checking its details. A chill runs up Noor's spine. She edges away. At a nearby P.I.A. counter a police officer is talking animatedly with an airline manager. Noor scans the hall. As if by magic the number of rifle wielding soldiers has multiplied by a factor of five. They scan the hall like a group of prison guards searching for an escaped convict. A soldier turns his gaze Noor's way and she steps beside the Chinese businessman in an attempt to obscure the soldier's view.

They're on to you.

Noor glances at the entrance doors. Out on the concourse a bus has pulled up.

You need to go. Now.

A couple of soldiers position themselves at the door. Noor hesitates.

"Next, please."

The Chinese businessman strolls up to the window. A shout punctuates the air. Noor spins in its direction. A man is pointing directly at her.

It's over.

The soldiers charge in Noor's direction. Noor closes her eyes. The soldiers' boots pound towards her only to carry on past like a passing thunderstorm. All around the hall men cheer and women shriek. Noor opens her eyes. A group of young men in green and yellow tracksuits are sauntering into the departures hall. On either side of them a phalanx of soldiers holds back a rabid crowd.

The Pakistani cricket team.

"Ma'am."

Noor spins towards the bureau de change. The clerk is gesturing her forward.

Go. This is your chance.

Noor plunges through the crowd and slips out the entrance. Down from the bus a taxi driver is handing a businessman his suitcase. Noor slides into the backseat of the taxi. She places her bag and purse beside her. The taxi driver gets behind the wheel and does a double take.

"The train station," she says in Urdu.

"Most certainly ma'am."

The taxi driver accelerates into traffic and turns on some jarring Indian disco music. They come down an onramp onto a highway. Noor has never seen such traffic, the four lanes on either side chock full of cars, buses, trucks and motorized rickshaws. Noor spies a sign proclaiming the highway's name. Shara-e-Faisal. King Faisal Road.

Even here I can't get away from the Saudis.

The traffic inches along past modern office buildings yet it doesn't stop the drivers, including her own, from blasting their horns and continually shifting lanes for the slightest advantage. Noor glances at her watch. It is two-thirty in the afternoon. She leans forward.

"Is it already rush hour?" she asks.

The taxi driver grins while cussing at a rickshaw driver.

"Oh no, ma'am, in Karachi it is rush hour all the time."

Noor slumps back in her seat. She finds herself yearning for the peace and quiet of Blowing Rock. She thinks back to the days when she and Charlotte would walk to school and would be shocked if more than ten cars passed them.

"Where's everyone trying to get to in such a hurry?" Charlotte would say.

Oh, Charlotte, if you could see the heart pounding chaos of Karachi.

To Noor's relief, the exit to the train station is not far down the highway. The cab driver turns off it and leaves the mayhem behind. They enter a part of town from an earlier era, made up of sandstone buildings from the English Raj. Karachi Cantonment, the train station, has the look of a faded palace with two red roofed towers on either end and a series of arched windows and doors. Outside its main entrance a small army of beggars lingers; desperate mothers with children, blind children with terrible burns, legless men, armless women, little girls and boys with deformed jaws and cleft lips. Noor hands her driver a twenty-dollar bill. She knows it's far too much but she just wants to get inside the station. Noor exits the taxi. Like a mythical hydra, the beggars' heads swivel in her direction and as one they rush towards her. Noor clings to her purse and suitcase and forces her way through the scrum.

"Please, ma'am, please, just a little something for my baby," a blind woman pleads.

Her baby starts bawling as if on cue. Noor fights the urge to give her some money. It would cause a tsunami. At the main entrance, a couple of soldiers shout at the beggars and the beggars shrink back. Noor takes a deep breath and gathers herself. Inside the paint is peeling on the walls and the tile floor is chipped but otherwise everything feels orderly. At the ticket office there is only one solitary line. Twenty people stand in it and it takes an hour before Noor gets to the front. She enquires about a ticket to Peshawar and is told that a train leaves in half an hour.

"I'd like to go first class," she says.

"I'm sorry, ma'am," the ticket agent says, "but first class is sold out."

Noor buys a second class fare. It's at least better than third. She makes her way to the platform and now understands why there were so few people in the main hall. They're taking up every available square foot of the platform. A street seller persuades her to buy a couple of samosas. From another she purchases a copy of the Dawn newspaper. She reads the main article about a train that was passing through Silbi yesterday. A passenger had spilt some gas from a container and decided to clean it up by lighting it with a match. It hadn't worked, or to be exact it had worked only too well. The carriage had gone up in flames and ten people had died in the inferno.

A horn blasts and Noor looks up to see a train lumbering into the station. The crowd surges. Noor spies her carriage twenty yards away. It might as well be a hundred for the deluge of people coming her direction. Gripping her suitcase handle, she fights her way towards it. Passengers jostle her. One yanks her violently on the arm. She spins around towards a man with blazing eyes. He tugs on her purse.

"Hey," she screams.

Behind her someone kicks the back of her left knee. She tumbles forward and puts her hands out to break her fall. The man wrenches her purse free.

"Thief," she screams. "Stop him."

No one pays her any heed. Noor scrambles to her feet. She spies the man's head bobbing through the crowd. She already knows it's too late. The money is gone as well as Samina Qari's passport. And then it occurs to her.

My suitcase.

Noor twists around and realizes it's gone too.

No.

She feels around her waist. The money belt is still there. She doesn't know whether to cry with relief or mourn the loss of her purse and bag. A conductor blows his whistle.

Just keep going.

Noor staggers towards her carriage and grabs hold of an iron handle. She pulls herself inside. The coach is a heaving sweating mass of humanity. On one side are single seats facing each other and on the other a set of benches with what look like cots hanging above them. Not only is every space on every bench taken but so are the cots whose occupants' feet dangle in the faces of those seated below. Noor pushes her way down the aisle only to discover a perspiring beast with a salt-and-pepper beard and a triangular sheepskin hat lounging in her seat.

"Excuse me," she says in Urdu. "That's my seat."

"Show me," he says.

Noor's hand reaches for her purse only to remember it's been stolen. The man smiles with satisfaction. The carriage shudders and the train edges out of the station.

Get out. You've still got more than enough money to hire a driver.

Noor shoves her way back down the aisle. By the time she makes it to the door, the train has picked up speed and is trundling past a slum.

Too late.

Through the door's open window, Noor catches sight of a girl gazing at the train. She stands at the entrance of a mud brick house. Her hair is mangy, her brightly colored sari frayed, but what strikes Noor most is the despair in her eyes as if she wishes she could be anywhere in the world but where she is right now. Noor wonders if the girl sees the same emotion in her own eyes. Noor turns away and leans wearily against the wall. Peshawar is still thirty hours away.

***

HOW THEY GOT on the raft, Noor hasn't a clue. But there they are; she, Charlie and Charlotte meandering down a lazy river under a scorching sun.

I've been here before. It's the Watauga River.

And then she remembers when. It was with Bert Donahue. He took her and Charlotte on a Saturday a little over six months ago.

Or was it a Sunday?

They'd had a guide with them, Bert was too old to man the paddle. They had floated downstream, Charlotte perched up against the side scanning the wooded banks with a pair of binoculars.

Today Charlie is holding the paddle. He smiles at her.

God I love that smile.

Charlotte lies back, her head arched so far over the side that her hair trails in the water. Noor closes her eyes and allows the sun to warm her face.

This is perfect.

The boat shakes and Noor's eyes start open. The water is no longer languid but rather a churning mass. Charlie fights the current with all his might. Charlotte sits there immobilized, staring at something up ahead. Noor twists around. Her stomach drops. It's a waterfall as wide and thunderous as the Niagara Falls. She screams at Charlie to do something. He gives her the same look he gave her in Riyadh Airport all those years ago. There's nothing he can do.

"Hold on," he shouts.

Noor feels herself falling, her view of the others obscured by the cascade of water around her. She hits the water and is tossed about so violently that she has no clue what direction the surface could possibly be.

"Charlotte."

To her surprise she is able to scream despite being underwater.

"Charlotte."

Her gyrations slow and the bubbles clear. Columns of lurid green kelp appear as well as brightly colored fish and sparkling coral. Charlie swims towards her with the grace of a mermaid.

"She's safe," he says.

Noor believes him. His hand reaches out and pulls her closer. She arches her lips towards his. His hand slips under her shirt. She eagerly anticipates its caress on her breast.

Instead it fondles her stomach with the rough, furtive quality of a policeman patting down a suspect.

"Stop it," she says.

"It's not me," Charlie replies and only then does she realize that she's in a dream.

Noor's eyes flash open. She is lying on the carriage floor. A mustached man with a milky right eye and a shock of curly, black hair kneels between her crooked legs. She follows the arc of his arm. It is snaked up underneath her kameez.

I'm being raped.

Noor goes to stand only for the man to whip out a knife and push it up against her throat.

"Nahi," he hisses.

The train's brakes screech and the carriage shudders to a halt. The carriage door opens. The man cuts the strap of the money belt and rips it away. He grabs a makeshift skateboard with his other hand and launches himself out the door past the embarking passengers. The last thing Noor sees are his legs or, more pertinently, his lack of them.

"My money," Noor screams.

No one pays her any heed. Noor scrambles to her feet and struggles past the surge of passengers who're now clambering on board.

"Watch it woman," a man yells.

She pays him no heed and pushes past. He shoves her in the back. Noor tumbles onto the concrete platform like a piece of tossed luggage. She lies there, her grazed elbows screaming in pain, the wind knocked out of her.

Get up.

She struggles to find a breath.

Get up or it's all over.

Noor staggers to her feet and catches a glimpse of the thief near the platform entrance, splayed on his skateboard, his rotating arms propelling him forward like a human centipede. He zips under the turnstile and disappears.

Noor sprints after him weaving between the passengers coming in her direction. A ticket collector stands at the turnstile. She barrels past him and out into the domed ticket hall. The thief is three-quarters of the way across it. Noor spies a couple of policemen

"Thief," she screams. "Thief."

The policemen are bemused while the thief looks back and only redoubles his efforts. Noor sprints after him. The thief reaches the entrance. He flies off its top step and disappears. Noor arrives twenty seconds later. At the bottom of a set of stairs, the thief lies sprawled on his back, his right hand still gripping the money belt. The thief spots Noor and twists back onto his front. Noor bounds down the steps. The man grabs his skateboard and jumps back on. He takes off across the parking lot towards a street shrouded in exhaust fumes.

Noor bolts after him. She closes the gap. A motorized rickshaw scoots past her. The thief grabs ahold of its bumper. Noor throws herself at the man and manages to slam her right hand down on the edge of his skateboard. The board upends and the rickshaw drags the man along on his stumps. He loses his grip and tumbles onto the asphalt. The two of them stare at each. Noor wobbles to her feet. The man twists around and crawls towards the busy street.

"Give me my money," Noor screams in Urdu.

The thief keeps going. Noor grabs a hold of his kameez and yanks him backwards.

"Help me," the thief screams to nearby onlookers. "Save me from this crazy bitch."

Noor bends down to grab her money belt. The thief rears his elbow back and catches her on the jaw. Noor reels backwards. The thief crawls forward once more. Noor shakes her head to clear it. She stalks up to the thief and kicks him in the small of the back. The thief howls in pain. She raises her foot and kicks him again and again until his screams turn to moans. Noor spins the thief onto his back and rips her money belt from his grasp. A whistle shrills. She spies the policemen racing down the station steps. She spots a motor-ized rickshaw idling nearby. Its driver stares at her, his mouth agape. She extracts a hundred dollars from the money belt and waves it in his face.

"Can you get me out of here?"

He nods. Noor climbs into the back and the driver spurts into traffic. Noor glances back at the thief still sprawled on the ground.

Who the hell have I become?

She no longer has an answer.

TWENTY-ONE

CHARLIE STARES AT Charlotte. She looks so like Noor it's uncanny. He wonders what she's dreaming about. Her mother no doubt. Maybe her old life; her friends, Betty, walking around Bass Lake. Or perhaps she's in the midst of a nightmare, conjuring up a fantastical version of the men who are after them. Unfortunately, she is probably not far off.

They're not going to stop till they find us. Not this time.

Charlie feels it in his soul. It's like they're in purgatory just waiting for Judgment Day to arrive.

We won't stay here long. We'll leave right after New Year.

Charlotte's eyes drift open.

"Morning you," he says.

Charlotte sits up in her bed and grimaces.

"I thought we could go get some pancakes," he says.

"I'm not hungry."

"Ice cream too if you want."

"I'm not four."

"I get it, but I'm sure as hell gonna have some."

"For breakfast?"

"I went nine years without ice cream. Hell, I'm going to have an ice cream sundae for breakfast, lunch and dinner."

Charlotte stifles a laugh.

Just.

"I thought we could go down to the ocean after," he says.

Charlotte purses her lips as she ponders her options.

Just like her mother.

"It's nice out," he says.

"Fine but I need to pray."

"Go for it."

"I need privacy."

"Course."

Charlie grabs his wallet and a couple of beach towels, and steps into the dim corridor. In the room opposite a couple of women are chatting away in German.

At least she's talking.

After their chat outside Fort Stockton her answers had returned to being monosyllabic at best. It was as if she were castigating herself for having had a conversation with him. Fort Stockton had been a small, spread out town but Charlie would have had a hell of a time describing it. It was dark when they drove in and dark the next morning when they left. He had driven another thirteen hours that day with pit stops only to buy food and pee. From time to time a police car had come wailing up behind them and he would stiffen but they always sped by. In fact, the greatest danger they'd faced were his drooping eyes. On more than one occasion he'd had to catch himself from falling asleep, and every time, when he looked in the rearview mirror, he saw Charlotte staring back at him with the same look of disapproval that Noor often used to give him. They had finally stopped on the outskirts of Palm Springs at another cheap motel. This one, at least, had a pool and in the morning they had gone to a nearby strip mall and he'd bought Charlotte a bathing suit.

"You want to have a swim before we leave," he had asked her.

She had shaken her head but he could tell she was tempted. That day, yesterday, they had continued on all the way to the Pacific Ocean and as they had walked down the Venice boardwalk with its fortune tellers and weightlifters, its henna artists and street dancers, he had reasoned that it was probably a better place than most to hide. Amidst the weirdoes and freaks, this bi-racial pair seemed almost normal.

The door swings open. Charlotte stands there in a T-shirt and shorts, the bathing suit he'd bought her underneath.

"Let's go," she says.

The elevator creaks and jerks down four floors. In the lobby the receptionist is engrossed in a martial arts film playing on a small TV. They step outside. Most of the stores are closed and the street artists are yet to appear. There is a chill in the air but not a cloud in the sky. The palm trees stand tall while an assortment of rollerbladers and bicyclists hurtle down the bike path. Beyond the beach, the pale blue water rolls gently towards shore. Charlie knows there's no land for thousands of miles.

Not until you hit Japan. Then China. Then India. Then Pakistan.

He wonders if Noor ever got there. If she is still alive.

"So we going?" Charlotte says.

Charlie smiles.

"Which way do you think the restaurant is?" he says.

"I don't know. It was your idea."

Charlie looks up and down the boardwalk.

"Let's take our chances and go this way."

It sounds like a metaphor for their journey.

He ambles along. He closes his eyes and breathes in the salty air.

That's something I never thought I'd smell again.

Then something miraculous happens. Charlotte slips her hand in his. He is tempted to look at her and smile. However, he doesn't. He just continues on walking as if it's the most normal thing in the world.

TWENTY-TWO

"WE LEAVE TOMORROW," Rashid says.

"Why risk it?" Tariq says.

Rashid rips off a piece of naan and shoves it in his mouth.

"The Americans are coming."

"To Pakistan?"

"This isn't Pakistan, this is the tribal areas and they'll do whatever they please in this God forsaken land."

"Then why haven't they come yet?"

"Because they're still mopping up in Afghanistan."

"Rashid's right," Nawaf says. "It's safer in the cities."

Since the moment Tariq had arrived two weeks ago, half frozen to death, there hasn't been a glimmer of daylight between the two Egyptians. They had gotten this mud walled tribal compound a couple of days before he had and as such had thought of Tariq as something of an intruder. Not once did it cross their minds that their early arrival meant they had fled Tora Bora before the Emir had even given them permission to.

Typical Egyptian blowhards.

The compound's impoverished inhabitants had treated them like their own sons. It was the Pashtun way, yet Rashid and Nawaf had never once shown any appreciation. If anything they had treated the tribes people with high-handed haughtiness as if they were the rulers of this land and not rats scuttling for safety.

"Where are we going?" Tariq says.

"Karachi," Rashid says. "Who knows after that. But first we need to get to Peshawar."

A trickle of fear passes down Tariq's spine.

Of all the places in the world to return to.

"Why do we need to go there? It'll be crawling with Americans."

"This lot are only prepared to take us that far," Rashid says. "Besides there's a safe house there."

"Whose cover's most likely blown."

"It shouldn't have been, inshallah. Few people know of it."

That hardly reassures Tariq. After all few people knew of the caves at Tora Bora.

"Besides we need money," Nawaf says. "New identities. How else are we going to get those?"

Tariq shovels the last of his naan into his mouth and washes it down with some lukewarm tea.

"Fine," he says, "tomorrow it is."

He lies down on his rope bed and stares up at the mud encrusted ceiling.

Oh, how did you ever find yourself in this situation?

It is a rhetorical question. He knows the answer.

Noor.

If it hadn't been for Noor, he would be living thousands of miles away. He would be a man of importance in the richest kingdom on earth. Instead he had spent the last eight years as a reluctant and itinerant holy warrior, first in Sudan and then Afghanistan. By the time he got to Afghanistan, he knew bin Laden and Zawahiri well. They treated him with respect and gave him ever increasing responsibilities. 'You are part of the greatest movement in human history,' bin Laden would tell him and Tariq would nod as if he believed him. He was trapped. Al Qaeda was going from being a nuisance to being America's enemy number one. First came the embassy bombings in East Africa then the attack on the U.S.S. Cole. After the embassy bombings, the United States launched a series of cruise missiles at their training camps. From then on they moved from one desultory compound to the next. There were rumors of Saudi and C.I.A assassination teams, that even the Taliban had decided to turn on them. He hardly saw Badia, his wife, or their two daughters. They lived with the other women on the outskirts of Jalalabad. The facilities there were little better than that of a rundown orphanage. So much for bin Laden's vaunted wealth! In eight years Badia had gone from a dazzling beauty to a haggard crone. The last time he saw her was three months ago. She told him she was taking the children back to the tribal areas. She had contacted her brothers and they were sending a nephew to fetch her. 'Righteous women are devoutly obedient' to their husbands, that's what the Quran proclaims, yet the idea that Badia was a righteous woman was laughable.

She's nothing but a two bit whore.

Tariq had punched her to the ground and kicked her shrieking form while his two daughters cowered against the walls. It was the least she'd deserved. When he had returned home the next day they were gone.

God knows what she told her brothers about me.

It's that fear that stops him from seeking them out and asking for refuge.

In the distance there's a crescendo of loud booms from across the border in Afghanistan.

Bin Laden never thought it would come to this. Not once.

No, in bin Laden's mind, the Americans were weak and once proven the Muslim world would rise up against them.

"It's coming," he'd remark cryptically. "Mark my words."

No one knew what he was talking about, yet the men began having dreams about jetliners and when they remarked upon this to bin Laden he would nod with a knowing smile. An air of excitement built amongst the men yet all Tariq felt was dread. On September 10th, Ahmed Shah Massoud, the lion of Panjshir, was killed by a couple of al Qaeda suicide bombers.

Oh no, Tariq remembers thinking. *Here we go.*

Bin Laden gave the order that they should drive up to the caves of Tora Bora. They were primitive affairs, no better than hollowed out stone chambers with tarpaulins and mattresses over their entrances to keep the rain and wind out. They had brought a television and a satellite dish but no one could make the damn thing work, and so they clustered around a short wave radio. As the sun dipped over the mountains to the west, the first exultant cry went up. A plane had hit one of the World Trade Center towers. What a victory! However, all bin Laden did was put a hand up as if to say 'wait'. A second plane hit the second tower, another rammed the Pentagon and a fourth was reported to have crashed in Pennsylvania. And then one tower and then the next crumbled to the ground. 'This is the moment we've been waiting for,' bin Laden said and for a moment even Tariq had been swept up in the euphoria. Perhaps his old dreams might still come true. Perhaps there would be a revolution across the Arab world. Perhaps bin Laden would become the new Caliph with his capital in Mecca. Tariq would be given a position of power. He would make sure the Prince was beheaded alongside his apostate relatives. But then, to their ever increasing dismay, nothing happened. Rather the Muslim world contorted itself into a protective ball. Bin Laden still professed a quiet confidence that if the Americans attacked they would find themselves bogged down in Afghanistan. Instead the Americans swept in with briefcases of cash and in a matter of days turned the majority of the country against al

Qaeda. Before they knew it, they were stuck in the caves of Tora Bora with Afghan militia and American special forces closing in from below as American aircraft dropped bombs from above. Bin Laden exhorted the men to keep fighting but Tariq could tell he knew the game was up.

Oh Noor, how you must laugh at my predicament.

In Sudan he'd heard the rumors that Noor had somehow managed to escape with the Prince's unborn son. It had hardly seemed credible especially considering the resources the Prince had at his disposal.

She truly must be the devil's spawn.

He wonders where they ended up. The child must be eight years old now, the age in Saudi Arabia when a boy is taken from his mother and goes to live with his father. He wonders if Noor will ever tell her son the true story; how he could have been a Prince, a man of untold wealth and influence. He wonders how her son will take it.

If it was me, I'd be furious.

Perhaps, one day, that will be Noor's undoing. Unbeknownst to her, her son will reach out to the Prince, the only man she hates even more than her brother.

Oh wouldn't that be the cruelest of ironies.

Tariq chuckles and wonders where Noor is right now. America? Canada? Australia even?

One thing's for sure, that bitch is far away from this madness.

TWENTY-THREE

"IS IT IN there?" Charlotte says.

Charlie looks up from scanning the New York Times' marriage announcements.

"It's too early," he says. "I'm sorry. It was stupid to even look."

Charlotte shrugs as if it's no big deal. She uses her straw to vacuum up the last of her Coke.

"It's okay to miss her," Charlie says.

"I know. I just don't get why she had to leave me."

Because I selfishly came back into your lives.

"Have you heard of a book called *The Lord of the Rings*?"

"The movie just came out. I wanted to see it but Mom said it wasn't suitable."

"Well it's a trilogy, you know, three books—"

Charlotte rolls her eyes. Duh.

"And in it is this hobbit called Frodo and he's been given this ring which has magical powers. He doesn't know that to begin with, but he soon learns that if it falls into the hands of this evil wizard, Sauron, that's basically it for Middle Earth. In fact, the only way he can ensure the world's safe is if he throws it into this volcano called Mount Doom."

"Sounds scary."

"The scariest. So he plucks up the courage and with a friend called Sam journeys there with the help of elves, dwarves, and this amazing wizard called Gandalf. All the time the bad guys are trying to steal the ring off him but somehow he manages to get to Mount Doom and throw it away. Middle Earth is saved, Sauron and the evil forces are destroyed, and Frodo returns home a hero."

"And Mom is Frodo?"

"You're too smart."

"And my father is the evil wizard?"

Way too smart.

"Your mom has no choice, Charlotte. Just like Frodo, only she can throw away the ring."

Charlotte munches on her last slice of pepperoni pizza and ponders Charlie's words.

"Did you ever meet my dad?" she says

"Just once."

He was holding Malaya's decapitated head and relishing the opportunity to cut off mine.

"He's done some pretty bad things, hasn't he?"

"He treated your mom very badly."

"And you?"

"Can't say I'm his favorite."

"And if he catches me he'll do bad things to me too, won't he?"

Charlie takes Charlotte's hand in his.

"You need to know something. When I make a promise I keep it. I promised I'd rescue your mom from Saudi Arabia and I did. I promised her I'd see her again and that happened too. And most of all I promised her I'd keep you safe."

"So I've got nothing to worry about."

"Not a thing in the world."

Charlotte smiles. Charlie feels like a fraud. Last night he'd hardly slept. Some sixth sense is telling him that their pursuers are close.

We'll leave first thing in the morning. Head north.

Charlotte yawns. Charlie realizes she's exhausted. They had spent the whole day in the sun, jumping waves, building a gigantic sand castle and bicycling up and down the coast. A loud cheer goes up in the restaurant. Charlie glances at one of its many TV screens. The quarterback for the Green Bay Packers has just thrown a touchdown against the Minnesota Vikings.

"You like Brett Favre?" Charlotte says.

"Brett who?"

"Oh, come on, Brett Favre. He's only like the most famous quarterback in the N.F.L.?"

Charlie smiles.

"He is, is he?"

"My favorite's Tom Brady though. He's so cute."

"Who does he play for?"

Charlotte rolls her eyes.

"Hey I've been cut off for almost a decade."

"Then I 'm going to have to tell you everything that's happened."

"Everything?"

"It will be my pleasure."

Charlie laughs. He jumps to his feet.

"Come on you. Time for bed."

He lifts Charlotte off her stool. Hand in hand, they walk out into the seething mass of humanity on the boardwalk.

"So where do you want to begin?" Charlotte says.

"I don't know. How about the internet?"

"But that's so easy."

"Not for me. I come back and it seems the whole way people communicate has changed."

"You mean like A.O.L.?"

"A.O. what?"

"You know email, instant message."

"Exactly. What's that all about?"

"You can send letters to friends over the internet."

"Sounds cool."

"But you need an email address?"

"How do I get one of those."

"You sign up and choose a name that no one's taken already."

"Okay like superman?"

"That's definitely taken."

"Then how about coolestguyintheworld?"

"That's stupid."

They come upon a group of tourists watching a man in a leopard skin G-string. He is balancing on one leg at the top of a twelve-foot ladder.

"Not as stupid as that guy," Charlie says.

Charlotte giggles.

"You know what," she says. "You're not so bad."

It's the greatest compliment Charlie's ever received.

***

ABDULLAH INHALES THE smoky aroma of his thirty-year-old single malt. At the Beverly Hills Peninsula, a glass costs almost a hundred fifty dollars. This is his second.

Enjoy it. In a week you might not have the chance to savor such a drink again.

Abdullah scans the dimly lit bar. It is populated by a couple in their sixties sipping the last of their wine before turning in for the night, a table of earnest looking executives discussing a business deal and a red-faced man in his fifties who, in a booming Southern accent, is telling a couple of acolytes a tall tale. As of yet, however, there is no sign of the person he's waiting for. Abdullah goes back to thinking about Charlie Matthews and the girl.

Where the hell could they be?

Barnes had put out an A.P.B. on Matthews' car yet nothing's come up so far. In Jacksonville Abdullah had surmised that Matthews had gone either south or west. The story about meeting up with the girl's mother in Miami was either a slip of the tongue or a calculated feint. Abdullah suspected the latter and so he had stationed himself and Barnes' team here in Los Angeles where the 10 freeway ended and another team in Miami at the denouement to the 95. If Matthews' car pops up on their screens they need to be able to move fast.

Last night the Prince had called asking for a progress report. Abdullah had nothing more than what he had relayed three days earlier. What a conversation that previous one had been as the Prince digested the news that his long lost eight-year-old son was actually a girl. Right there, on the phone, the Prince had gulped for air like a landed fish while denying that it could possibly be true. After Abdullah had assured him that it was, that they had even done a DNA test to make doubly sure, the Prince had transitioned swiftly into anger. Any interest in his child was gone. All he cared about was finding Princess Noor so he could exact his revenge. Three days later his anger was still burning bright and Abdullah had found himself its target.

"The trail has gone cold again, Abdullah," the Prince had said, and Abdullah had cursed this fucking country for being so vast and free.

"Do I need to send someone else out there?" the Prince had asked.

"No," Abdullah had said. "Inshallah, we'll have them in a couple of weeks."

"You have one," the Prince had replied and hung up.

Six days. Tick tock. Tick tock.

Abdullah wonders if Matthews and the girl have reunited with Princess Noor by now. He suspects so. He imagines them hanging out on the verandah of some isolated hunting lodge, Matthews and the Princess raising a glass and toasting the fact that once again they had got the better of him. Abdullah downs the rest of his Scotch to quell his mounting fury.

"Mr. Abdullah,"

Abdullah looks up. A young woman with cascading blonde hair and an impossibly curvaceous body smiles down at him. Abdullah stirs.

"That's correct."

"I'm Katie."

"How very nice to meet you, Katie."

He gestures for Katie to sit and she squeezes into the booth beside him. She smiles.

More perfect American teeth.

"Would you like a drink?" he says.

"A vodka martini would be great," she says with an assurance that belies her years.

Abdullah severely doubts she's of a legal age to drink. He had told the agency he wanted a young woman and they had promised him one of their very youngest. He doubts she's more than a week over nineteen, and for that he will see scant change out of four thousand dollars.

Who cares? If this is my last hurrah I might as well enjoy myself.

After all the Prince is paying.

TWENTY-FOUR

PESHAWAR IS UTTERLY the same and yet totally different. The same madness of humanity, the same chaotic traffic, the same intoxicating smells, the same dilapidated infrastructure, the same shalwar kameez and shawl wearing men, the same burqaed women. Yet the atmosphere feels different. Ten years ago there had been a sense of malaise, of a city that had lost its relevance and was drowning under the burden of its refugee population. However, now Peshawar is once more on the front lines. It's going to be just like the Eighties. There is a buzz about the city as the merchants sense an imminent deluge of American dollars and the officials once more contemplate being able to pocket foreign bribes and funnel them to Dubai. Yet, as ever, the city is schizophrenic. People wonder whether the conflict will spread. Already there is a noticeable increase of military personnel on the streets with checkpoints manned by jittery soldiers. Harassment of the Afghan refugees that remain has increased and I.S.I. agents seem to be lurking around every corner. For the average man it is especially confusing. Osama bin Laden was a source of pride, someone, unlike their corpulent and corrupt elite, who'd led an ascetic life and pulled off the greatest attack ever perpetrated on American soil. He had made the unbelievers quake in their shoes yet now his organization is fleeing in their direction. Every neighborhood is rumored to have an al Qaeda operative hiding out in it. From looking invincible bin Laden suddenly seems curiously feeble. He can't be, the locals reason, and so the whole thing has to be a conspiracy. No longer is 9/11 the celebrated work of al Qaeda. No, it was an American, Indian, Zionist plot. How else did every Jew survive the attacks? It was nothing more than an excuse to wreak havoc on Muslim lands. 'Fuck America' appears in graffiti across the city yet everyone hopes the Americans arrive soon with their briefcases of money. Yes, only in Peshawar could everything be utterly different yet totally the same.

It had taken just under twelve hours for Noor to get from Multan to Peshawar. At Multan bus station she'd found a minivan driver who was more than happy to bring her here for two hundred dollars. They had driven through the night. Every thirty minutes or so, Noor would startle awake certain that she was about to be robbed and left for dead by the side of the highway. However, she hadn't been.

Why didn't you just take a minivan in the first place, you fool?

However, now is not a time for regrets and recriminations. She is safe. She still has money. She has a job to do.

She asks her driver to drop her off at Dean's Hotel. It isn't nearly as luxurious as the Pearl Continental, which she daren't go near, but it will be somewhere she can rest and plot her next move. They find it no longer exists and has been replaced by a monstrous shopping center.

"Where now?" her driver asks.

Noor's mind unravels. The only places she's ever lived in Peshawar was Kacha Gari refugee camp and Charlie's house in University Town.

"Qissa Khwani," she says.

The driver asks for directions. It all comes back to Noor and she rattles them off. Soon they are in the midst of the ancient, claustrophobic bazaar. Noor steps out of the van.

"Good luck," the driver says.

He roars away. Noor feels eyes on her; the chapli kebab seller, the policeman directing traffic, the soda boy, the candy store owner, the dull eyed patrons at the corner cafe. She had forgotten what it feels like to be a single woman in a land like this. She plunges into the bazaar, past the jewelers and gold sellers, beyond the spice sellers and butchers, down the alley of bookstores where storytellers used to read aloud to throngs. The buildings encroach in on her, a man smacks his lips while another undresses her with his eyes. She makes it to the clothes bazaar and spies an open fronted store with an array of burqas hanging out front. She approaches the storeowner and points at a light blue burqa. The storeowner uses a stick to bring it down.

"How much?" she says.

"A hundred rupees."

She realizes she only has dollars.

"One minute," she says.

She edges further into the store and unzips her money belt. She extracts a hundred-dollar bill. She senses his presence. She turns. The storeowner is halfway down the aisle peering at her.

"I'm going to need more clothes," she says.

It's the truth. She has nothing but the clothes she's wearing. She swipes four pairs of underwear, a couple of bras, three shalwar kameez, and a pair of sneakers. At the till the storeowner is on the phone, his voice too quiet for her to hear what he's saying.

Who's he talking to? The I.S.I? His buddies intent on a gang rape?

He hangs up and smiles. Noor hands him the clothes. He takes meticulous care folding them.

"It's okay, you don't need to do that," she tells him in Pashtu.

He keeps on folding them. Noor grabs the clothes and shoves them into a plastic bag. She slaps the hundred-dollar bill down on the counter.

"Here," she says.

Noor hightails it out of the store.

"Hold on, ma'am," he shouts after her. "Your change."

Noor doesn't look back. She cuts down one shadowy alley after another. She bursts out onto a street overflowing with long bearded young men. Down the way a preacher stands in the back of a pickup, a megaphone to his lips, denouncing the Americans as the spawn of Satan. She pushes her way through the crowd drawing vicious looks. She arrives on the other side of the street. She drops the plastic bag and pulls out the burqa. She throws it over her head and finds herself enveloped in darkness. She twists it around until the grille is in front of her face. She picks up the bag and heads down the street. Her foot catches on the hem and she topples onto her knees. The crowd surges around her. She forces herself up. Ahead an effigy of George W. Bush is set aflame. A roar goes up. Noor fights against the flow. She bursts free and spies a motorized rickshaw. She bundles her way over and slips into its backseat. The driver spits on the street.

"Where to?" he says.

She sits there paralyzed. At any second she expects a hand to reach in and grab her.

"I said where to, woman?"

"The Red Crescent hospital."

The driver accelerates away and already Noor feels safer.

TWENTY-FIVE

"WHEN I HEARD about the bombing in Khartoum I was filled with sadness," the Prince says.

You probably had a goat slaughtered in celebration.

"So senseless. How many Sudanese died?"

"Thirty-eight," Ivor says.

"But you, of course, were lucky. Just the leg if I'm not mistaken."

Ivor wonders whether the Prince knows about his balls. He detects the slightest of smirks and suspects the bastard does.

"How are your children, your Highness? I trust they're all well."

The smirk vanishes from the Prince's face.

I'm not the only one who has a well known 'secret'.

The Prince sips his tea.

"It is a strange world. Both of us back in Pakistan after all these years. Working once again for the same team."

Same team. Bullshit.

Yes, the Prince has discarded his fixation with creating a caliphate and is now only working with the interests of the Saudi royal family in mind, but that didn't mean they are on the same team. If a Martian came down to Earth, he'd believe the United States and Saudi Arabia were mortal enemies. After all, even if the Martian discounted that fifteen of the nineteen 9/11 hijackers were Saudi, Saudi Arabia's greatest export other than oil is an extreme Wahhabi doctrine that's infected every Muslim country and the minds of millions of young Muslim men. How could an ally spend billions exporting a philosophy that labelled America as evil and denounced the pillars of its liberal democracy? What ally turned a blind eye to members of its royal family sending money to some of the world's most extreme terrorist groups? One report, Ivor had seen, even stated that a top Saudi diplomat had checked into the same Marriott Inn as three of the hijackers on the eve of the attacks and had claimed it was a mere coincidence before hightailing it back to Riyadh.

Same team. It's as if America's a quarterback and before each play we never know whether the Saudi offensive line is going to protect us or step aside and allow our opponents to take their best shot.

For all this, 9/11 had rattled the Saudis. For a brief moment, they had feared that their elaborate shell game was going to fall apart, that even the reliably insouciant American public would see through it and demand their government take action. However, the Saudi network in Washington D.C. had soon swung into action. Only two days after the attacks the Ambassador, Prince Bandar, a man so close to George W. that he was nicknamed Bandar Bush, had smoked cigars with the President on the White House balcony and convinced him that the Saudis would be as ruthless as the Americans in going after al Qaeda. Yet barely two months after the attacks the Saudis are already back to their old games and the Prince is in the thick of it. Ostensibly he's in Islamabad to facilitate cooperation between Saudi intelligence and the C.I.A. However, Ivor knows his true remit. He's here to mop up and expatriate back to Saudi Arabia as many Saudi al-Qaeda operatives as he can get his hands on. The last thing the Saudis want is for these men to fall into American hands.

"Just like the old days," Ivor says.

"I assume you're happy with the result of our latest operation."

The Prince is referring to two Algerian operatives caught in Rawalpindi who were so far down al Qaeda's totem pole that they'd been cleaning out latrines back in Jalalabad.

"It went very smoothly," Ivor says.

"Off to that brand new prison of yours in Cuba."

"I hear it's just like Club Med. Sand, palm trees, great views of the sea."

"You make it sound so enticing, I'm tempted to go."

I'd love nothing more than to throw your fat ass in it.

"So I'm assuming you've not heard anything about bin Laden's whereabouts," Ivor says.

"Oh come, Mr. Gardener, if I had you'd know already."

Sure I would.

There had been a great deal of speculation within the Agency as to what the Saudis or the Pakistanis would do if they captured bin Laden. The consensus was that they would hide him. Killing him was too risky. After all it could foment such a backlash in their respective countries that it might instigate a coup. No, out of sight, out of mind will be their strategy while they feed the Americans spurious intelligence.

"And Tariq Khan?" Ivor says.

"Same story," the Prince says.

Ivor leans forward.

"Just to be clear, I want this man."

"I would presume so," the Prince says.

Again that fucking smirk.

Ivor hands the Prince his business card.

"If you get the slightest whiff make sure I'm the first person you contact."

"Of course."

The Prince leans back and places his flabby hands over his even flabbier belly. The meeting is over. Ivor ponders whether he should eke it out another fifteen minutes just to piss the Prince off. He decides not to. He wants to be around the Prince even less than the Prince wants to be around him. Ivor stands. A shard of pain zigzags from the stump of his right leg all the way up his back. He forces himself not to wince.

"Stay in touch," he says.

The Prince smiles.

"Happy hunting, Mr. Gardener."

TWENTY-SIX

NOOR EDGES HER way down the gloomy corridor. In a room to her right a young child is screaming, a couple of nurses restraining him as a doctor tends to a bloody stomach wound. In a room to her left, a man sits up in bed, his head bandaged, his gaze rigid as if he were staring off at the horizon. In another there is nothing but a white sheet on the bed, the outline of a body underneath it. In the corner a burqaed woman wails while a little girl sits cross-legged at her feet. Noor shivers. She'd forgotten how much she hates hospitals.

She passes through a set of double doors and crosses a scrubby courtyard before coming to another set of doors. Above them is a hand painted sign in both English and Pashtu. Amputee Rehabilitation Center, it proclaims. Noor enters a waiting room with brightly colored murals painted on the walls. They are of limbless men performing all manner of tasks. An assortment of Afghan men sits on a set of couches. Some miss a leg, others an arm. They drink tea and smoke. A couple play backgammon. In the background Indian pop music plays.

"Excuse me, Ma'am, but the women's department is on the other side of the building."

Noor turns to find a stocky orderly behind her. Noor attempts a smile only to remember that the orderly has no way of seeing her face.

"I'm here to see Wali Mohammad," she says. "I'm a relative."

"Of course. Please, follow me."

The orderly leads Noor down another corridor. Off it are rehab rooms. In one a double amputee is learning to use his prosthetics on a set of bars. It reminds Noor of the set her father built in Charlie's garden. In another room eight one legged men are doing strength building exercises. At the very end they come to a closed door.

"This is his office," the orderly says.

The orderly walks away. Noor hesitates. Inside she hears Wali typing away like he's hitting the keys of an old fashioned typewriter. She hesitates.

Don't do this. You're only putting him and his family at risk.

The typing ends with the flourish of a pianist concluding a concerto. Noor starts back down the corridor. The door swings open.

"Ma'am."

Noor freezes. She recognizes the timbre of Wali's booming voice.

"Is there some way I can help you?" he says in Pashtu.

"Na," Noor says.

She hustles down the corridor only for the class of one-legged men to emerge on crutches and slow her progress. Wali comes past her and turns back in her direction.

"Please, ma'am. It's clear you came here for help. For a husband, a son perhaps. Who knows maybe I can assist you."

Noor puts a hand against the wall to steady herself. Apart from a little gray around his temples, Wali hasn't changed. His hair is still jet black, his mustache is ridiculously thin, his shalwar kameez is perfectly pressed and above all his eyes still sparkle. He is also standing which seems an impossibility until

Noor stares down at his feet and notices his sneakers are connected to two metallic prosthetic legs. Before she can stop herself, she is weeping. Her legs buckle and she slides down the wall until she is slumped on the floor.

"Ma'am, please wait here. I'll go find a female member of staff to assist you."

Wali hurries off in the direction of his office.

"No, please," Noor calls after him in English. "I'm fine."

Wali halts. Noor realizes her mistake. She struggles to her feet and scurries towards the waiting room.

"Noor?"

Noor stops.

"Noor, is that you?"

Noor hears the squeak of Wali's prosthetic footsteps on the linoleum floor. She turns and lifts up the front of her burqa. Wali takes an instinctive step backwards.

"Oh, my word, it is."

Wali throws his arms open and wraps Noor in a fierce hug.

"How glorious it is to see you. Like a returning angel no less."

Wali steps back to take Noor in again. His smile is broad, his cheeks damp with tears. He wipes them with his sleeve.

"I don't understand," he says. "Why are you here?"

"It's a long story."

"But you are married to the Prince, no?"

"Not for a long time. I live in the United States now."

Wali clenches his fist as if he's just sunk a putt.

"I knew it! When I read about Mr. Matthews being arrested in Saudi Arabia, I said to Bushra, 'there is no way on God's green earth that that marvelous man could have done such a thing.' No, I knew Mr. Matthews must have gone there to save you, but all these years I thought he had failed."

"No, Wali, he succeeded."

Wali grins.

"I tell you, Miss Noor, that Mr. Matthews is the cleverest, bravest man, I've ever known."

"You won't get any argument from me."

"But not lucky. Dear God no, he has the luck of an Afghan. Worse I would say and that's saying something."

"But he's free now."

Wali cries out in delight.

"I cannot believe it. Two miracles in a day. Have you seen him?"

"Yes."

"Then why in God's name would you come to Peshawar of all places?"

"I'm here to kill the Prince."

"That truly is a most wonderful joke."

Noor holds Wali's gaze.

"I'm serious, Wali, I'm here to assassinate him."

Wali's smile evaporates.

***

WHO'D HAVE EVER thought?

Noor is back in a jam packed bus trundling down the Jamrud Road. All around her men natter away in Pashtu while the mud huts of Kacha Gari refugee camp whip by. This time, of course, no one is leering at her. She is, after all, wearing a burqa and Wali is sitting next to her.

"I'd have thought, given your position, you'd have a car," she says in Pashtu.

Wali laughs.

"King Wali of Rehab Kingdom, is that what you think?"

"Don't be modest."

"Please, trust me, I'm not. When Miss Elma Kuyt first got me the job, yes, I had a car and driver. I'm telling you when you have no legs it is essential. And the salary, well I couldn't imagine such money. Truly, I did feel like a king. But every year that passed, the amount of foreign aid we received dropped, not just for us but for every N.G.O., until today it is little more than a dribble. Now it is just me, Iqbal, my faithful assistant, and two part-time therapists. The men you see in the waiting room, they come because they have little else to do. My little kingdom is as much a social club as it is a rehab clinic. We haven't had any new prosthetic legs in over two years. We mend our clients' old ones the best we can but with no spare parts it is a dicey business. No, do you know what my main job is nowadays? Keeping my ear to the ground for dead clients."

"To attend their funerals?"

"So I can grab their prosthetic legs. During the good times thousands of amputees passed through our doors and we were giving legs away like sweets at Eid. So as soon as I hear that an old client has died, I jump on a bus and make my way to wherever they might live whether it be Kacha Gari or even Jalozai. Sometimes I get there in time and return victorious but more often than not, I am too late and it has already been sold by the man's family to a scrap dealer for less than a day's wages."

Wali leans in and lowers his voice as if he is telling Noor a well guarded secret.

"I hate to say this, but the Americans only have themselves to blame. They used the Afghans to defeat the Soviets then left us to the wolves. In Afghanistan it got so bad that people yearned for the return of the Communists. Can you imagine? When the Taliban appeared out of nowhere, well what would you have preferred, a bunch of religious maniacs who enforced Sharia law but at least maintained order, or a bunch of murderous warlords who'd rape your wife and daughters in the morning and come back in the evening to burn down your home and slit your sons' throats?"

"And al Qaeda?"

"Well they provided the money."

The Prince's money.

Noor rests her head against the chilly windowpane. She spies the bicycle shop and alleyway down which Charlie had once chased her, and the marketplace where she and her father would always catch the bus. She screws up her eyes and imagines Baba at the side of the road, dressed in his proud but tatty blue blazer, negotiating with a stall owner, hoping he can bargain him down enough that he can bring two mangos home to his daughters rather than one.

The bus drops a gaggle of refugees off and turns left into the new suburb of Hayatabad.

"We're almost there," Wali says.

Noor remembers watching from Kacha Gari as Hayatabad mushroomed during her time in the camps. It is the suburb of the relatively well-to-do in Peshawar. It is split into seven phases and behind it the brown and barren Khyber Mountains rise out of the plain like a protective wall. Phase IV, the one nearest the camps, was little more than an expanse of dull dirt when she left. All it contained were roads, a half built school and the odd house standing behind a high wall like a British outpost during the Raj. Now it is built up, filled with shops and schools, parks and tree lined avenues.

"How long have you lived here?" Noor asks.

"Almost eight years," Wali says. "When I first started working at the rehab clinic my salary justified it, but now I am paid less than a bus driver. Our landlord, however, is a good man. An Afghan businessman who admires the work I do and allows us to live almost rent free these last three years. If he didn't, I dare say, we'd be living in your old hut back in Kacha Gari."

Noor thinks of the four and half thousand dollars in her money belt and hopes she'll have enough money left over to ease Wali's worries. The bus zips past a large park. Noor stares at a Ferris wheel at its center. Its multi-colored lights twirl around and around and it can't help but make her think of Charlotte.

Dear Allah, please keep her safe.

The bus slows.

"This is us," Wali says.

Wali squeezes past Noor and guides her down the packed aisle. They clamber down the stairs. Wali offers Noor a hand. Outside a fine drizzle mists the air.

"Please, this way," he says.

Wali hobbles away from the ring road and turns down a narrow street.

"This is our street," Wali says.

The houses on either side are all of a similar design. Each house abuts the next and has a large corrugated gate, a metal door and a windowless ground floor. Like a pyramid, the next two floors recede backwards creating two verandas. For the most part the owners have constructed brick walls around them to keep prying eyes out. Each house abuts the next. A hundred yards down they come to a pale yellow house. Wali takes out his keys. Noor's heart races. Wali unlocks his metal gate. He pulls it open and they step into a small courtyard. Four young children come running in their direction.

"Baba," they shout.

"My little ones."

Wali lifts each of them into the air and swings them around. How he accomplishes the feat in a pair of prosthetic legs Noor has no idea. Only afterwards do the children notice her.

"Children, do I have a surprise for you," Wali says. "This is your Aunt Noor."

Noor removes her burqa and the four children stare up at her.

"Now this is Aamir," Wali says. "He's eight, our oldest."

"The same age as Charlotte," Noor says. "Your cousin."

Aamir grins. He is the spitting image of his father and has an identical twinkle in his eyes.

"It is wonderful to meet you, Aamir," Noor says.

"And you," Aamir says. "We have heard many stories about you."

"Only good ones I hope."

"And this is Mariam," Wali says. "After your mother."

A serious looking six-year-old steps forward.

"You look just like her," Noor says.

"That's what Mamaan says."

"You're lucky, she was an amazing woman."

"And these are Noor and Chawki. Our twins."

A wide-eyed four-year-old boy and girl cling to Wali's legs.

"Chawki was the closest Muslim name we could find to Charlie."

"I know he'd be honored," Noor says. "As am I."

"Now, please, come inside. Bushra won't believe it."

"I don't."

Noor turns. Bushra stands in the doorway with an infant in her arms. She is plumper than ever, the rolls of her belly covered by a table cloth sized shalwar kameez. However, she also looks alive. Her eyes might not sparkle with the intensity of Wali's but they shine nevertheless. Noor approaches her.

"And who's this?" she says.

"Parveen," Bushra says. "We named her after Wali's mother."

Parveen stares up at Noor with her large brown eyes.

Once upon a time Charlotte looked not much different.

"She's beautiful," Noor says.

Bushra touches Noor's cheek.

"How?" she says.

"It's a long story," Noor says.

At dinner, over a simple meal of daal and chicken, Noor tells it. Wali and Bushra hang on her every word while the children are unable to take their eyes off their exotic aunt. When she reaches the part where Charlie arrives in Blowing Rock, she tells Bushra that the rest is inappropriate for the children. Wali claps his hands and announces it is time for bed. The children rise and clear the dishes. They kiss their parents and long lost aunt and go upstairs. Bushra serves Noor and Wali chai, and Noor tells them about the killings and their subsequent escape. Wali, now sitting on a love seat, his prosthetic legs lying next to him, leans so far forward that Noor fears he is going topple over.

"So if the Prince is in Islamabad," Bushra says, "why are you in Peshawar?"

"I'm going to lure him here," Noor says.

"And what if he can't be lured?" Wali says.

"Then, yes, Islamabad is where I'll have to go."

"How are you going to kill him?" Bushra says.

"I'm going to shoot him."

"You have a gun?" Wali says.

"No, but I'm going to buy one."

Wali shakes his head.

"You have been away too long, my dear. In Peshawar, for a woman, that is impossible. Don't worry, I'll buy it for you."

"No," Noor and Bushra say at the exact same time.

Wali's head swivels between the two of them.

"I don't want you involved in any way," Noor says. "This is my responsibility not yours."

"Well then let me at least point you in the right direction," Wali says. "Guns aren't hard to come by in this town."

"Not the gun I'm needing."

"And what type of gun is that?"

"One that I'm going to need to go to Darra Adam Khel to buy."

TWENTY-SEVEN

CHARLIE AND CHARLOTTE exit the diner and take one final stroll down the Venice boardwalk. Beyond the pale yellow sand, the Pacific Ocean is so placid that Charlie wonders why the wet-suited surfers have even bothered to venture out. A warm breeze brushes his cheeks. 'It's called a Santa Ana,' their waitress had informed them. It is meant to be the middle of winter but already it is in the seventies and by midday it will be in the high eighties.

Enjoy it. Where you're going next is sure to be a lot colder.

Charlotte stops next to the Muscle Beach gym and leans over its railing. Charlie joins her and together they watch two men with bulging muscles take turns doing bench presses.

"They look like freaks," Charlotte whispers.

"You know Arnold Schwarzenegger used to train here," Charlie says.

"Who?"

"Oh, come on, the Terminator. 'I'll be back.'"

Charlotte laughs at Charlie's imitation.

"Nope," she says.

"Philistine."

"That's what Mom always says."

"Well come on, I want to beat the morning traffic."

"Where we going?"

"I'm not sure. North for sure."

"Do I get a say?"

"Don't see why not?"

"So what are the options?"

"Well I guess there's Seattle. It's —"

"I know, in Washington. It rains all the time there, doesn't it?"

"So they say."

Charlotte screws up her nose.

"What else?"

"Denver perhaps."

"It snows there, right?"

"Charlotte, we're not going to find anywhere with good weather this time of year."

"But we could ski, right? I'm really good."

"Nice to know you're so modest."

Charlie thinks. In all honesty a ski resort might not be the worst idea. The arrival of two newcomers wouldn't raise any eyebrows and they could spend their days on the slopes and their evenings in a snug rental.

It's the last place the Saudis will think to look.

"Sure, why not?" he says.

"Yes!"

Charlotte jumps in the air only to freeze as she's seized by a notion. She looks up at Charlie with her wide brown eyes.

"Could we go to Disneyland first?"

"I don't think that's a good idea."

"Mom always promised to take me and it's so close. There was this leaflet in the hotel that said they're even having a promotion right now."

Of course they are.

"Please, please, please."

Charlie glances at his father's watch. They could get there at close to opening time and leave by three.

What's the harm?

He looks down at Charlotte and frowns. Her smile droops.

"Let's do it," he says.

"You serious?"

"Totally."

Charlotte jumps into his arms.

"You're the best."

Charlotte drops to the ground and sprints off down the boardwalk. She looks back.

"Hurry up," she yells.

***

ABDULLAH STARES AT Katie's back, at the curve where her waist ends and her hips begin, at her round, elegant buttocks.

And to think there are those who don't believe in God.

He and this delectable creature had gone late into the night. It had been his first time using Viagra.

What an invention! I fucked like I was twenty.

Back in Saudi Arabia his male friends and relatives always wondered why he didn't take a second wife, or even a third or a fourth. 'A man needs variety,' they would say with a wink, however, Abdullah's observations led him to believe that the novelty of a new bride quickly dissipated. His friends ended up bemoaning the multi-directional nagging they were now subjected to, the hordes of children under their feet, and the draining of their bank accounts. No, it was much better to have one wife whom he cherished, three children, whose names he didn't get mixed up, and, on foreign trips, kafir whores like Katie that could take him to places no wife could reach. Abdullah reaches out a hand and strokes the cleft between her buttocks. She lets out a soft moan. Katie, even when half asleep, has mastered the fundamental requirement of being a great whore; that before you make a man feel good, you need to make sure that he feels good about himself. It's as if she's been dreaming about him all night.

No wonder you cost so much.

On the side table, his cellphone rings. His hand pauses mid-stroke. He rolls over and answers it.

"What is it?"

"We've located them," Barnes says.

Abdullah's heart beats faster than at any time the previous night.

"Where?"

"Disneyland. The F.B.I.'s been tracking cars going into the place since 9/11. The license plate popped up."

"Do you have eyes on them?"

"No, but a team's almost there."

"Come pick me up."

"I'm already on my way."

Abdullah hangs up to find Katie sitting up, her perfect breasts defying gravity, a soft smile on her lips that suggests there's no one she'd prefer to wake up beside.

"You need to go," Abdullah says.

"I thought you'd want to—"

"Now!"

Katie scrambles off the bed. Never has a black dress been put on so quickly. She retrieves her shoes and scurries out the door. It slams shut behind her. Abdullah springs from the bed like he's twenty years old.

Here we go.

***

ROUND AND ROUND the carousel they go, Charlotte strapped onto the white horse next to Charlie's. Her eyes are wide with delight and have been ever since they arrived at the park. They have been inside the Haunted Mansion and sauntered along the Jungle Cruise, ridden helter-skelter through Space Mountain and been up the Matterhorn, got soaked on Splash Mountain and hurtled along the Big Thunder Mountain railroad. At the end of each ride Charlotte would grab ahold of Charlie's hand and hasten him towards their next port of call, only stopping to fuel up on hot dogs, popcorn and multi-colored icees. The carousel slows. Charlie glances at his watch. It's four-thirty.

"We gotta go."

"Oh, please," Charlotte says. "Just one more ride."

"Sorry. We should've been on the road an hour ago."

The carousel stops. Charlie climbs off his horse. He undoes Charlotte's leather strap and lifts her to the ground.

"Thanks," she says. "I've had the best time. Ever."

Charlie smiles.

"You deserve it."

The two of them wind their way between the horses and exit the ride. Ahead of them is the iconic castle with its multitude of pink turrets.

"That's Sleeping Beauty's castle," Charlotte says. "Come on."

Charlotte races ahead. Charlie starts after her but finds his progress thwarted by a group of tourists all wearing the same bright yellow T-shirts. By the time they've passed Charlotte is nowhere to be seen. Charlie quickens his pace.

"Charlotte," he shouts.

He barrels through the three arched passageway. On the other side is the circular plaza and Main Street.

"Charlotte. Charlotte."

Nearby four acapella singers serenade an adoring crowd.

O Jesus, where she's gone?

The ragtime song comes to an end and the crowd bursts into applause.

"Charlotte!"

Charlie strides towards the circular plaza. A horn beeps. He steps back and an open topped fire engine trundles past. He strains on his tiptoes and looks further down Main Street. Charlotte's purple T-shirt is nowhere to be seen amongst the throngs. His head begins to swim.

"Charlotte!"

"I'm right here."

Charlie swings around to find her standing in front of him.

"Where were you?"

"I went inside the castle."

"Why the hell would you do that? I told you we were leaving."

Charlotte's eyes tear up.

"I thought—"

"Well next time don't, okay. You can't run off like that."

The tears cascade down Charlotte's cheeks. Charlie feels like the biggest shit in the world. He crouches down.

"I'm sorry," he says. "I was just scared that's all. The last thing I want is to lose you."

He wraps his arms around her. Charlotte buries her head in his shoulder and he strokes her hair. Finally, her tears subside. He wipes them away from her cheeks.

"I love you, you know that."

"As much as Mom."

"Just as much."

"We're not going to see her again are we?"

"No, we will. You and I just have to stick together till we do. We can't be apart even for a second. Can you promise me that?"

Charlotte nods.

"Then how about we get some ice cream before we go."

"Really?"

"Whatever flavor you like."

Charlotte's smile returns. Charlie takes her hand and together they walk down Main Street towards the exit.

***

THE RADIO COMES to life.

"We have a visual."

Abdullah sits up and grabs the mike.

"Is she with them?" he says.

"No, it's just Matthews and the girl."

Abdullah takes a deep breath.

Don't worry, they'll lead you to her.

For five hours now, he's been sitting in the back of an S.U.V. in the parking lot of a Best Western. He hadn't sent anyone into the park. There was no need. Barnes' initial team had found Matthews' car and stuck a magnetic transponder inside one of its wheel wells.

"They're on the move," Barnes says. "Not long now."

Barnes holds a navigation device. On it a red dot is moving along a street. Abdullah stares out the windshield towards Disneyland Drive and its perfectly arranged palm trees.

I might as well be in Riyadh.

"Here they come."

Abdullah leans forward. The light turns green and a bevy of cars turn off it onto a six lane street.

"I can't see them," Abdullah says.

"Don't worry," Barnes says. "We're on it."

Barnes' driver glides out of the parking lot and navigates his way through the traffic.

"They're a hundred feet ahead," Barnes says. "There. You see? The white Toyota in the right lane."

"Pull alongside them."

The driver slides into the middle lane and accelerates. Abdullah stares out his tinted window. In the back of the Toyota, he makes out the girl. She is licking an ice cream, her mouth running a mile a minute. Behind the wheel, Matthews is laughing.

"You can pull back," Abdullah says.

The driver eases off and the Toyota carries on under a freeway overpass and past a medley of fast food chains.

The height of American cuisine. No wonder so many people want to burn this country to the ground.

A couple of miles further along the Toyota takes a curved onramp onto another freeway.

"Where does this one go?" Abdullah says.

"North," Barnes says.

Abdullah closes his eyes. He suspects it's going to be a long ride.

TWENTY-EIGHT

"WHAT ARE YOU looking to buy?"

The storeowner wouldn't be out of place in a Bollywood gangster movie with his slick black hair, his bushy mustache, the wad of tobacco under his lower lip and the pistol on his hip. Noor is already regretting that she chose this store.

"I need a rifle," she says in Pashtu.

"Then why doesn't your husband come and buy one?"

"It's not safe for him to travel at this time."

"Then why not send someone else? Why you? A woman. This isn't a jewelry bazaar."

"There's no one he trusts more."

The store owner allows a globule of tobacco stained saliva to plop into a metal cup. He picks up a steel pistol and twirls it about his finger.

"What kind of rifle?" he says.

"A Ruger 10/22, or a close imitation."

"That should be possible."

"It should have a ten round rotary magazine, a detachable rifle scope, a steel mounting base and a silencer."

"You have memorized his instructions well."

"It needs to break down into two components. The barrel and the receiver."

"And you want this today?"

"Yes."

"Impossible."

"So be it."

Noor stands and shuffles in her burqa towards the door.

"Wait," the man says. "Perhaps my cousin can put such a gun together, but it won't be cheap."

Of course it won't.

"Please," the owner says. "Give me a moment."

The man strolls out of the store and Noor returns to where she was sitting. She looks about the store. On one wall hang a row of AK-47s and two rows of shiny black Uzis. They are all imitations and made here in Darra Adam Khel. In one corner is a tall wicker basket filled to the brim with bullets and on the far wall row after row of pistols wrapped in clear plastic bags. Noor is tempted to take one and load it just in case the owner tries to pull something. She closes her eyes and forces herself to stay calm.

"This is Sayyid, my cousin. He says it can be done."

Noor opens her eyes to find a bearded man in a grimy shalwar kameez standing beside the storeowner.

"Now, tell me," the storeowner says, "how much did your husband tell you he was willing to pay."

"He didn't. He trusted me to negotiate."

The two men look at each other. Their opening gambit has failed.

"Can you at least say whether you'll be paying in dollars or rupees?"

"Dollars."

The storeowner nods. That's good. He turns to his cousin.

"If the rifle didn't need to be broken down it wouldn't be so hard," Sayyid says.

"Like I said I am happy to go somewhere else."

"Five thousand dollars," Sayyid blurts out.

Noor laughs and heads for the door.

"Wait," the owner says. "You must understand these are complicated times. 9/11 has made selling guns very difficult."

"Which I'd assume would make my business even more valuable."

"But risky. If this gun were to be used for some terrible purpose."

"It won't be."

"But if it were and it were traced back to us. This would not be good."

"So you're saying you don't want to sell me a gun."

"No, I just need an insurance policy. You understand?"

For the next hour Noor negotiates with the two men until a price of two thousand three hundred dollars is agreed upon. For that she'll get not only the rifle but also four cellphones. The owner seems pleased. Too pleased. Noor consoles herself that, as a woman, it was probably the best deal she was going to get. Sayyid says it will take six hours to put all the components together and hurries away. The storeowner, meanwhile, returns a few minutes later with four bulky cellphones. Noor thanks him in Arabic. He gives her a blank stare.

Good, you don't speak a word.

Noor turns on one of the phones and dials the Prince's number from memory. It rings and rings and eventually goes dead. There is no option for leaving a voicemail. She tries again and gets the same result. The storeowner grins.

"Your husband not home?"

"He must be too busy killing people."

The storeowner's grin remains frozen in place. Noor sits there entombed inside her burqa.

Perhaps the Prince's already gone back to Saudi Arabia.

If so it has been all for nothing. Noor stares out the window and watches a tribesman march out of the store opposite theirs and raise a semi-automatic rifle. For a moment she thinks he's aiming at her. She ducks. The tribesman lets off a volley of shots but not a single bullet passes through the window. Noor realizes the tribesman was testing it by firing over their building. The tribesman returns inside the store. Noor goes to stand. Her whole rationale for being here makes no sense anymore.

The phone rings. Noor startles. She glances at the incoming number. It's not the one she dialed.

"You promised me this was a new phone," she says.

"It is," the storeowner says.

Oh my God.

Noor picks up the phone and presses answer.

"Who is this?" the Prince says. "Hello?"

Out on the street the tribesman tests another rifle. Rat-a-tat-tat. The shots jolt Noor out of her stupor. Just in time she remembers to heighten her voice by a couple of octaves.

"I am calling on behalf of the Emir," she says.

There is a long pause on the other end of the line. Noor fears the Prince has hung up.

"How did you get my number?" he says.

"The Emir has an important package that he insists you pick up personally. Something he knows your government will be keen to get their hands on."

"I don't understand"

"That's all I've been instructed to say."

"When? Where?"

"Details will follow. Right now all he wants to know is if you'd be willing to do this."

"I have no way of knowing if you truly speak for him—"

"If the 'little prince' would be willing to help."

On the other end there's a sharp intake of breath. Back in Saudi Arabia, Asra had once told Noor that 'little prince' had been the Prince's nickname growing up. It referred in part to the French children's book and in part to the Prince's pudgy physique. The Prince despised the name and only a very few people had gotten away with calling him it, even in affection. One of them had been a contemporary, a boy called Osama bin Laden. Outside there's another barrage of rifle shots.

"I must go," Noor says. "We have to move position."

"No, wait," the Prince says. "Tell him, I'll do it."

"He will be most gratified to hear that. Ma'a as-salamah."

Noor hangs up. Her whole body trembles. She turns to the storeowner.

"My husband thanks you for your assistance. He says you are doing Allah a great service."

The storeowner attempts a smile but it turns out to be more of a wince.

Good. He's convinced my husband's al Qaeda.

"I need a set of pliers," she says.

The storeowner scurries to the back of the store. Noor opens the back of the cellphone and takes out the SIM card. The storeowner returns and hands her the pliers. Noor crushes the SIM card and the cellphone's screen. She hands the astonished storeowner the mangled phone.

"Please dispose of this."

Over the next six hours Noor only leaves her spot to use the bathroom or pray. Other than that the storeowner just sits with her. They don't speak. She has nothing to say to him and he is now too afraid to start up a conversation. Eventually Sayyid returns. He lays out the rifle in front of Noor as if it is a work of art. He shows her how to break it down. It's as simple as pulling the bolt back, pushing a recessed lever and twisting the barrel and receiver apart.

"It's beautiful," she says.

Sayyid grins. She assumes he built it himself.

"I need to test it."

The two men laugh. Noor doesn't. Their smirks fade.

"Hurry," she says, "the sun will be setting soon."

The storeowner dashes to the back of the store and returns with a small stack of paper. The two men guide her down Darra Adam Khel's dusty main street. On either side gun shops abound. Some have a similar selection to the storeowner's, others sell even more exotic fare like mortars and grenade launchers. Noor remembers reading once that the arms dealers of Darra Adam Khel pride themselves on being able to acquire any weaponry you might want, and that a drug lord had once asked them to find him a tank. Sure enough a week later they delivered a refurbished Soviet T-55 to the gates of his compound. Sayyid and the storeowner turn down a side alley. In dim workshops, on either side, teenage boys sit in front of sparking lathes and file down gun barrels. They emerge into a grass field. At its far end lies an apple orchard. Down either side are tree lined irrigation ditches.

"We can test it from twenty yards," the storeowner says.

"No, a hundred," Noor says.

The storeowner sighs and marches down the field. He nails a piece of paper to three different trees and traipses back towards them. Noor takes the rifle from Sayyid. She assembles it and loads the magazine. She lies down on the ground and lifts up the front of her burqa. The approaching storeowner stares at her, struck dumb by her beauty.

"You may want to get out of the way," Noor says.

The storeowner hurries to join his cousin. Sayyid pulls out a pair of binoculars. Noor looks down the scope and zeroes in on the first piece of paper. Five concentric circles expand out from a quarter sized circle in the middle of George W. Bush's forehead. Noor can't help but chuckle. Back in North Carolina everyone uses an identical target except the face they're aiming at is Osama bin Laden's. Noor fixes the crosshairs on the quarter. Her heart beats fast. She fires. The piece of paper is untouched.

"You missed," Sayyid says.

The storeowner snickers. Noor remembers Betty's words the first time she took her to the range.

Relax and breathe slowly.

Noor fires again. The bullet strikes just below the 43rd President's left ear. She adjusts the scope up and pulls the trigger. The bullet pierces his left eye. She adjusts the scope one more time. She fires. The bullet strikes the quarter. Behind her the two men gasp. Noor zeroes in on the second target. Noor fires off the remaining seven bullets. Each of them is within an inch of the quarter. She rises and faces the gaping gun sellers.

"I won't be needing the third target," she says.

***

IVOR LISTENS TO the call.

"The Emir has an important package that he insists you pick up personally."

Ivor pauses the recording. He turns towards Evans, their hulking tech guy.

"Were you able to pinpoint where the call came from?"

"It pinged off a tower near Darra Adam Khel, so basically anywhere in a fifteen-mile radius."

"Like the tribal areas?"

"Sure."

Where everyone's convinced bin Laden's hiding.

Ivor looks across at Rick Townley, his protégé.

"Go and see if Wright's around."

Townley hurries away. When you have a lead on U.B.L. you don't keep it from your local station chief or Langley for that matter. Not if you want to keep your job.

Ivor presses play.

"Something he knows your government will be keen to get their hands on," the shrill voice continues.

Ivor pauses the recording. He wonders why bin Laden is taking the risk of reaching out to the Prince personally.

It must be someone high up.

He assumes bin Laden has as much to lose as the Saudis if this man falls into American hands.

This could be huge.

Ivor presses play again.

"I don't understand." the Prince says.

"That's all I've been instructed to say."

"When? Where?"

"Details will follow."

Ivor pauses the recording.

Who the hell is the woman? Clearly someone he trusts. A wife perhaps.

Ivor wonders if it is Amal al Sadah, the teenage Yemeni bride bin Laden married a year ago.

Maybe, but this one sounds too assured.

He gives up trying to work it out.

The woman is of no importance. She's nothing but a messenger.

TWENTY-NINE

TARIQ SITS CROSSLEGGED on the roof and watches the sun dip below the Khyber mountains. When he lived in Kacha Gari refugee camp, Tariq would pray in their direction and beg Allah to deliver him from his hellish existence. He had despised the mud hovel he shared with his sisters and father, the bland food they ate, the ragged clothes they wore, the stifling heat in the summer, the stench of shit coming off the dried up river bed. Most of all he had despised his father's perpetual optimism, his belief that brighter days lay ahead.

What lies.

They had arrived in Hayatabad earlier in the day, all three of them lying squished in a hidden compartment in the back of a truck. Above him, through crevices in the wooden floor, Tariq could make out the hooves and bellies of the sheep that had been crammed in the back. In one sense, it had been a clever ploy. The Pakistani soldiers, who manned the checkpoints along the way, had been loathe to empty out the whole herd. However, the genius who'd come up with the plan hadn't taken into account that sheep piss and shit. Every few minutes, Tariq would hear the pitter patter of warm piss hitting the wooden boards and from time to time it would seep through the cracks and drench his clothes and face.

This is what I've been reduced to. Even those Greek gods, Baba was so fond of talking about, couldn't have devised a worse punishment.

Tariq climbs down onto the second floor balcony and rejoins Rashid and Nawaf. They are ensconced in a couple of deck chairs. Ashraf, their host, sits opposite them and plays with a set of prayer beads. Tariq slumps into his own chair. A brick wall encircles the balcony. Every few feet a brick has not been laid so the inhabitants can look out but prying eyes can't look in. He stares through one of the gaps towards a park in the distance. At its center is a twirling Ferris wheel.

"We have decided to journey south tomorrow night," Nawaf says.

"Surely it'd be better to leave at dawn," Tariq says. "There are more cars on the road during the day. Less chance of being stopped."

"He has a point," Ashraf says.

"Well it's too late to go tomorrow morning," Nawaf says.

"Then how about the day after tomorrow," Tariq says.

Nawaf spits on the ground.

"Fine. Just the sooner I'm out of this city the better. It gives me the creeps."

"Just wait till you reach Karachi," Ashraf says.

Ashraf extracts a pack of Benson & Hedges from his shirt pocket. He offers them up. Nawaf and Rashid decline. Tariq grabs one as if it is the last drop of water in the desert. Ashraf lights Tariq's cigarette and lights one of his own. Tariq inhales. The nicotine floods his brain and he feels better.

"You lived here once, didn't you?" Ashraf says.

"For a while," Tariq says. "First in the camps and then in the Prince's compound."

Tariq doesn't need to say the Prince's full name. Everyone in Peshawar knows to whom he's referring.

"Tariq's sister married the Prince," Nawaf says. "Then she fled to America with his unborn son and this one got the boot."

Tariq reddens. All he wants to do is charge across the balcony and pound Nawaf's face into the cement floor.

"Don't forget," Ashraf says, "that the Prophet Yousuf's brothers threw him down a dark well expecting him to die and look what happened. He became the King of Egypt."

"I severely doubt that'll be Tariq's fate," Rashid chuckles.

"How would you know? Only Allah is privy to such knowledge."

It's Rashid's turn to blush.

"So you came here from Afghanistan originally?" Ashraf says.

"I fled with my father and two sisters," Tariq says.

"Is your father still alive?"

"He died some time ago."

"And your other sister, what happened to her?"

"I heard she got married. To an amputee."

"Not a very propitious match."

Tariq tries his best not to wince. Propitious is the type of word his father liked to use.

"It's funny, they probably still live in Peshawar."

"What was the amputee's name?" Ashraf says.

"Wali."

"Wali Mohammad?"

"You know him?"

"Of him. Everyone does. He runs a rehabilitation clinic in University Town. Give me a moment."

Ashraf lumbers out of his chair and heads inside.

So Bushra's done well. Of all of us who'd have thought she'd be the one to come out on top.

Ashraf returns with a phone book. He flips through it.

"Here we go."

Ashraf runs his finger down the page.

"Wali Mohammad. He lives right here in Hayatabad."

THIRTY

CHARLIE FIGHTS TO keep his eyes open.

Come on, don't tempt fate. Pull in for the night.

They've travelled close to four hundred miles. A mile back they passed a sign welcoming them to Utah.

Out of Los Angeles the cars had been bumper to bumper as if everyone in the city were fleeing some apocalyptic event. Charlotte was oblivious and had recounted in endless detail every attraction she had done and lamented every one they hadn't had time for.

"But that's okay," she'd said. "We can do them when we go back with Mom."

Charlie was happy Disneyland had put her in a hopeful frame of mind.

It was the right decision to go.

Once they had reached the I-15 the traffic eased. By the Nevada state line, with its tawdry casinos, Charlotte had fallen fast asleep. Twenty miles on, they had come over a rise and Las Vegas materialized below. It looked like an alien colony that had been dropped in the desert. At one end the Luxor's black pyramid shone a beam of light high into the night sky while at the other the Stratosphere with its red radio antenna towered over them all. For most travelers the flashing casinos beckoned like modern day Sirens. It's New Year's Eve. The city was surely packed with revelers. However, Charlie was immune and had driven right past and on into the darkened desert.

Ahead he spies a sign for a city called Saint George and another for a Holiday Inn. He indicates and takes the off ramp. Before long he is pulling into the Holiday Inn's parking lot. He turns to look at Charlotte. Her chin is raised towards the ceiling, her mouth open as if she's hoping to catch a drop of rain from above. Charlie smiles.

Just like her mother.

He gets out and pops open the trunk. He shoulders their solitary bag and opens the back door. He gently unclasps Charlotte's seat belt. She stirs and he lifts her into his arms.

"Where are we?" she says.

"Halfway there."

"Is it New Year yet?" she says.

Charlie glances at his father's watch.

"Two minutes past midnight. Welcome to two thousand and two."

"Happy New Year."

"It's going to be a great one, just you wait and see."

Charlotte throws her arms around his neck and lays her head on his shoulder. Charlie kicks the door shut and locks the car. A black S.U.V. pulls in and parks on the other side of the lot, its trunk facing them. Charlie calculates how quickly he can get Charlotte back in the car. A clean cut white man gets out and ambles towards the motel. Charlie shakes his head and breathes easier.

Even you can be too paranoid sometimes.

***

THROUGH THE TINTED back window, Abdullah watches Matthews carry the girl towards the motel.

"You want to do it tonight?" Barnes says.

Why not? It won't be hard.

In a couple of hours, once Matthews and the girl are fast asleep, they'll pick their door lock and inject them with a fast acting sedative. After that it will be a short journey down the emergency staircase to the second S.U.V. From here they'll drive to the nearest Saudi government residence where he and Matthews will get reacquainted.

However, right then an overwhelming weariness comes over Abdullah. He yawns.

You're not as young as you think. Last night's exertions have caught up with you.

"This is just a stopover," Abdullah says. "It will be simpler if we let them lead us to the Princess."

"Okay, I'll go book you a room."

Barnes clambers out of the S.U.V. and closes the door. Abdullah sits alone in the dark. He's already looking forward to calling the Prince in the morning and giving him a progress report.

He'll be pleased. Ecstatic even.

Once Matthews and the girl meet up with the Princess things will move fast. He will dispatch Matthews to a shallow grave and ship the Princess and her daughter off to Saudi Arabia on a jet.

"You're lucky, Matthews," he says as if he were sitting right beside him. "I'm saving you from a host of pain."

THIRTY-ONE

NOOR KNEELS IN the dark and finishes her Fajr prayer. She creeps out of Aamir and Mariam's bedroom. (The two oldest children had slept with the twins last night.) Noor tiptoes downstairs and enters the sitting room. She goes over to a cupboard. Stashed in the back is a wicker shopping basket bulging with dirty laundry. At the very bottom is one of her three remaining cellphones as well as the rifle and its component parts. Noor picks up the burqa lying beside it and puts it on. She grabs the basket and heads into the hallway. She unlocks the wooden door and then the outer metal one. She steps outside and locks them behind her. She shivers. It's freezing.

Noor makes her way down the street and crosses the deserted four lane ring road. She enters Tatara Park just as the city's muezzins wail out the call to prayer. Dawn is fast approaching. Noor works her way around a pond, past its paddling boats and the somnolent Ferris wheel before arriving at the river. To call it a river is as much of an oxymoron as it was a decade ago. Only the barest stream trickles down its center. The rest is nothing but a football field wide expanse of gray silt that only fills when it rains. Noor picks her way down the worn path that works its way along the bank. The odd man comes the other way but they pay her no heed. Twenty minutes later she is at the Jamrud Road. On the other side is Kacha Gari refugee camp.

Noor waits for a break in the traffic and scurries across the road. Her right foot steps on the hem on her burqa and she trips. A horn blares. A bus is bearing down on her. Noor scrambles to her feet and swoops up her basket. She forces her legs forward. A blast of air from the passing bus propels her into the dirt. Noor lays there, her heart pounding.

Still alive. Just.

Noor struggles to her feet and takes in the street market. The sellers are setting up their wooden stalls. Watermelons are piled high on one, on another are an assortment of nuts. Smoke rises from the cafes as their cooks make the first samosas and chapli kebabs of the day on open fires. Groups of young boys try to get as close as possible to warm themselves and every so often a cook will shoo them away like they're a swarm of flies. Once the early morning crowds arrive the boys will accost them with offers of cigarettes and cups of tea. By the side of the road, a small cluster of men, woolen shawls wrapped tight around their torsos, wait for a bus to take them into the heart of the city. A woman in a green burqa stands to the side. In the dim light she looks like a statue. Noor remembers coming here every morning in order to take the bus to University Town. She was invariably the only woman whose face was uncovered and there was scarcely a day when some man wasn't leering at her.

Yet there wasn't a day that I ever thought of wearing a burqa. Baba taught me too well.

Noor knows Baba would understand her present predicament. However remote the possibility she daren't be spotted.

"But, promise me, my dear, that you will burn that despicable garment once it's over," she hears Aamir Khan say.

"I promise, Baba," she whispers.

Noor winds her way through the market. She crosses the bridge that spans the concrete water channel and heads down the camp's main thoroughfare. She turns off it and navigates the warren of narrow, mud-walled alleyways. Left here, right there, ahead forty yards before another right. It's as if she never left. She bursts out of a final alleyway and finds the graveyard before her with its burial mounds and fluttering flags. She looks to her left and her heart lifts. By some miracle the eucalyptus tree is still standing. She gathers up her burqa and races towards it. Her father's bench sits right under the tree. She drops to her knees and wraps her arms around it like it's a long lost friend. Her fingers trace her father's intricate carvings. She hears a cough and twists around. An elderly man stares down at her.

"Are you all right, ma'am?" he asks in Pashtu.

Noor rises to her feet, her cheeks flushing.

"Yes, I was just … my father made this bench. Many years ago."

The old man frowns.

"You are Aamir Khan's daughter?"

Deny it, a voice inside her says.

Noor finds she's unable to.

"You knew him?" she says.

"I am proud to say I did," the old man says. "He had a Scrabble game, the pieces carved magnificently out of wood—"

"The board the back of a Hekmatyar poster."

The old man chuckles.

"How we enjoyed rubbing Gulbadin's face in the dirt."

The old man gestures to the bench.

"Please, take the weight off your feet."

Noor sits and pats the bench beside her.

"I'd be honored if you'd join me."

The old man sits down next to her.

"We used to have tea here every morning," Noor says.

"Other than praying it was the most important ritual in Baba's life."

"And a very sound one too. This younger generation, I find they have lost the ability to sit still."

If only you could see the kids in America.

The two of them stare out across the graveyard.

"Your family left Kacha Gari very abruptly," the old man says. "No one knew where you had gone. And then a few months later I heard a rumor that Aamir Khan had been murdered, by his son no less, and that one of his daughters had been married off to a Saudi prince. I am sure it is nothing but gossip. You know how people love to spin tales."

"No, it's true," Noor says.

The old man turns his gaze towards her.

"All of it?"

"Oh, that's just scratching the surface."

"And your sister, the one that married the Prince."

"She escaped."

"Where to?"

"If only I knew. I hear the Prince continues to look for her to this very day."

"Well I pray he fails. Those Saudis, they think they can have anything they desire. My word, they and their imams even had the audacity to steal the souls of our people."

Noor laughs.

"I now understand why you and Baba were such close Scrabble partners."

"He was a superb player. Said his youngest daughter was the only person who could beat him, that she was, in his unbiased opinion, the smartest person he'd ever known. It's no wonder you've managed to stay one step ahead of the Prince all this time."

Noor starts. The old man gives her a gentle smile.

"Don't worry, Noor, your secret is safe with me."

"How did you know?"

"Your hands. They aren't those of a woman who's lived in Peshawar all these years."

Noor shakes her head and thanks God the old man's an ally.

To think I could be undone by something so simple.

"I apologize I never learned your name," she says.

"Abdul Qadir."

"I was wondering, Abdul Qadir, could you do me a favor?"

"Whatever you ask."

"Would you mind sitting on this bench for the next twenty minutes."

"At my age sitting could be considered my greatest skill."

Noor smiles and picks up the wicker shopping basket.

"Thank you. I'm so glad we met."

"Likewise. May God be with you."

Noor heads out across the graveyard. She doesn't diverge from her path and two thirds of the way across she counts out her hundred and thirtieth step. She knows from her time at the Blowing Rock shooting range that that's equivalent to a hundred yards. In front of her is a raised grave with a yellow flag at the end of a reed pole. It flaps in the wind like a clacker at a football game.

It should be easy to find.

Noor turns around. The old man is still sitting under the eucalyptus tree. She looks about to ensure she isn't being observed and squats down. She pulls out the laundry and deposits it on top of the grave. She assembles the rifle and lies down. She rests the barrel on a pile of clothes and peers down the telescopic sight. The old man comes into view. His eyes are closed. Noor positions the crosshairs over his forehead and imagines a bullet pulverizing the Prince's brain. It's the perfect spot.

All you need now is get him here.

She pulls out the cellphone and powers it on.

***

"IT'S ME AGAIN," the woman says.

Inside a secure room deep within the U.S. Embassy, the assembled C.I.A. officers listen as Townley provides a simultaneous translation. Apart from Ivor, no one else speaks Arabic.

So much for the C.I.A. being prepared for 9/11.

"I was wondering when you were going to call," the Prince says.

"It needs to happen tomorrow morning. In Peshawar."

A buzz permeates the room.

"Quiet," Steve Wright, the station chief, barks.

There is a pause at the other of the line as if the Prince has somehow heard them.

"Why Peshawar?" the Prince says.

"That's what the Emir's decided. Why? Are you having second thoughts?"

"Of course not."

Ivor smiles.

This woman's good.

When you challenge a man's masculinity he's liable to put caution aside, and that's doubly true if he's Arab.

"The Emir will be heartened to hear that," the woman says. "I will call you at six a.m. Be ready."

The woman hangs up.

"Do we have a trace on the call?" Steve shouts out.

"It pinged off a cell tower in Hayatabad," a tech replies.

"Hayatabad?"

"It's a suburb of Peshawar," Ivor says.

"Which means the woman and the high value target have already journeyed in from the tribal areas."

Ivor doesn't reply. Steve has a habit of reiterating the obvious.

"So here's what we're going to do," he says.

Ivor leans back and pretends to listen. It's no longer his show. This one's gone to the top. There are conflicting agendas at play. At the White House, and especially within the Vice President's office, there is growing frustration that not a single high level al Qaeda member has been captured. The Vice President is convinced a dirty bomb attack is around the corner and they've been advised that they can do 'whatever's necessary' to extract information from this high value target. On the other hand, this operation has the potential to seriously ruffle the Saudis' feathers.

"On no account is the Prince to be hurt," Steve says.

No shit, Sherlock.

"To that end, when we move in, I want Ivor to get out first."

Ivor sits up. This is news.

"He has the closest relationship with the Prince and the greatest chance of persuading him that we're only interested in the target."

And the greatest chance of being riddled with bullets by the Prince's bodyguards.

Steve glances in Ivor's direction.

"I assume you're okay with that?"

Ivor nods.

You reap what you sow.

"Good, then let's get to work."

The meeting breaks up. Steve wanders over to Ivor.

"It's an excellent plan," Ivor says.

Steve smiles. Ivor's known this cocksucker on and off for the last fifteen years and there's nothing he likes more than having his own attended to.

"We wouldn't be in this position without you."

Just in case it all goes south.

"It's a team effort," Ivor replies. "I'm just happy to do my part."

Steve lights a cigarette. He offers one to Ivor. Ivor shakes his head.

"I wonder who the hell it is," Steve says.

"I can't wait to find out."

It's the first honest thing Ivor has said to Steve all day.

THIRTY-TWO

BRIAN STARES AT his computer screen with bloodshot eyes and types with one deliberate finger stroke after another.

Someone clearly had a fun New Year's Eve, Charlie thinks.

"So how long were you folks planning to stay?"

Charlotte gives Charlie a look. She is equally intrigued to learn the answer. Charlie hasn't a clue. All he knows is there wasn't an announcement regarding the marriage of Olive Dean and Michael Daniels in the New York Times this morning. He's beginning to doubt there will ever be.

Something's happened. I can feel it.

"Bro?" Brian says.

"A month," Charlie says. "Perhaps longer."

Brian strokes his scraggly goatee.

"Not gonna be easy. We got Sundance in a couple of weeks. Place is gonna be filled to bursting."

Charlie hadn't thought about that. Rather, this morning, as he had studied a ski resort guide over breakfast, Park City had seemed ideal. It was only four-and-a-half hours from Saint George compared to eight or more for the Colorado resorts.

"I can pay in cash," Charlie says. "Throw in a little extra commission."

Brian swings his legs off the desk and types away with a sense of purpose as yet unseen.

"No way. A lodge just popped up. Four bedrooms though and two grand a week."

"That's doable," Charlie says.

Brian grins.

"What you say your name was again?"

"Mike. Mike Daniels."

Charlie hands Brian the fake driver's license he procured from a tattoo parlor off the Venice boardwalk.

"And you have a name, little lady?"

"Katie," Charlotte says before Charlie can intervene. "Katie Daniels. He's my dad."

"Course. You guys are the spitting image."

Brian grabs a set of papers and springs from his chair. He heads over to a key rack. Charlotte rolls her eyes at Charlie. Charlie muffles a laugh. Brian swipes a key and bounds in their direction.

"I'll catch a ride with you. If you like it, we can fill in the paperwork right there and then."

Brian hustles Charlie and Charlotte out of the office. The Toyota Corolla is right outside and he guides Charlie up Main Street past the pioneer buildings that nowadays contain ski stores, clothing boutiques and high end restaurants. At the far end the mountain looms, skiers dotted all over its slopes.

"Hang a left," Brian says.

The Corolla turns and struggles up a steep, slushy lane.

"Now a right."

They creep down another lane with pastel colored lodges on either side.

"Here we go," Brian says. "The blue one on the right. The ski lift's only a couple of minutes down the hill."

Charlie pulls in. Brian jumps out before Charlie has even turned off the ignition. He leads them down a set of stairs to a brick patio. Charlotte squeals in delight.

"It has a hot tub."

"Thought you'd like that, little lady."

Brian musses Charlotte's hair. He unlocks the door and throws it open.

"Voila."

Charlie steps into a pine walled living room with a large fireplace, a cowhide rug and a bevy of antlers and ancient skis on the walls.

"Ski resort chic," Brian says.

"I love it," Charlotte says.

She races up the stairs to explore the rest of the house.

"I guess I love it too," Charlie says.

THIRTY-THREE

THE FERRIS WHEEL carries Tariq's pod ever higher. Tariq closes his eyes. It reminds him of his early childhood, a time when life was carefree and innocent, the only time he's ever felt truly loved.

No one's ever loved me the way Mamaan did.

Tariq will never understand why Allah took her from him.

Why couldn't it have been my fool of a father?

His pod reaches its apex and begins its descent. Tears course down his cheeks.

I was happy then. I even loved Noor.

He and Noor had had a complicated relationship. He was two years older than her and she was constantly battling to keep up. He would beat Noor up yet she never backed down and as a result she won his grudging respect. At school he was protective of her. He even bashed in Mohammad Kadir's nose when Mohammad called Noor an ostrich on account of her long neck. Blood spurted everywhere. So much in fact that Tariq wondered if Mohammad was going to bleed to death. He didn't, of course, and Tariq received a thrashing from the principal. Yet it was well worth it. After that all the boys in his class thought he was a God, and for the next week

Noor did anything he asked before they settled back into their familiar and adversarial relationship. They were like opposing Afghan tribes. Constantly warring on their home turf but united if ever threatened by an outside entity.

And then Mamaan died and everything changed.

When they arrived in Peshawar, bedraggled, heartbroken and penniless, Tariq was consumed with anger. He pushed back when his father tried to get him to keep up with his studies. Instead he would wander the camp and hang out with a group of kids who dabbled in petty crime and smoked hashish. He remembers, back in Afghanistan, an imam once saying that no two children in a family can hold the same role at the same time. Growing up in Kabul he had been the undisputed leader while Noor had been the scrappy rebel.

It's why she climbed higher on the apricot tree than me. She had more to prove.

However, after their arrival in Peshawar he allowed that leadership position to become available. Noor seized it and refused to let their family be crushed by their newfound circumstances. A couple of times he attempted to wrestle it back, yet it was too late. By then Baba and Bushra looked to Noor not him.

Tariq's pod rises again. When it reaches its apex he opens his eyes. Peshawar is spread out before him as if he were its king. Tariq realizes why he despises Noor so much. It's not because Noor destroyed his relationship with the Prince. No, he hates her because if she hadn't misappropriated that leadership role he wouldn't have felt the need to join the Prince's mujahideen group. He would have returned to the fold and allowed his father to teach him. He would have gone to university and gotten a visa to the United States. He would have ended up being someone; a doctor, an engineer, a tech entrepreneur perhaps.

Instead I'm nothing but a desperate fugitive forever destined to run.

The Ferris wheel slows. Tariq wipes away his tears. His

pod comes to a halt and he steps off. It's time to get back to Ashraf's house. He meanders down the stone flagged path that encircles the boat pond and passes a number of families out for an afternoon stroll. Here in Hayatabad most of the women don't wear burqas though every one of them wears a headscarf. One of the women smiles at something her husband says. Another calls out after a couple of rambunctious girls in party dresses. He stops and stares at them. He thinks about his own two daughters, Mehnaz and Shazia. Mehnaz will be turning seven in a week. She's a beauty, smart as a whip too. Back in Afghanistan, he'd often stare at his daughters when they were asleep and feel a love that came close to that he felt for his mother.

I wasn't a good father but I could have been.

"Hey," a man says. "Keep your eyes to yourself."

Tariq jerks his gaze away. Their father is eyeballing him. Tariq hurries on before the situation develops. Rashid and Nawaf had considered him a fool when he told them he was off for a walk.

"If someone recognizes you, don't you dare come back," Rashid had said.

However, Tariq doubts anyone will remember him now. The mujahideen who'd been his constant companions when he had lived here had either returned to the Middle East or joined al Qaeda.

And the C.I.A.? Ivor Gardner?

To this day he can't fathom how thirty-eight Sudanese died in the bombing in Khartoum yet Ivor, his target, had somehow survived. Ever since he's had a creeping sense that Ivor's just around the corner waiting to exact his revenge. Yet the last place he suspects Ivor or the C.I.A. are hanging out is Tatara Park in Hayatabad.

No, the only person who'd probably recognize me would be Bushra.

Tariq slows and searches his memory for her address.

It's in Phase I, that's for sure. What was it?

It comes to him. He approaches a gardener weeding a nearby bed of roses and asks directions. The gardener points.

"It's just on the other side of the ring road."

Tariq strides away with renewed purpose. At the ring road he waits for a break in the traffic. It takes forever. It's as if the whole of Peshawar is on a constant loop around the city. A gap appears. Tariq jogs across the road in his lopsided manner and heads down a couple of streets before coming to Bushra's. He counts off the house numbers. His heart beats steadily faster. He comes upon it. Tariq retreats to the other side of the street and squats between two parked cars. From within he hears children playing and a woman reprimanding a child in Pashtu. He recognizes Bushra's husky timbre.

Her tone's different. She's more assured.

He smiles.

A new role opened up for you too, Bushra.

Tariq is tempted to knock on the door. He'd love to see his nephews and nieces. He wonders how many he has. He imagines a tearful scene as he and Bushra reconcile. Yet he soon disabuses himself of the fantasy. However justified he might have been, he doubts Bushra will ever forgive him for killing their father.

Tariq is about to leave when he hears someone approaching. He waits. A woman in a light blue burqa appears. She is carrying a wicker shopping basket. To his surprise, she walks up to Bushra's front door and unlocks it. Tariq wonders who she might be.

Perhaps it's the mother-in-law.

The woman unlocks a second door and steps inside the house. She closes the doors behind her. Tariq stands and hobbles down the street. Back at the house, the children scream out in excitement.

"Aunt Noor, Aunt Noor."

Tariq halts in his tracks.

THIRTY-FOUR

ABDULLAH NURSES A Scotch and stares out the vast bay window at the lights of Deer Valley below. Their orange glow stands in stark contrast to the ghostly blue mountains that surround the resort.

Trust the royal family to own a ski lodge close to Park City.

The front door slams. Abdullah turns. Barnes comes down the sweeping staircase into the grand reception room below.

"A drink?" Abdullah says.

"Why not?" Barnes says.

Abdullah wanders over to the wet bar and pours a generous finger of Scotch into a crystal tumbler. He hands it to Barnes. Barnes takes a healthy slug.

"So?" Abdullah says.

"The two of them went to a Thai joint on Main Street a couple of hours ago."

"And the Princess?"

"I sent a couple of guys into the house. There's no sign of her or anyone else for that matter."

Where is she? She must be on her way.

Abdullah knows he can't wait. The Prince had called him an hour earlier asking for a progress report. 'I tracked down

Matthews and your fucking daughter, isn't that progress enough?' Abdullah had wanted to say.

"Are they back now?" Abdullah says.

"Girl's tucked up in bed."

"And Matthews?"

"Reading a book the last I heard."

Abdullah downs the remnants of his glass.

"Go in once he's asleep and bring them here. I've dismissed the staff. There won't be any problems."

Barnes heads for the staircase.

"Oh and Barnes."

Barnes turns back.

"Don't underestimate, Matthews. Trust me, it's been my undoing in the past."

***

CHARLIE CREEPS DOWN the darkened corridor, Noor at his side. She holds her gun out in front of her like an actor in a TV cop show. At the far end is a closed door. Light spills underneath it as does the voices of men speaking Arabic. None is more distinct than that of the Prince. Charlie steps on a floorboard. It creaks and Noor spins in his direction. She frowns.

"What are you doing?" she says.

"I'm here to help."

"But where's Charlotte?"

"She's fine. I promise."

"That's not good enough, Charlie. Where is she?"

Down the corridor, the voices quiet. Noor stiffens.

"Quick. Go and protect her."

Charlie hesitates. The door bursts open. Three men carrying submachine guns appear.

"Go!" Noor screams.

Charlie scrambles the other way. A barrage of gunfire erupts.

Charlie startles awake. He sits upright and gets his bearings. He's in the lodge's master bedroom. Light from the streetlamp outside slashes across the ceiling. His pillow is drenched in sweat. Outside a couple of late night revelers yell drunkenly at each other. He takes a couple of deep breaths.

Nothing but a dream.

He turns his pillow over. He hears a creak on the landing outside his room. He stares at his bedroom door.

Relax. It's only Charlotte going to the bathroom.

His doorknob turns. A cold sweat bathes his forehead.

It's turning too slow.

He pulls the duvet cover back and slips out of bed. He searches for a weapon. He spies a set of mounted antlers. He lifts them off the wall and holds them above his head. The door creeps open to reveal two darkened silhouettes.

Do it.

Charlie charges at them.

"Watch out," a man shouts.

The warning comes too late. Charlie brings the antlers down and embeds a tip in the other man's skull. The man howls in pain. Charlie's momentum takes him out the door and onto the landing. He puts out a hand to stop himself from tumbling over the banister into the living room below. He twists around. The first man is holding a glinting object.

A knife?

The man stabs Charlie in the leg. Charlie swings the antlers. They rake the man's face. The man screams worse than his compatriot. His hands fly up to his face and press up against his right eye. Blood pours through his fingers like water through the crevices of a cliff. Charlie takes off down the landing. Charlotte's door is open.

No.

He barges into the bedroom. A man stands by the bed holding her limp body in his arms.

"Give her to me," Charlie says.

The man goes in and out of focus. Charlie's face tingles.

"I said give her to me. Now."

Charlie attempts to grab Charlotte. The man evades his grasp. Charlie tries again but this time he's hardly able to swing his arms. Charlie looks down and sees a depressed syringe sticking out of his leg.

No.

From behind someone barrels into him. Charlie tumbles to the floor. The man twists Charlie over. It's the first man he struck.

"You fucking bastard," the man says.

He thrusts a syringe into Charlie's arm and as its contents enter his bloodstream, a single thought enters Charlie's mind.

I've failed.

***

"WHY THE HELL are we hearing these only now?" Ivor says.

Houghton, the station's deputy, takes a step back as if he's worried that Ivor will deck him.

"We didn't think they were relevant?"

"Don't you think Steve and I should be the judge of that?"

Steve leans back in his chair as if the three of them were going over a seating arrangement for an upcoming embassy event.

"The Prince makes tens of calls a day," Houghton says.

"Yet how many others are to the States?"

Houghton doesn't reply. Ivor already knows the answer. None.

What is it with Matthews and this bitch? Why do they keep rearing their ugly heads?

When Ivor had listened to the call he knew exactly who the Prince was talking to. Abdullah's gruff Arabic drawl was so distinct he could pick it out in the midst of a crowded bazaar. It had been made a couple of hours earlier and its contents were serious enough that even an idiot like Houghton knew it had to be brought to his station chief's attention. Abdullah had abducted Matthews and Noor Khan's daughter. Abdullah still had no idea as to the location of Noor Khan but he had told the Prince that he'd learn it shortly.

"And then you're to slit Matthew's throat," the Prince had said.

"As you desire," Abdullah had replied.

Fuck, why did they have to go there?

The C.I.A. now had a preemptive warning regarding a potential murder on American soil. They even had a fix on Abdullah's location, some lodge the Saudi royal family owned in Deer Valley.

"We're obliged to inform the F.B.I.," Steve says as if he's pursued the priesthood all his life rather than foreign intelligence.

And so the game of covering your ass begins.

Everyone knows if the F.B.I. bust into the lodge that it will derail the operation. The Prince is jittery enough as it is. Yet if it ever gets out that the C.I.A. allowed the murder of an American citizen to occur on U.S. soil then those who'd been in the know would find their careers in the toilet and could possibly end up in jail.

"Ivor, I want you to call the F.B.I. office in Salt Lake City and inform them of this development," Steve says.

Steve now has deniability and Houghton will testify to that. Yet from the way Steve is holding Ivor's gaze the insinuation is clear. Steve no more wants to upend this operation than Ivor. If need be Ivor will have to take the fall.

"Of course," Ivor says.

But not for another sixteen hours. Not until the operation's gone down. Who knows maybe Matthews will be able to hold out until then.

Ivor doubts it. Abdullah is one of the finest practitioners of his art.

Ivor stares out the eighth floor window across the embassy gardens and the compound's reinforced blast walls to the mammoth King Faisal mosque and the lush, green Margalla Hills.

What kind of mother would abandon her daughter? Especially one who'd gone to such lengths to protect her in the first place?

It doesn't make sense.

There has to be another piece to this puzzle.

Yet before Ivor can consider what that might be, an operative rushes into the room.

"The Prince just left the Saudi embassy," he says. "He's on his way to Peshawar."

THIRTY-FIVE

NOOR DOUBTS SHE could eat another mouthful. Bushra has cooked all day and for the last hour has brought dish after dish to the table. A platter of crispy samosas, a chunky shorwa soup, a delicious Kabuli Pulao with tender lamb and crunchy pistachios, moist chapli kebabs, soft yellow saffron rice and stewed okra.

"You're as good a cook as Mamaan," Noor says.

Bushra blushes.

"She is amazing, isn't she?" Wali says patting his belly. "Even with the scant resources we possess, I come home every night to the most delectable of meals."

Everyone around the table takes a moment as their bodies digest the monumental amount of food they've devoured. Despite what Wali just said, Noor knows they must have spent a small fortune on this particular meal.

Don't worry, you'll make it up to them tomorrow.

Noor remembers a similar dinner many years ago at Charlie's house. She and Mukhtar had cooked it. It was a night filled with hope. Wali had just proposed to Bushra. Charlie's father had called to say there was a man at the American embassy who could get Noor a visa.

And then the next day everything changed.

Noor prays this dinner isn't an omen.

"We would've done this last night," Wali says, "but I must admit you caught us by surprise."

Noor laughs.

"Just a little, right?"

"A soupçon as the French would say."

"How do you know the French say that?"

"Because your friend, Miss Elma Kuyt, told me."

"When?"

Wali shifts in his chair so that he is sitting up straighter.

"Now I'm sure you're aware that once upon a time Miss Kuyt was having an affair with the French ambassador. Everyone knew, everyone but his wife that is."

Wali chuckles.

"Wali!" Bushra says.

With a flick of her head, Bushra indicates the children. They are all staring wide-eyed at their father. Wali winces.

"Anyway one day, I would say approximately six months before I had the great fortune of becoming Mr. Skeppar's assistant at Mine Aware, I worked as a waiter at a reception at the American Club. It was a large event and they required extra hands on deck. At the time I was most close to Iqbal, the assistant manager, that is before he was arrested for stealing member dues. Anyway he stationed me at the soup station, and sometime during the evening Miss Kuyt, looking like a sex goddess—"

"Wali!" Bushra hisses.

Wali offers up a plaintive smile.

"I am sorry, my dear, truly I am, but there is no other way to describe Miss Kuyt that night, none that I am capable of at least. However, children, you boys especially, I forbid you from ever using that expression, at least until you are married, and perhaps then you'd be better advised not to."

Wali turns back to Noor and gives her a sly wink.

"Anyway I saw Miss Kuyt slinking her way towards me and right behind her was this grey haired man. He looked like an ugly gnome but his eyes sparkled like those of a young boy who'd secretly devoured the dessert before anyone had had a chance to eat their main course."

Bushra lets fly with another exclamation but this time Wali refuses to look in her direction.

"So they arrive at my station and he asks me, 'What are ze flavors of ze soups?' I tell him and he chooses the spinach soup. So I pour him a bowl and am about to whirl some cream on top when he says, 'Just a soupçon, please.' I stare at the gnome and Miss Kuyt remarks that in French that means just a very little. What a marvelous expression! Oh, I can't tell you how tickled pink I was. As soon as they moved on I wrote it in my phrase book, and ever since I have tried to use it whenever I have the opportunity."

Noor laughs.

"Oh, Wali, you don't know how much I've missed you."

"And Mamaan too, of course," Aamir says.

"Of course. Just in a different way."

"What do you mean?" six-year-old Mariam says.

Noor looks down the table at Bushra.

"Your mother is my dearest sister, my blood. I feel drawn to her like the moon's drawn to the earth."

"And Baba?" Aamir asks.

"One of your father's greatest qualities is his ability to make me laugh and lighten my spirit."

"Just like Mr. Matthews," Wali says.

"Yes, just like Charlie."

Bushra notices Noor's pained smile.

"Children, it's time for bed," she says.

The four children say good night to their mother and father before coming over to Noor. Noor grips each of them by the shoulders and stares into their angelic faces before giving them a hug. She knows she's unlikely to see them again. The children troop out of the dining room. Noor turns back to Wali and Bushra.

"Tomorrow's the day," she says.

Bushra's hand flies to her mouth.

"Why so fast?" Wali says.

"Because the longer I stay with you the greater the danger I put you in."

"That is of no concern to us."

"But it is to me. I never meant to involve you. Circumstances just led me here."

"But this plan of yours is crazy," Bushra says. "Please, I beg you, take a few more days to think it through."

"I've already had plenty of time. It's the only option."

Bushra wants to argue further, however, Wali shakes his head.

"Noor's made her decision, Bushra."

Fat tears well above Bushra's plump cheeks.

"Whatever happens tomorrow," Noor says, "I won't be coming back."

"No," Bushra says, the tears now flowing down her cheeks. "Please don't leave me again."

"I'm sorry but I must."

Bushra drops her head on the table and sobs. Noor goes over and puts her arm around Bushra's broad shoulders. After a while Bushra's sobs subside. She raises her head and stares into her sister's eyes.

"I believe in you, Noor. You're going to succeed tomorrow, I know it. Allah is on your side."

Noor smiles.

"Now those are exactly the words I needed to hear."

Bushra laughs.

"You're not going to bed straight away, are you?" she says.

"No, I can stay up a little longer."

"Good. I'll be right back."

Bushra rises from her chair. Wali's loving gaze follows her out of the room. He turns back.

"I have one final request," Noor says.

"Anything?" Wali says.

"I'm going to write a couple of letters before I leave. One to Charlie, the other to Charlotte. If I die tomorrow and you hear of it, which I assume you will, please make sure they get to Elma Kuyt. There will come a time when she'll be able to give them to them."

"I will make it a point of honor to do so."

"Thank you."

Wali takes Noor's hand in his.

"This life we've been given by Allah is a funny thing, isn't it?" he says.

"It's certainly not what I expected."

"Yet the hardships we must endure, that we have endured, they have not defeated us. No, if anything they have made us wiser."

"Sometimes I'd dearly give up a little wisdom for a little more peace."

"You say that but I don't believe you. After all, I know I wouldn't be the man I am if I still had my legs. Trust me, I much prefer this version of myself."

"So life's about continual sacrifice?"

"Yes, perhaps it is, or at least perhaps it should be."

Bushra bustles in carrying a large tray. On it is a steaming teapot as well a plate stacked high with bright orange, fried jalebi.

"I hope you still have room." Bushra says.

"Of course I do," Noor says. "Jalebi was Baba's favorite."

Bushra pours each of them a cup and Noor senses her fears melting away.

I'm ready for whatever happens next.

THIRTY-SIX

ON AN ESCARPMENT above the lodge, Abdullah trudges through knee deep snow. Some years ago his doctor had warned him that he needed to take more exercise and change his diet if he didn't want to die of a heart attack like his father. He had done the former but found it impossible to do the latter. He was too fond of his food and drink. However, since coming to America, he had spent too many days in cars and airplanes, and as they had tracked Matthews and the girl through the Martian looking landscape of Utah, he had felt that with every mile his arteries were getting ever more clogged.

No, this is what I need.

He forces himself on a final twenty yards before coming to a halt. He gulps down huge lungfuls of cold, crisp air. He already feels less stressed. Throughout the day the Prince had called him and he had ignored every single call for one very good reason. He had nothing new to report. Matthews' abduction had come close to being a fiasco with one of his team losing an eye and another suffering a serious head wound. Matthews' resistance, meanwhile, had led him to receive two doses of the sedative not one. It meant that he still wasn't awake and so instead of the two them getting reacquainted, Abdullah had only had the young girl to question. After a couple of hours, she hadn't divulged anything that brought him closer to discovering Princess Noor's whereabouts. According to the girl, the Princess had been with them until South Carolina where she had gotten on a bus. Since then they hadn't heard from her.

"Not even a phone call?" he had asked.

The girl had shaken her head.

"Where did she go?"

The girl had no idea and he believed her. He had succeeded in convincing the girl that he was a friend of her mother's and that they had saved her and Matthews just before the bad guys were about to snatch them away. When she had asked to see Matthews he'd told her that Matthews had been injured and was presently in hospital. Her eyes had gone wide.

"Don't worry, he's fine. I'll take you to see him tomorrow," Abdullah had said.

When Abdullah realized that the girl had no more to offer, he had told her that she had to stay in her room for her own safety. The man standing in the hallway was there to protect her. She had accepted his explanation without the slightest hesitation and after that had seemed far more interested in the bedroom's massive dollhouse.

What will become of her?

He suspects the Prince will marry her off within a few years. She'll be tainted goods but she'll still be of royal blood. Most likely she'll become the fourth wife to an older family member or a political ally of the Prince's, one no doubt with a predilection for young women. He almost pities her. She reminds him of his own daughter when she was that age.

Abdullah stares at the distant mountains. With the sun setting behind him their snowy slopes are an amalgam of pinks, purples and dark jagged shadows.

Not a sight you'd see in Saudi Arabia.

He takes a moment to cherish the view. By tomorrow evening he hopes to be a long way away from here.

Someone shouts his name and Abdullah looks down the slope towards the lodge. One of Barnes' men is wading up it. Abdullah meets him halfway.

"What is it?"

"It's Matthews, sir," the man says. "He's awake."

***

CHARLIE'S GAZE JERKS around the room. Two sides of the room are lined with chrome tool chests. On the third side is a lathe and a gleaming table saw, and on the fourth, close to where he lies, is a ski waxer and a boot fitter. His hands are cuffed behind his back while his ankles are cuffed and connected by a six-inch chain to a metal ring that's embedded in the polished concrete floor.

I'm screwed.

After he had woken, and the young man, who'd been watching him, had scurried out of the room, his memory of the previous night had returned. He had tried to work out how they had managed to track them down but soon gave up. It was a fruitless task.

What does it matter now?

He wonders if Charlotte's already on a plane to Saudi Arabia. The thought makes him nauseous. She must be petrified. He knows the only reason he's still alive is that they want to find out where Noor is as well.

If there's one last thing I can do before I die, it's resist telling them.

The door opens. A man enters. Charlie recognizes him despite the fact that he is wearing a blue blazer and jeans rather than a thobe and ghutra. Charlie's throat constricts. Abdullah grabs a folding chair and drags it over to Charlie.

"It's been far too long."

Charlie refuses to give him the satisfaction of a reply.

"I see, so this is how you want to play it."

Abdullah strolls over to a chrome tool chest. He opens a variety of drawers as if he were a cook looking for the perfect ingredients.

"I know what you're thinking," Abdullah says. "That this time you'll be able to hold out. That you won't betray the Princess. That our fine Saudi jails have hardened you to such an extent that you can endure any level of pain."

Abdullah returns with a small butane torch and a pair of garden shears. He sits back down.

"But I've dealt with men and women who've had it far harder than you. Filipino maids whose employers beat them black and blue from the day they began working for them. Bangladeshi laborers who've endured the kinds of deprivation that made that prison of yours seem like a five-star hotel. Sudanese drug dealers whose upbringings were so brutal it was a miracle they even made it to adulthood. And allow me to let you in on a little secret. Eventually they all told me their deepest and darkest secrets. It may take a few hours, perhaps even a day, but, mark my words, you will tell me where Princess Noor is."

Abdullah cradles the butane torch and shears in the palms of his hands as if he were offering Charlie the holy sacrament. Charlie feels his insides twist,

"Here's what I'm going to do," Abdullah says. "One by one I am going to cut off each of your toes and use this torch to cauterize each wound."

Abdullah puts the torch on the floor. He bends down and grasps a hold of Charlie's right ankle. Charlie tries to yank it free but the chain has no give. Abdullah positions the blades around Charlie's pinky toe.

"Where is Princess Noor?"

Charlie's heart pounds in his chest. His head feels as if it is about to explode. Abdullah snaps the pliers. Charlie screams. Blood spurts onto the floor. Abdullah lights the torch and brings the flame up against its stump. The stench of burning flesh wafts into Charlie's nostrils and he vomits down the front of his shirt.

Abdullah positions the shears around the next toe.

"Just so you're aware, after your toes are gone I'm going to move onto your fingers, then your ears. And if that hasn't worked, well you know where I'll eventually end up."

Abdullah's gaze drifts towards Charlie's groin.

"Where is Princess Noor?"

"Fuck you."

Charlie screws his eyes shut. There's a knock on the door. Abdullah sighs. The chair scrapes backwards. Charlie hears muffled voices and by the time he unclenches his eyes, Abdullah's gone.

***

ABDULLAH STRIDES INTO the paneled study. Barnes stands at the desk with the phone. Abdullah throws him a thunderous look. Barnes places his hand over the mouthpiece.

"I'm sorry but he insisted we find you."

Abdullah holds out his hand and Barnes hands him the receiver. Barnes goes over to a side table and picks up a second phone.

"Your Highness," Abdullah says.

"Where have you been?" the Prince says.

"Speaking to our erstwhile friend."

"He still hasn't told you where she is?"

Abdullah grimaces.

"Matthews is a tough customer, your Highness. We have Buraydah prison to thank for that."

"Sounds to me as if you've lost your touch, Abdullah."

Abdullah focuses on a spot of Matthew's blood on his pearl white cuff. He takes a deep breath.

"Don't worry, your Highness, he was on the verge of breaking when you called."

"I'm flying home from Peshawar in a couple of hours and I want to know where she is before I take off."

Peshawar. What the hell's he doing there?

"That shouldn't be a problem, your Highness."

"Use the girl."

"Excuse me, your Highness."

"Torture her in front of Matthews. That'll pry his lips loose. Just make sure you don't kill her. I'm going to do that in front of her mother."

The Prince hangs up. Abdullah replaces the receiver. Barnes has paled considerably.

"I didn't sign up for this."

"Neither did I but you're in too deep to back out now, Barnes."

Barnes stands with his fists clenched. Abdullah stares him down. He knows Barnes will bend.

He has the moral fortitude of a Nazi collaborator.

Barnes swallows. He nods.

"Let's go get her," Abdullah says.

The two men head out of the study and down a corridor lined with Western landscapes. They reach an elevator. Barnes presses the up button. Abdullah notices Barnes' hand is shaking.

When you dance with the devil …

The doors open and they step inside. The doors close and the elevator rises. Neither man says a thing. Abdullah contents himself with the thought that Matthews won't want to see the girl suffer.

The threat should be enough.

The doors open and they step into a plush sitting room.

They head down another opulent corridor. At the far end, one of Barnes' men stands guard outside the girl's room.

"Why's the door closed?" Abdullah says.

"She was getting changed. She wanted privacy."

Abdullah feels his heart race. He flings the door open and notices a chill in the air.

"Charlotte."

Abdullah marches over to the en-suite bathroom. He tries its handle. It's locked.

"Kick it down," he shouts.

Barnes' man smashes his foot against the door. It flies inward. Cold air blasts their faces. Abdullah races over to the open window and leans out. Beneath the window is a small roof. Its pristine snow covering looks like it's been disturbed by an animal.

Or an eight-year child.

Abdullah leans further out. The next three stories down have a small roof of their own. Like stepping stones each is just a little further out than the one above. The snow on each has been disturbed by the same set of footprints.

Abdullah twists around.

"Find her," he screams at Barnes.

THIRTY-SEVEN

THEY SIT IN silence in Ashraf's living room, each in their own thoughts. For all their bravado, Tariq knows that Rashid and Nawaf are scared shitless. Tariq takes a sip of his tea. He grimaces. It's lukewarm and too sweet for his liking. He puts his cup back down and feels for his pistol with his only hand. It is concealed in a holster beneath his kameez. There are twelve bullets in its magazine, a paltry number if they get into a shootout with the authorities.

But one's all you'd need to blow Noor's brains out.

Outside, over the constant patter of pelting rain, Tariq hears the rumble of an engine. Rashid and Nawaf jump to their feet.

"Let's not be too eager," Ashraf says.

Rashid and Nawaf sit back down like scolded children. Ashraf slips out of the room. Soon after Tariq hears muffled voices and a high pitched whine as the metal gate opens and closes behind the vehicle. Ashraf pokes his head in.

"All clear."

Rashid and Nawaf spring up. Tariq follows them outside. The rain descends in a fury from the black sky above. Tariq pulls his threadbare shawl tight. The driver, a young man with a thin mustache, jumps out of a white minivan. His eyes flit between the three of them. He introduces himself. Tariq doesn't register his name. His thoughts are elsewhere. Rashid and Nawaf hug Ashraf goodbye and race for the shelter of the van. Rashid grabs a seat and waves at Tariq.

"Come on," he says.

Tariq doesn't move.

"What's your problem?"

"I can't," Tariq says. "There's something I need to take care of."

"The only thing you need to care about right now is saving your skin."

However, Tariq knows that's not true. He no longer cares whether he dies.

Not as long as Noor does too.

"Go," he tells his erstwhile comrades.

They don't need another excuse. Rashid yanks the passenger door closed. Ashraf opens the metal gate. The van reverses and heads off down the street. Tariq follows it out and stares after it until its red lights are swallowed up by the deluge.

"Would you mind telling me what this is all about?" Ashraf says.

Tariq walks over to Ashraf and embraces him.

"Thank you for your hospitality, Ashraf. May Allah bless you."

Tariq strides away.

"Where the hell are you going?" Ashraf yells after him.

Tariq feels no compunction to reply. This is now purely between him, Noor and Allah.

***

My Dearest Charlotte,

I'll never forget the first time you asked me if I was going to die. It's the question every parent dreads. You were five and it was one of those gorgeous summer days in Blowing Rock where the sky's a seamless blue blanket and there's just enough of a breeze to make the blazing sun tolerable. We'd been at the park, you were so proud of yourself for having finally mastered the monkey bars, and we had gone to Kirwins to celebrate where you ordered that rainbow colored ice cream that, much to your delight, always turned your poop bright blue. And so there we were, walking back home, each of us licking our cone, when you came to a halt in front of the Episcopal church and asked me. I wasn't prepared for the question but I soon gathered my wits and crouched down in front of you and said, "One day, my love, but not for a very, very long time." You took my answer, as you do pretty much everything in life, in your stride. "Good," you said, "make sure you do," and on you skipped up the hill.

Yet now, if you're reading this letter, you will know that I have indeed died much earlier than I said I would back then. In that regard I have failed you miserably and for that I am very sorry. However, please know, that the only reason I have is because you are the most precious thing in the world to me.

People often say "I love you more than life itself", especially to their children, yet it's rare for anyone to actually put those words to the test. I wouldn't call myself fortunate, that's entirely the wrong word, but I'm blessed to have had two people who have. Mamaan, my dear mother, who sacrificed her life to save her children's and Charlie who was prepared to lose his so mine and yours might be saved.

Now it's my fate to lose mine so that you can live the life I was never able to. A life in which you can pursue your dreams and desires. I beg you to seize this gift. Be brave but also kind. Be confident but always remain humble. Be tenacious but never forget to ask for God's help. And most of all, never be afraid to love those who accompany you along the way. I know this will be a major hurdle for you. It was for me growing up. "Why love," I'd wonder, "if those you love the most seem to always be taken from you?" The only answer I can offer is that love once given, unlike almost everything else in life, is something that no one can

take away from you, not even when you are in the darkest of circum-
stances. It is the true elixir of life, Allah's greatest gift to humanity, and
as I sit here now, the rain battering my window, I can feel not just your
love but Charlie's and Baba's and Mamaan's and Bushra's and Wali's
and Betty's and Bert's and so many others' swirling around me.

Be good to Charlie. (Forgive me, I know you will.) Let him guide
you. He is as wise and kind a man as my father and that's saying
something. I meant to write him a letter as well but time has gotten away
from me. Tell him, will you, that I love him so unbelievably deeply and
thank him for reawakening in me that capacity to love and be loved.
Outside of you, it is the greatest gift I've ever received.

I hate to go, my love. I wish I could keep writing and writing.
Moreover, I wish I could have achieved my goal without dying and been
able to come back to you. Just know this. While I might not be able to
return to you in body, I will always be there in spirit, in every breeze that
brushes your cheeks, every ray of sun on your brow, every piece of music
that delights your ears and every book that engrosses your mind. I will be
in your tears as well as your laughter, with you in your triumphs and in
those moments when you fail and have to pick yourself up. I will always
be there whether you realize it or not, and I'll always love you with a love
that is far greater than life itself.

Mommy.

A tear drops and smudges Noor's signature.

"Damn."

Noor wipes her eyes and folds the letter. She places it in an envelope and seals it. She leaves it perched on the desk alongside the other that she's addressed to Wali. It contains a thousand dollars. She hopes it can tide him and Bushra over in their time of need. She glances at the clock next to her nephew's bed. Five o'clock.

Just one thing left. The most important thing of all.

Noor rises from her chair and stands in front of a prayer rug. She raises both of her hands and touches the lobes of each ear with her thumbs.

"Allahu Akbar."

Noor performs the Fajr, every movement and word suffused with significance. She turns her face to the right.

"Assalum alaikum wa rahmalullah."

She turns her face to the left.

"Assalum alaikum wa rahmalullah."

Noor kneels there and does her best to picture Charlie. His wise eyes, his contemplative gaze, his proud, unbreakable countenance. She does the same for Charlotte. Her vivacious smile, her infectious energy, her piercing, intelligent eyes.

Whatever happens I'll always love you both.

Noor glances at the bedside clock. A quarter past five.

Time to go.

She rises and picks up the wicker shopping basket lying at the foot of the bed. There will be no farewells this morning. Last night, despite Bushra's vehement protests, she had made Wali and Bushra promise not to see her off. Noor opens the bedroom door and glances down the corridor towards Wali and Bushra's bedroom. Their light is on. They must be up but they're being true to their word.

"God bless you," she whispers. "God bless you all."

***

TARIQ HUDDLES AGAINST the wall opposite Bushra's home. His clothes are drenched, his shawl sodden and heavy.

If you're going to do it, you need to do it now.

It won't be easy. With his sole hand he will have to pull himself up over the metal gate before breaking in through a downstairs window. However, in an hour, the call to prayer will blast out across the city. The inhabitants of the house will awaken and the street will fill with men heading to morning prayers, and his task will become exponentially harder.

Tariq prepares to cross the street when the metal door opens. A woman in a light blue burqa steps outside. She is carrying a wicker shopping basket.

Noor.

She hastens down the street and soon her burqa melds with the pouring rain.

Go you fool. Don't you see, Allah has presented you with an opportunity.

Tariq scuttles after her.

***

WHAT A DIFFERENCE one night of rain makes. The river is a churning mass of water. It reaches halfway up the bank and every minute is getting higher. The path is now a sloppy and sludgy mess. Noor slips and slides along it. She grips her wicker basket tight. If it were to slip into the river her plans would be ruined. She wonders if the Prince will even come.

What are the chance in this sort of weather? What were the chances to begin with?

Noor attempts to banish such thoughts from her mind.

Focus on the job at hand. That's all you can do.

Noor uses her free hand to pull up the hem of her burqa and carries on slogging through the mud.

One step at a time. Isn't that what life's all about?

***

TARIQ PEERS AT the ungainly figure as she stumbles through the blinding rain. He wonders if there's a part of Noor that wishes she'd never fled Saudi Arabia.

Surely there must be.

He could probably get closer without revealing himself. After all she hasn't looked around once and if she did what would she see but some other poor soul forced to endure this misery. What's ironic is that there's probably no better time than now to kill her. He could walk right up behind Noor, shoot her in the head and with one swift kick send her tumbling into the river. Her body would wind up tens of miles downstream and no one would ever identify her.

I could board a bus to the Cantonment and be on train to Karachi by dawn.

Yet Tariq maintains his distance. His curiosity has gotten the better of him.

Where the hell are you going at this time in the morning, in this sort of weather?

***

NOOR COMES UPON the Jamrud Road. A truck barrels past and blankets her with a deluge of icy water. Noor staggers backwards and just manages to retain her footing. She sees another truck approaching.

Enough with this.

Noor staggers across the road, her drenched burqa dragging behind her like it has lead weights sewn into its hem. The truck blasts its horn. She reaches the other side. Today only a couple of stallholders are present, each of them crouching under the tarpaulins they've hastily arranged over their produce. Noor approaches the first stall holder, a gnarled old man.

"Salaam alaikum. May I take shelter a moment?"

The old man nods and returns to gazing out into the darkness. She places the wicker basket under his cart and pulls out a plastic bag containing her last cellphone. She takes it out. Its display indicates it's three minutes past six.

Damn, I'm late.

She pulls up her sodden burqa. Water trickles down her face. She dials the Prince's number. He picks up.

"Hello."

"Are you in Peshawar?"

"Of course."

"There's a package waiting for you at the front desk of Green's Hotel. It contains a phone. Retrieve it and drive along the Jamrud Road towards Hayatabad. I'll call you on it in exactly thirty minutes."

Noor powers off the phone. She places it back in the plastic bag and returns it to the wicker basket.

"Thank you," she says to the old man.

Noor drops the front of her burqa back down and scurries towards the mud huts of the Kacha Gari refugee camp. Behind her a truck blasts its horn. She ignores the commotion and soon after slips down the alleyway Charlie chased her down all those years ago.

***

RICK TOWNLEY SPINS towards Ivor in the back seat.

"Fuck me, it's really on."

Ivor keeps his eyes trained on the front doors of the Pearl Continental hotel.

Come on you bastard, it's show time.

The Prince had arrived late last night in an unobtrusive manner. There was no convoy of S.U.V.s nor a grand arrival ceremony. The Prince hadn't taken over the top floor of the hotel either, as he was wont to do, but rather had just booked a couple of suites.

He doesn't want to make a splash.

For Ivor and the C.I.A. team that's all for the better. As far as they can tell a large contingent of I.S.I. agents hasn't been assigned to protect him. They have identified no more than a couple and have a team ready to block them from following the Prince.

Ivor spies a couple of white S.U.V.s pull up in front of the hotel.

"Bandit's on the move," their agent in the lobby hisses over the radio.

Here we go.

Ivor leans forward. A couple of turbaned doormen scurry to open the lobby doors and the Prince strides out accompanied by four gun-wielding bodyguards. They usher him into the rear S.U.V. Two jump in with him while the other two get into the vehicle in front.

Four bodyguards and two drivers.

Ivor likes his odds. The S.U.V.s tear away. Ivor's driver allows two other C.I.A. vehicles to take the lead. The C.I.A. team has seven vehicles in total. Whoever set up the meet was clever enough to create a phone drop. Whatever conversation transpires next they won't be in a position to listen in on. However, that's not an issue.

We aren't going to lose the Prince. Not now.

THIRTY-EIGHT

TARIQ STILL CAN'T quite believe it happened. He'd been right across the road. Noor was talking on a cellphone, his heart pounding as he got his first glimpse of her face in a decade. He had assumed she would be as withered as Badia. Instead she was more beautiful and vital than ever. It only made him despise her more. And then the burqa was back down and Noor was on the move. He had hurried to follow her, only for a truck to blare its horn. If he had stepped back a second later he would be lying on the Jamrud Road now with a bunch of refugees gawking at his broken body. By the time a gap in the traffic did appear and he had managed to race across the road, Noor was at the entrance to an alleyway. He had sprinted after her and soon came to a fork.

Left or right?

Had a question ever held such significance.

Of course, I chose wrong.

He has no idea where she's gone. Tariq staggers on taking one turn after another. The alleys are funnels of flowing mud. It's as if the huts are melting. Tariq emerges into a small square. Four dilapidated mud huts face each other. Flapping cloths are draped across their openings and earth piled up at their entrances to keep the water from entering.

To think, after all these years, I'm back in the hellhole we first made home.

Home. Of course.

He races up to one of the huts and pulls back the cloth. A woman kneels over an earthen pot. She screams. A barrel-chested man springs up and rushes at Tariq. Tariq scuttles backwards so fast that he tumbles into a puddle.

"What in God's name are you doing?" the man shouts.

Tariq holds up his hand.

"I apologize, I just need to be pointed in the direction of the graveyard. My father's being buried."

"Right now?"

"I swear to Allah, as we speak."

The man squints at Tariq as the very first rays of dawn bleach the sky. He offers Tariq a hand and pulls him up.

"Come, I'll show you the way."

The man marches off and Tariq hastens after him. Down alley after alley they go, like rats in a sunken ship. Finally, they emerge into the open. The man peers out across the graveyard. Tariq looks down the way towards his old mud hut.

"I don't see anyone out there," the man says.

Tariq's spirits soar. In her light blue burqa, Noor is gliding towards their old home like a spectral entity. However, much to his surprise, she continues past it.

"It's all right," he says. "I see my sister. She'll know where it's taking place."

Tariq scurries along the row of huts. Noor heads towards the bedraggled eucalyptus tree and sits down on the bench their father crafted. With her back to Tariq, she raises the front of her burqa once again and retrieves the cellphone from her wicker basket. Tariq slips his hand underneath his kameez and grasps his pistol.

***

NOOR DIALS THE cellphone she left at Green's Hotel the previous day. The Prince picks up.

"Now what?" he says.

"Where are you now?" she says.

"Where are we?" the Prince barks out.

"Just past the airport," someone replies.

"Does your driver know the Kacha Gari refugee camp?" she says.

"Yes."

"Tell him to turn down its main thoroughfare and drive to the very end. There you'll come upon a graveyard."

"I know it."

"Then that makes things easier. A hundred yards to your right is a Eucalyptus tree. There is a bench underneath it. Go and sit on it. The Emir insists it be you, no one else, do you understand?"

"I understand."

"As soon as you sit down the package will be delivered. Ma'salaama."

Noor hangs up. She grabs her basket and stands. A dull object taps her on the shoulder. She spins around.

"Surprised to see me," Tariq says.

Noor's brain grinds to a crawl.

How?

"Trust me," Tariq says, "I had a similar reaction when I stumbled across you yesterday."

"What are you doing here?"

"The more pertinent question is what are you doing? What package are you here to deliver? Why put on that high pitched voice?"

Noor spies a couple of men exit a mud hut and head in their direction. Tariq steps around her and shoves the pistol into the small of her back. Noor's mind scrambles for a solution. To her despair none comes.

"Walk towards that abandoned hut," Tariq says.

Noor complies. The hut is four down from their old home. Its door is long gone, the timbers from its roof stripped, its interior open to the elements.

Keep him talking. There's still time.

They pass the two men. The men offer up salaams and Tariq returns one of his own. Tariq shoves Noor into the hut.

"Turn around."

Noor swivels in Tariq's direction.

"Get on your knees."

"Please, Tariq, if you only knew—"

"I said get on your knees."

Noor thinks about rushing him, however, her legs refuse to comply. She sinks into the muddy floor.

"Toss me your basket."

Tears spring in Noor's eyes. She throws the basket at Tariq's feet. With the gun still in his hand, Tariq grabs a hold of one of the handles and backs away like a coyote caught feasting on a carcass. He upends the bag. The laundry and the rifle's constituent parts plop into the mud. Tariq frowns.

"This is the package?"

"Yes. It's how I make my living nowadays."

"Who's it for?"

"A tribal elder."

"Then why were you speaking Arabic?"

"He's a learned man."

"I don't believe you."

Noor casts her gaze over Tariq's bedraggled frame.

"Tariq, all your life you've disregarded the advice I've given you, that Baba gave you, and it hasn't served you well."

Tariq's eyes bulge as if someone were throttling him.

"I beg you, for once listen to me. Turn around and walk away. You'll be better off, I promise."

Tariq strides over to Noor and shoves the barrel of his pistol into her skull. He forces her head down into a puddle. Noor snorts water through her nose. She struggles to breathe.

"I'm going to ask you one last time. Who are you giving this to?"

Never.

Noor lunges upwards. Tariq slips and tumbles to the ground. A blast rings out. Noor has no idea whether she's been shot or not. She doesn't care. She throws herself on top of her brother. He brings the pistol up. She bites down on his wrist. He screams and it drops from his hand. Tariq grips Noor's throat and squeezes. She rolls over yet somehow he holds on. She drives her elbow into his face. He cries out and lets go. She crawls through the mud towards the pistol. She grasps it. Her index finger finds the trigger. She twists around only to see the rifle barrel come arcing towards her. It catches her on the cheek and sends her tumbling onto the ground. Noor forces herself back up only for the silencer to smash into the back of her skull. She tries to assemble a coherent thought. Only one comes to her.

He's finally won.

It's the last she has before everything goes black.

***

SOMEHOW ABDULLAH HAS managed to control himself. On discovering the girl was missing he'd been tempted to cut off every single one of Matthews' nineteen remaining digits. However, thankfully, the more rational part of his brain broke through. The pain would have surely caused Matthews to pass out and by the time he came around the Prince would be in the air. Instead Abdullah has waited in the lodge's reception room and trusted that Barnes and his ludicrously expensive team have the ability to track down an eight-year-old girl. Abdullah glances at his watch.

Where the hell are they?

He wanders over to the wet bar and pours himself a second whisky. He downs it.

What if they don't find her?

Abdullah doesn't know which would be worse; the girl finding sanctuary at some nearby lodge or wandering off into the snow and dying of hypothermia. In either case any hope of his career being rehabilitated will be over.

Who knows? Perhaps the Prince will throw me in Buraydah prison just like he did Matthews.

He hears the growl of an S.U.V. and soon after a child's high pitched wail. The front door opens and Barnes appears at the top of the staircase. He holds the girl by the arm.

"We found her just before she made it to the main road."

Abdullah couldn't care less about the particulars. Barnes frog marches the girl down the stairs. Her pants are soaked through and she whimpers like an abused puppy. Abdullah takes her by the arm and leads her towards the elevator.

It's time to get this over with.

***

CHARLIE WAITS. AFTER all these years he'd have thought he might have gotten used to it, but this wait has been the most agonizing he's ever had to endure. After Abdullah left a false hope had grown inside him.

Perhaps we've been saved.

However, he'd soon disabused himself of that notion. No one knows they're in Park City.

It's over. You used up your nine lives a long time ago.

The only question that remains is whether he'll be able to hold out. He closes his eyes and prays to God to give him strength. He hears footsteps approaching. The door flies open and Abdullah enters dragging Charlotte behind him. A chill runs through Charlie's veins. Abdullah shoves Charlotte down on the chair and picks up the shears. Charlie catches Charlotte's gaze. It's blank as if her soul has retreated deep inside her in order to survive.

"She's in Pakistan," Charlie says.

"Liar."

Abdullah grabs Charlotte's left hand and positions the open shears around her thumb. Charlotte's eyes roll to the back of her head.

"I promise you," Charlie screams. "She's gone there to kill him."

"Kill who?"

"The Prince."

Abdullah stands there motionless.

"Peshawar," he mutters under his breath.

He drops the shears and sprints from the room.

***

TARIQ SITS WITH his back against the wall. Noor lies prostrate before him. Blood seeps from a gash in her head and tints a puddle of otherwise murky brown water red. He's been sitting here a while now like a victorious boxer at the end of a long and grueling fight.

Finally, it's done.

Noor coughs. Tariq wonders if it is nothing more than a death rattle. On the battlefield, in Afghanistan, he'd witnessed such a phenomenon on a couple of occasions. Noor coughs again. Her sodden body shakes.

No.

Tariq grabs the rifle barrel and staggers over to her. He raises the barrel over his head like an Eskimo about to club a seal. He hears the thrum of a vehicle approaching.

Who could that be?

He edges over to the doorway and peers out. Two high end S.U.V.s pull up beside the eucalyptus tree.

Maybe Noor was telling the truth about the tribal leader.

Four men, dressed in dark suits and carrying sub-machine guns, step out of the lead vehicle.

Arabs?

One of the guards gives a signal and another guard emerges from the back door of the rear S.U.V. He opens an umbrella, and a man in a white thobe and a red and white ghutra steps out. The man takes the umbrella and walks towards the eucalyptus tree. Tariq's mouth drops open.

Why? How?

It comes to him.

Noor didn't come here to deliver a package. She came here to kill him. And I'm the one who's saved him.

A tremendous warmth wafts through his body.

Allah's finally answered my prayers.

The Prince sits down on the bench. Tariq drops the rifle barrel and steps out of the hut. A guard shouts out a warning. The others swing their guns in Tariq's direction.

"Wait," Tariq shouts in Arabic.

Tariq holds his hand up. The Prince turns in his direction. The two men hold each other's gaze.

"Tariq?"

"Yes, it's me, your Highness."

"It's all right," the Prince says to the guards. "He's a friend."

Friend.

Tariq has never heard sweeter words. The Prince rises and makes his way over to him.

"Are you the only one?" the Prince says.

"Excuse me, your Highness."

"Are you the only one the Emir sent?"

Tariq hasn't a clue what he's talking about.

"The Emir did send you, didn't he?"

Say yes, you fool!

"He asked that you take care of me," Tariq says.

"And I will, I promise."

The Prince kisses Tariq on both cheeks. Tariq can't remember being this happy in years, perhaps ever.

"Come. Let's get you home to Riyadh."

The Prince leads Tariq towards his S.U.V. Tariq cries tears of joy. He wipes them away and sees three vehicles come speeding around the corner towards them.

***

IVOR JUMPS OUT of the lead vehicle. His prosthetic leg jars and sends a shaft of pain up through his stump. Ivor grimaces. He hobbles on, his cane stabbing the muddy ground before him. The Prince's guards scream at him to halt while another hustles the Prince and the target into the rear S.U.V. Three more C.I.A. vehicles roar in from the other direction. The Prince's guard whirl their weapons about. Ivor throws away his cane and raises his hands.

"We're not here to harm the Prince," he shouts in Arabic.

The guards continue to scream. Ivor drops to his knees. Once more his stump erupts in pain.

"You hear me? I only want to talk to his Royal Highness then you're free to go."

The guards arrange themselves in a protective cordon around the Prince's S.U.V. Ivor knows that unaided it's going to be next to impossible to stand back up.

If the target comes out blazing you're screwed.

No one says a word. Rain pelts the ground around him. The vehicles' windshield wipers clunk back and forth. The passenger door of the Prince's S.U.V. opens. A guard climbs out and opens an umbrella. The Prince emerges and they head in his direction. The Prince glowers at Ivor.

"You've made a terrible mistake, Gardener."

"You mind helping me up?"

Ivor holds out a hand. The Prince nods at the guard. The guard grabs Ivor's hand. Ivor stands unsteadily. He wipes his hands on his pants.

"Not the best of days, is it?"

"I suspect it will be your last at the C.I.A."

"Sure, if the Crown Prince makes a stink. But if he does, I suspect it'll be your last as Deputy Foreign Minister."

The Prince's gaze flickers.

"We know you have a senior al Qaeda operative in that vehicle."

The Prince chuckles.

"Sadly your vaunted intelligence is once again flawed."

"Really? Then why did bin Laden go to such lengths to have you rescue him?"

The Prince purses his lips.

"I can only imagine the phone call between President Bush and Crown Prince Abdullah. The President indignant that a member of the Saudi royal family was aiding the escape of a senior A.Q. member only months after 9/11. Jesus, if it leaked to the press, can you imagine the outcry? U.S. Saudi relations will be in the toilet. The Crown Prince humiliated."

The Prince's face reddens.

"But it doesn't have to be that way. Just hand him over and we'll pretend you were never here."

The Prince stares Ivor down. Ivor doesn't flinch.

"Go get him," the Prince says.

The guard heads for the S.U.V.

"I wonder if you can guess who it is," the Prince says.

"Khalid Sheikh Mohammad."

The Prince shakes his head.

"Al Zawahiri."

"Better yet."

Better than al Zawahari?

The guard yanks Tariq from the backseat.

"You gotta be shitting me," Ivor says.

Tariq wrestles free and blunders across the graveyard.

"Get him," the Prince shouts.

The guard races after Tariq and tackles him from behind. The two men flail about on the ground. It reminds Ivor of a mud wrestling tournament he once attended in Louisiana. The other guards rush over and pin Tariq down.

Finally, you're mine.

Out of the corner of his eye, Ivor sees a woman stagger out of an abandoned mud hut. Her left cheek is a swollen mess, her shalwar kameez splayed with blood.

What the hell?

Ivor spies a pistol at her side.

"Your Highness," he yells.

The Prince spins in the woman's direction and puts out a hand. The woman raises her pistol and fires three times before a shot sends her spiraling to the ground. The Prince gazes at his once pearl white thobe. An ever expanding circle of blood is staining it bright red. He frowns as if none of this makes any sense and drops face first into the mud.

Fuck.

***

ABDULLAH BARRELS INTO the study. Barnes, a glass of whisky in his hand, is sitting with his feet on the desk,

"The phone," Abdullah screams.

Barnes lurches to his feet and hands it to Abdullah. Abdullah punches in the Prince's number.

Come on. Pick up, damn you.

Someone finally does.

"Your Highness," he says.

"Abdullah?" a voice on the other end says.

It's not the Prince's. It's American.

"I need to talk to the Prince immediately."

"It's Ivor."

"Ivor? Thank God. You need to warn the Prince—"

"It's too late, Abdullah. He's dead."

Abdullah grasps the side of the antique desk.

"She killed him, didn't she?" he says.

"Three shots to the heart."

Abdullah swallows.

"Look I gotta go, Abdullah. It's a shit show over here. Call me later if you want the details … oh, and Abdullah, please tell me Matthews and the girl are unharmed."

"What did you say?"

"We know you abducted Charlie Matthews and the Prince's daughter. Are they still alive?"

"Yes."

"Make sure it stays that way."

The line goes dead.

"What's going on?" Barnes says.

Abdullah chuckles.

"Seriously what just happened?"

Soon Abdullah's bent over, his whole body shaking as deep throated laughter erupts from within.

Of course. How could it end any other way?

Abdullah suspects that Allah is laughing equally hard. Abdullah lurches out of the room. At the elevator he presses the button for the basement. The elevator purrs down two levels. He steps into a bare utilitarian corridor and marches to the workroom. There he discovers the Prince's daughter clinging to Matthews. Abdullah picks up the shears.

"No," Matthews cries out.

Abdullah ignores him. He snips Matthews' plastic cuffs

and unlocks his ankle cuffs. Abdullah gestures towards the open door.

"Go, before I change my mind."

Matthews struggles to his feet. He lifts up the girl and hobbles out of the room.

***

WITH CHARLOTTE IN his arms, Charlie stumbles down the moonlit road towards the lights of Deer Valley.

"I can walk if you like," Charlotte says.

"No, I got you."

He means it. The way he's feeling right now he could carry her another fifty miles.

Noor did it. She had to have. There's no other explanation.

He hears the thrum of a car engine and looks back. The blazing lights of a black S.U.V. are coming their way. Charlie freezes. The S.U.V. slows as it comes alongside them. The window lowers to reveal a bearded man in a ski instructor's jacket.

"You folks all right there?"

"Sure," Charlie says.

The man glances at Charlie's feet and frowns. Charlie realizes he isn't wearing any shoes.

"On second thoughts, you mind dropping us off in Park City."

"Course not."

Charlie opens the back door and deposits Charlotte in the S.U.V.'s warm interior.

"Where we going?" Charlotte says.

"Home," Charlie smiles.

THIRTY- NINE

"MISS KHAN? MISS Khan?"

Noor forces her eyes open. The blurred outline of a man hovers above her. He leans in and a Pakistani doctor with a trim mustache comes into focus.

"Where am I?"

"Lady Reading Hospital."

"So I'm not dead?"

The doctor laughs.

"No, though it was touch and go there for a moment. You lost a lot of blood."

Noor attempts to sit up. The room spins and she collapses back onto her pillow.

"Please, take it easy. I need to examine you."

Noor closes her eyes. The doctor opens her hospital gown and pulls back a swathe of bandages that are taped to her chest. A shard of pain passes through her body as if she's been speared by a lance. The doctor replaces them and with the help of a nurse turns Noor over and pulls away more bandages on her back.

Noor plays over the moment she came to in the abandoned hut. She remembers voices piercing the drumbeat in her head and gazing out the open doorway and spotting the

Prince standing there. He had come. It seemed so cruel to be so close yet so far. And then she saw Tariq's pistol lying beside her. She grasped it and teetered to her feet. There was a man next to the Prince, however, she was so focused on the Prince she never took him in. She recalls the other man screaming, "Your Highness." The Prince turned and raised a hand as if he were commanding her to stop. She brought the gun up and held it steady, just as Betty had taught her, and fired off three rounds before she was hit so hard she felt like a horse had kicked her in the chest. She tumbled into the mud and lay there as men ran about and screamed in English and Arabic. After that she remembers nothing.

The doctor and nurse turn her back over and the doctor untwists the bandage that's wrapped around her head.

"Did he die?" she asks.

"I beg your pardon."

"The Prince. Is he dead?"

"I'm sorry, Miss Khan, but I haven't the faintest clue what you're talking about."

If the Prince were dead he'd surely know. I missed. I must have.

She closes her eyes and cries.

"Is something the problem, ma'am?" the doctor says.

Noor shakes her head. Her tears flow. To have come so close and failed is almost too much to bear. The doctor wraps a fresh bandage around her head.

"Be gentle with her," he says. "She's still very weak."

The doctor and nurse exit the room. The door closes behind them. Noor hears something metallic click its way towards her. She senses a presence.

"Go away," she cries. "Please, I beg you."

"I wish I could, Noor, but I'm catching a plane in an hour."

Noor's eyes fly open. Ivor Gardener looms over her.

"And in answer to your question, yes, the Prince's dead. You're quite the shot."

Other than the Prince and Tariq there's no one Noor has ever despised more. Yet, at this exact moment, Ivor might as well be an angel delivering a message from Allah. A smile creeps across her face.

"It's no laughing matter," Ivor says. "You've no idea what trouble you've caused. Not just with the Saudis but the Paks too. To say they were pissed about us conducting an operation on their soil without their knowledge … well, you lived here long enough, you know how sensitive they can be. The only saving grace was that they were just as mad at the Saudis, and as mad as the Saudis were with us, well our government was even madder at them. The Saudis denied any knowledge of the Prince's activities. They claimed the whole incident was a family dispute and that you should be extradited to Riyadh."

So be it. All that matters is that Charlotte and Charlie are safe.

"But then some genius in the Vice President's office had a brainwave. What if it was announced that the apprehension of Tariq Khan, a high ranking al Qaeda operative, was a joint operation, a shining example of cooperation in the War on Terror. We, Americans, can trumpet that we've finally nabbed one of the bastards responsible for 9/11. The Saudis' can see their reputation in the West transform overnight, especially given a member of the Saudi royal family, no less, gave his life. And the Pakistanis can get what they always want. Money from the Saudis, and arms from us. Everyone wins. Hell, I even get to keep my job and you, well, you get to keep that pretty little head of yours."

"I'm not being extradited?"

"No, you're getting this instead."

Ivor hands Noor an American passport. She opens it. At the back is her photo, the same hopeful one Charlie took years ago. She glances at the surname. Naipaul. Below it is her given name. Indira.

"How did you know?" she says.

"Let's just say an old friend of mine was looking for you."

Noor trembles.

"Don't worry. Your daughter and Matthews are safe. Never been safer in fact."

A moan escapes from deep within Noor.

It's over, a voice says.

Noor recognizes it as her mother's. Noor weeps and soon her cries turn into sobs. It's as if she's finally able to cleanse herself of all the worries, fear and agony she's endured all these years. By the time she calms down and looks about the room, Ivor is long gone.

FORTY

TARIQ LIES ON the sloped board. His feet are tied to one end. His black mittened hand cuffed to a chain wrapped around his waist. He wears a bright orange jumpsuit and shivers uncontrollably. The room is even colder than the passes above Tora Bora. He has no clue where he is. They've flown him somewhere he knows that. Despite the blacked out goggles they clamped over his eyes and the headphones they fastened over his ears, there was no way to disguise the sensation of lifting off into the air. When he was led off the plane a bitter wind seared his face and crept under his jumpsuit. In fact, the first room he ever saw was this one and that was only after they had tied him down to the board. The walls are constructed out of large cement blocks. The floor made of rough concrete. On the ceiling are a couple of fluorescent lights. In one corner is a video camera with a blinking red light. Two guards, dressed head to toe in black and wearing balaclavas, stand either side of the door. They've not moved since he's been here. He swallows. His parched throat feels as if it's being rubbed with sandpaper.

"Water. Please," he croaks.

The men don't respond.

"I promise, I had nothing to do with the attacks."

For once he is telling the truth. Like most people in the training camps he had no idea it was coming. At times he believes this is nothing but a nightmare and at any moment he will awake. However, he never does, and deep down he knows he never will. As the hours have stretched by he's become ever more convinced that it wasn't just the Prince that Noor meant to lure to Kacha Gari camp.

It was me too.

She had to have been working with the C.I.A.

They used her as bait and, like a fool, I bit.

He thinks of Rashid and Nawaf. They'll be by the warm shores of the Arabian Sea by now. They might even have slipped out of Pakistan.

Why didn't I go with them?

Tariq retraces all the other decisions he's made in his life, all the instances of bad luck that have brought him here.

Oh, Allah, you must truly despise me.

His thoughts are interrupted by the clang of the door opening. A figure enters. Upside down he is tough to identify. However, as he limps ever closer, his cane clacking on the frigid floor, Tariq realizes who it is.

Ivor Gardener.

Tariq tries to pull himself up, however, the restraints around his chest won't allow him to budge an inch. Ivor stares down at him.

"It's been some time since our last meeting.

"I promise you," Tariq stammers, "I was forced to bring that bomb with me. If I didn't they'd have killed me."

Ivor looks towards the camera and back down at Tariq.

"Tell me, where have the leaders of al Qaeda fled?"

"I don't know. That's the truth."

Surely he believes me.

"Are we ready?" Ivor says.

Tariq realizes the two masked men have moved to the foot of the table.

"What are you doing?" Tariq says.

"You should feel honored," Ivor says. "You're our very first."

A guard shoves a damp cloth over Tariq's mouth and nose. The other picks up a jug and pours water onto it. The water trickles up Tariq's nostrils. Tariq screams and in the process the cloth clamps across his face like a vice. Tariq realizes he can no longer breathe and in his panic tries even harder. Water floods his throat. He feels like he's drowning. Just before he loses consciousness, he has one last terrifying thought.

I've gone to hell and I'm never going to leave.

EPILOGUE

extol

FORTY-ONE

Kabul, Afghanistan

November 28ᵗʰ, 2002

"IN MY HUMBLE opinion," Wali says.

"And let's remind ourselves that Wali's opinions are nothing but," Charlie says.

Noor laughs along with everyone else around the long kitchen table.

"I am glad, my dear Mr. Matthews, that after all these years you acknowledge that."

"Oh, get on it with it, Wali," Bushra says from the opposite end.

"I am trying, my love, but this gentleman keeps on interrupting me."

Charlie holds his hands up to indicate the floor is Wali's.

"As I was saying, in my humble opinion, this is the finest meal that has been prepared in the great city of Kabul in a hundred years."

"My mother would have something to say about that," Noor says. "As would Aunt Sabba."

"And the last thing I wish to do is denigrate the memory of those two wonderful women but unfortunately their meals were exclusively Afghan."

"You traitor."

"While this meal has been enthusiastically prepared by many people from many different cultures. After all, not only is the Afghan influence of you and my delectable spouse in evidence, but so are the Dutch sensibilities of my fine boss, the incomparable Miss Elma Kuyt."

"Suck up," Elma shouts out.

"I don't deny it. I have always been one of the best."

More peals of laughter ring out.

"There are also Egyptian dishes supplied by the distinguished Doctor Tahiran and Saudi Arabian ones influenced by her slightly less distinguished husband, Doctor Kadhim."

"Kadhim can't cook to save his life," Tahiran says.

"Guilty as charged," Kadhim says.

"I do not dispute that, however, you can't deny, Tahiran, that your husband's Saudi heritage was infused into that most delectable kabsa. So, if I could be so bold, I would like to ask everyone to raise a glass, you too children, and toast what is an indefatigable fact that when people of different cultures come together and eat, they enrich this world and make it a better place and for that I am truly thankful."

They all raise their glasses.

"To eating together," Wali says.

"To eating together," everyone roars back.

Noor turns towards her husband. Charlie is leaning back in his chair. He has a distant look in his eyes. Noor knows it well. Though he'll deny it, Charlie can't help but be pulled back from time to time to a not too distant past.

"You should say something," she says.

Charlie snaps out of his trance.

"I don't know if I could ever top Wali," Charlie says.

"Something else I'm glad you acknowledge," Wali shouts.

Charlie jumps to his feet.

"Right, that's it. Just a few words then."

A resounding cheer goes up. Charlie raises his hands for quiet and stares at all the beaming faces.

"I think the reason Thanksgiving is so special back in the States is that everyone celebrates it. It doesn't matter whether you're a Christian or a Jew, a Muslim or a Hindu, an atheist or a Buddhist, black, white, brown or none of the above. It's an occasion where we can all be thankful for all the wondrous things in our lives. And we have so much to be thankful for this year. Kadhim's release; the liberation of this great country; our health; this beautiful house that miraculously survived the civil war; the work we each do and which gives meaning to our lives; our beautiful children; the unborn son Noor and I have on the way to join our amazing daughter, Charlotte."

Charlie takes a moment. His eyes moisten. Noor reaches out and clasps his hand. No one says a word.

"Over the years, there have been days, many, many days, when I thought a night like this could never happen, yet here we are. Yes, here we are, and for that I am eternally grateful."

Charlie smiles.

"And now for pecan and pumpkin pie."

Another cheer goes up. Noor remembers that the pies are still in the old servant's quarters. She looks down the table hoping to catch Charlotte's eye, however, Charlotte and Aamir are already involved in a competition to see who can carry the most plates from the table. Noor heaves herself out of her chair. She crosses the kitchen and opens the door to the courtyard. There's a chill in the air.

There will be snow soon.

She stares up at the bare branches of the apricot tree.

"In all of Afghanistan there is no grander apricot tree," Baba would tell her with pride. "After all your great grandfather obtained the seed from the plumpest fruit of the tallest tree in the most acclaimed orchard in Herat, the greatest apricot growing region in the entire world."

Of course Noor had accepted Baba's explanation as she had accepted nearly everything else he ever told her.

You were the one who forced me to go to Charlie's house for lunch.

She now knows why. Though Baba never acknowledged it, he had always known that she and Charlie were meant for each other.

Noor walks up to the tree and strokes its rough bark. She digs her right hand into the first finger hold.

I've climbed this tree so many times I could do it with my eyes closed.

And so she does. Her hands find one branch after another, her feet ancient toeholds that lift her ever higher. She reaches the highest branch and sits down. Unlike in Charlie's garden, back in Peshawar, there is no view. Apricot trees, however magnificent, don't reach as high as oak trees. Rather she faces her old room, the one in which her mother had woken her that fateful night, the one that Charlotte now occupies along with her rabbit, Betty.

"Noor? Noor?"

Noor spies Charlie down below.

"I'm up here," she says.

Charlie cranes his neck back.

"I was worried about you," he says.

"Just thought I'd have a moment to myself."

"Okay. Just be careful on the way down."

Charlie heads towards the house.

"Why don't you join me?" Noor calls out.

Charlie turns.

"I thought you—"

"Charlie, surely you must have figured out by now that you're always the exception."

Charlie grins. Despite not being five months pregnant, his climb is a far more stuttering and labored affair. He reaches the highest branch and Noor scoots down. Charlie plops beside her and catches his breath.

"I don't know how you do it," he says.

"Didn't you know? I'm from a long line of Afghan ninja warriors."

Charlie laughs.

"I wouldn't be surprised."

He takes Noor's hand in his and they sit there like a couple of teenagers on a date. From within the house high spirited conversation and laughter leak out, yet Noor and Charlie might as well be in a different world. Noor can't help but think of Tariq. Not the Tariq of later years, but the prepubescent one. Her rival, her protector, her one-time best friend, the brother, who much to his chagrin, could never climb as high as she. She says a prayer for him.

She thinks of her father, how she used to curl up in his lap right here in the courtyard and how Baba would read to her and transport her to all manner of fascinating and marvelous places until her mother would burst out of the kitchen and demand that Noor hurry to bed.

"Here," Baba would whisper as he slipped the book into Noor's hands. "Tell me what happens in the morning."

She thinks of her mother, of how wonderfully willful Mamaan could be, how she had insisted her daughter play tennis, and when there wasn't a girls' tournament, she had initiated a sit-in in the club manager's office until he allowed Noor to take part in the boys'. Noor fell at the quarter final stage and when she came off the court, her mother grasped her by the shoulders and said, "Not to worry. With a little more effort you'll win next year." Noor didn't. A year later she was in Pakistan and Mamaan was dead.

Noor stares up at Venus, twinkling brighter than any other star in the inky sky, and imagines that it's heaven, and that her smiling parents are looking down at her.

Perhaps they are sitting hand in hand in a tree like this.

From within the house, Charlotte calls out her name.

"I guess we better get back in," Charlie says.

Noor turns towards Charlie. He is staring at her with such love and affection that she tears up.

"You okay?" he says.

She wraps her arms around him and holds him close.

"Yes," she says.

And, right then, Noor realizes she truly is, that all of them are, and there's no more wonderful feeling in the world than that.

ACKNOWLEDGEMENTS

When I first set out to write this story I had no idea it would take me eight years and three books to achieve. In all honesty if I had known, I would have thrown my laptop in a lake and run for the hills. It has been a long road, this third and final book especially arduous, but it has also been a journey with plenty of highs and my characters have become dear friends despite the occasional shouting matches we have gotten in to. Enormous thanks to Clarke, my wife, who when I was done and maintaining that I couldn't write another word, read the manuscript and calmly insisted I go back to the beginning and make it better. Thanks also to my mother, Georgie, who continues to be this book's fiercest advocate and guardian. And to all my readers. I can't thank you enough for coming on this journey with me. I know it has been a nerve jangling one at times with a couple of lengthy delays along the way. To stick with me until the bitter end is the highest compliment I could ever receive.

N.G.O

http://www.facebook.com/Refugenovel

http://www.ngosborne.com

Printed in Great Britain
by Amazon